The Last BEST Story

Also by Maggie Lehrman

The Cost of All Things

The Last BEST Story

MAGGIE LEHRMAN

BALZER + BRAY

An Imprint of HarperCollinsPublishers

Balzer + Bray is an imprint of HarperCollins Publishers.

The Last Best Story
Copyright © 2018 by Maggie Lehrman
All rights reserved. Printed in the United States of America.

ISBN 978-0-06-232077-3

Typography by Jenna Stempel-Lobell
18 19 20 21 22   PC/LSCH   10 9 8 7 6 5 4 3 2 1
❖
First Edition

FOR FREDDY

ONE

NEW TEAM TAKES OVER *GAZETTE* MANAGEMENT

Rose and Grant had heard all the possible variations on the joke that no one read the paper anymore. Anyone looking to take them down a peg or two would have to dig deeper for an insult. (For Grant, mention his late growth spurt. For Rose, imply plagiarism.)

"If it's true that no one reads us," Rose said, perched on Grant's editor-in-chief desk in the *Gazette* room, "then why do you care what we publish?"

Grant smiled from his seat at the desk behind her. Vice-Principal Hackenstrat, the newspaper's nominal adviser, stood in the doorway wearing a wrinkled suit and holding the proof pages that the *Gazette* was required to run past him before sending the issue to the printer. It was the last issue of the year, affectionately known as the grad issue, and since Rose and Grant were juniors, it was the first issue they'd worked on since Grant had taken over as editor in chief.

They hadn't discussed it, but both of them were willing to be expelled over the contents of the paper, though they suspected it wouldn't come to that. Hackenstrat didn't have nearly the same investment in his side of the argument; he was doomed before he began.

The vice-principal rubbed his forehead with the back of his hand. "You can't write this. You're advocating for leaving our school vulnerable."

"No, we're refusing to endorse your ridiculous plan to invade students' privacy," Rose said. "That's not the same thing."

"It's not ridiculous." Hackenstrat waved the papers to emphasize his words, but the pages flapped in his face. "After what happened in Columbine, at Virginia Tech, at Sandy Hook—"

"Those are all awful tragedies," Grant interrupted him. "But we already do lockdown drills, like every other school in the state. No one else does what you're suggesting."

"If you're innocent, you have nothing to worry about," Hackenstrat said.

Rose shook her head. "That's, like, the definition of a slippery slope."

Hackenstrat's proposal to the school board to increase the school's security included a requirement that all students give up their online passwords, along with more standard requests like regular random locker checks for any reason and metal detectors at every exit and entrance. Rose and Grant's editorial pointed out that Hawks High wasn't any different from any number of high schools in the state or the country—in the middle of suburban sprawl, a reasonable distance from Chicago and its uptick in crime, but not far enough into the country for students or their families to have any significant hunting culture. Although it was a big school with kids from all sorts of backgrounds, everyone had always gotten along fairly well. Treating every student as a potential threat seemed a huge overreaction.

"I know you think of yourselves as adults, but you're children, and you're under our care. We get to choose how to keep you safe."

Rose crossed her arms. "Where's your evidence that having our passwords would save anyone? Why not come up with ways to help kids who are struggling, instead of turning the school into a police state?"

"Watch it, Rose," Hackenstrat said sharply. "You're hardly in a police state. The fact is, you don't know who might crack. I don't know; no one knows. Maybe it'll be no one, or maybe it'll be the quiet kid in the back. So I want us to get all the information we can."

"You're treating everyone as if they're already guilty *just in case* someone snaps."

"Wouldn't you rather be safe and constrained than free and dead?"

"No," she said, sticking out her jaw.

"Oh, come *on*, Rose—"

"Mr. Hackenstrat, this is a super fun fight, but are you going to censor the paper or what?" Grant asked.

Hackenstrat sighed and ran his eyes over the proof pages. "The issue is not the paper itself, or even your right to publish facts," he said. "Editorials are opinion pieces. So it wouldn't be suppressing the *facts* for me to forbid you to publish it."

Grant leaned back in his chair. "So. The censorship road, then."

"We'll figure out a way to get our piece out there," Rose said. "And then everyone will know that you're responsible for stifling honest debate."

"You'll get more attention for censorship than the original editorial would get, for sure," Grant said.

"Is that really what you want?" Rose asked.

Hackenstrat went pale as the full ramifications of the story played out in his mind. Grant and Rose could see his thoughts dribbling out into a puddle on the ground.

There would be plenty of students and parents and teachers who agreed with Hackenstrat's argument, but there'd be a significant majority who would rally behind the paper. Freedom of the press, privacy of the student body. There'd be calls from parents. Calls from the superintendent. Maybe the hot-button topic of school safety would mean that outside reporters would jump on it. Hackenstrat saw his job security plummet. He saw the peaceful summer ahead of him, ruined. He slumped against the doorframe and gazed mournfully at Rose and Grant.

"Are you two going to be like this forever?"

"Yes," said Rose.

"When we're done with you," Grant said, "we're both going

to go to Northwestern and major in journalism and then hope-fully annoy editors and publishers together for the rest of our lives."

"Wait a minute, though. What do you mean? What are we 'like'?" asked Rose.

Hackenstrat struggled. "So . . . so . . ."

"Dogged?" Grant suggested.

"Clever?" Rose chimed in.

"Charming?"

"Beautiful?"

"Perspicacious?"

"Vivacious?"

"Enough," the vice-principal said. He tossed the page proofs onto an empty desk in the front row. "I have to get back to prom anyway."

"Oh, is that still happening?" Rose asked.

Hackenstrat rolled his eyes. "I'd threaten to write to North-western and warn them what a couple of insubordinates you are, but I suspect I'd only be making your case for admission for you."

"We appreciate, as always, your valuable input." Grant folded his hands in front of him on the desk and sat up straight. "I hope we'll continue to have a fruitful relationship over the course of my tenure as editor in chief."

"Be seeing you," Rose added, as Hackenstrat left without saying goodbye.

If there hadn't been a desk between them, Rose and Grant might've hugged. They might've finally kissed, too, which was something that had been threatening to happen for months now, the anticipation like the crackle of electricity in the air before a storm. But instead Rose picked up the proofs and held them over her head. "Victory!"

"Thanks to you for writing it."

"Thanks to you for publishing it."

Grant stood and came around to her side of the desk. He took the proofs from her and placed them on the desk, then reached over and pulled a piece of fiberglass from Rose's hair. "You have something there," he said, brushing the dust away and then tucking her hair behind her ear. "All better."

Rose smiled up into his face and he smiled back. They were the only two people in the room (literally) and the only two people in the world (as far as they knew or cared). They had the best high school newspaper in the Chicagoland area, and they had each other. Rose had Grant, her editor in chief, who made bad ideas sound good and good ideas sound like magic, and who would help her change the world. Grant had Rose, his right-hand reporter, the best writer he'd ever met, who was always there for him even in the darkest times.

This time next year, who knew what might happen?

Rose Regnero hadn't been back to the *Gazette* since she'd quit the paper two months ago.

"It'll only take a second," she said, squeezing JB's hand. "I kept meaning to pick it up earlier, but there are always so many people around, and now this could be the last time I'll ever be in this school, and no one'll be in the room anyway, so it's actually kind of perfect, as long as you don't mind."

Rose babbled when she got nervous or excited. Grant used to interrupt her when she got on a roll, but JB tended to let her get to the end of the thought, even when that thought had multiple endings piling up like a high-speed highway crash.

"It's fine," JB said when she took a breath. "Whatever you want."

Rose smiled up at JB and adjusted her wrist corsage. It was made of real flowers, bought for her by JB, with a rose and lilies of the valley and all that froufrou. It matched her 1950s-style sleeveless dress. Which, in turn, matched the vest of JB's rented tux. If someone needed a stock photo of "happy couple at prom," Rose and JB would be an ideal choice.

Last year during prom, Rose and Grant had stayed up until two a.m. finishing the grad issue of the paper. This prom would be better.

Hawks High's prom was held in the school gym, a cavernous room, like everything in the school: built huge in the 1970s to accommodate a booming population. Long hallways, constantly loud because of voices echoing off the high ceilings. This year the student council had attempted to move the prom to a fancy hotel, and promised to cut nonessentials in order to keep the ticket price low. Rose had covered the decision-making process extensively for the *Hawks High Gazette*. She'd been there every step of the way, as the committee gradually reinstated every luxury (photo booth, favors, DJ, catering) until she reported, with some glee, that the cost of a ticket to this year's prom would exceed the amount of last year's, and the committee was forced to relocate the festivities back to the gym to even out the expense.

It had been an interesting and effective series, but not particularly popular with the student body.

Rose and JB sneaked out through the interior gym doors that led to the rest of the school. They'd arrived with the other prom-goers through the doors connecting the gym to the parking lot, where most of the chaperones were posted.

"You sure it's okay we're leaving?" JB whispered. It was the type of dark and desolate that made people want to whisper.

"Positive," Rose said. "I mean, technically it's against the rules to leave the gym during prom, but that's mostly for people who would want to go to the parking lot and get drunk and then come back. Not for people like us, only doing a quick errand."

JB's pause seemed doubtful.

"And besides, I've been at school a million times at night," Rose said quickly to fill the silence. "I love it, actually. Walking down the halls in the dark. It's like floating in a lake at night, isn't it? It's like the walls could be super far away, as if the edges have disappeared."

She could hear herself waxing rhapsodic about a high school hallway. *Shut up, Rose.* She was trying too hard, and the entire point of this whole prom experience—her whole *life*, even—was that maybe she didn't need to work so hard to be happy.

They kept walking down the wide, dark hall. Their shoes clicked on the floor, much louder than the echo of a pop song coming from the gym behind them. Hawks High was H shaped, coincidentally, with two long buildings, lined with alternating red and green and orange and blue windows, connected by a short central hall. The ends of the two buildings housed the school's biggest gathering points: the gym, the small theater, the library, and the administration office. The *Gazette* room was located in the connecting hallway between the two buildings, commonly known as the bridge.

"Anyway," she said, attempting a breezy tone, "I'll grab it quick and we can go back—oh no."

They'd turned into the bridge and could see light spilling from the open *Gazette*-room door, a few feet in front of them.

"Rosie!"

Rose closed her eyes and stopped walking, but the voice got closer.

"Rosie, you here to file a late-breaking story? We sent off the grad issue already, but I bet you can convince the new editor to add something if you ask nicely. By the way, you look great. Oh-la-la, is that a corsage? Come on, open your eyes and tell me how great I look. Oh, hello, I'm Grant Leitch, Rosie's editor in chief."

Rose opened her eyes, and JB and Grant were shaking hands in front of the open door. Grant was wearing a tuxedo and he looked irritatingly good in it.

"You've met JB at least four times," Rose said. "And I quit the paper two months ago."

"That doesn't sound right." Grant did not stop smiling. "I'm sure I would've remembered."

"Hi," JB said.

"What are you doing here?" Rose asked.

"Checking on the new class. Making sure they haven't destroyed my legacy already."

"In a tux?"

Grant looked down at himself. "Oh, right. Well, it's prom, isn't it?"

"Why are you at prom?"

"Why am I—is there some reason I shouldn't be allowed at prom?" Grant furrowed his brow, mock concerned. "Did I get banned like Marty Caulfield but blacked out and forgot about it?"

Rose made a frustrated noise. "You've always said you hated prom. You think it's a joke."

Grant shrugged. "I must've changed my mind." He gestured to the open doorway. "Let's all go in and get comfy and let Rosie tell us all about her new story."

All of a sudden, there was no enticement that could get Rose through the *Gazette*-room door. "I don't have a story. I told you. I quit."

"Yes, but you can't really mean that."

"I can, actually. And I'd appreciate it if you stopped emailing me your thoughts on today's headlines, texting me about story assignments, and filling my mentions with your every spare thought."

"What about the telegrams? I write a great telegram."

"Leave me alone, Grant."

Grant rocked back and forth on his heels. "Mixed signals, Rosie. You say to stop bothering you, and then you show up here. . . ."

"We're here for the award," JB said helpfully, and Grant's face lit up.

"Of course! Rosie's Midwest Regional Excellence in Journalism Award. No way would she leave the MREJ lying around." Grant directed his words at JB, but they were meant for Rose. "Because she cares about the paper more than anything."

"Not anymore."

He leaned forward so that the sleeve of his tuxedo brushed her upper arm. This close, she remembered a little too late that his smile sometimes turned dangerous. Her heart beat without her permission. "You have to miss it. The thrill of investigation. The satisfaction of finding just the right words."

"No, I don't, actually."

"I don't believe you."

"What does it matter? School is over."

Grant didn't stop smiling, but the character of his smiles changed all the time. This one was conspiratorial. "School isn't all there is in the world. Something's bound to happen, and you'll want to write about it."

"You can write all you want at Northwestern. But don't bother me about it."

Grant nodded, as if she'd revealed the crux of the matter. "I knew it. It's Northwestern."

Rose's hand lifted to rub the space between her eyes, but she remembered her carefully applied makeup and clasped her wrist with the other hand. "It's *not* Northwestern. Screw Northwestern. And something *isn't* bound to happen, at least not tonight. It's prom. There will be dancing, they'll pick a king and queen, someone will throw up at an after-party. It's not news. It's normal."

"That sounds terrible."

"Then why did you come?"

For once, Grant didn't have an answer. She looked at him, waiting. She knew him so well: his silences and his jokes, his stubbornness and his enthusiasms. That's what happened when you spent every spare minute with someone for four solid years. They became a part of you. Even if she'd never kissed him (and they had kissed once and only once, that horrible wonderful time they never spoke about), she'd still know him better than anyone.

This particular silence meant that he was about to say something true.

"Rosie . . . ," he started.

"We should go," she said to JB, grabbing his arm and turning back toward the gym.

"What about the award?" Grant asked.

A winch twisted in Rose's chest and squeezed her heart. She blinked back tears. "Keep it," she called over her shoulder.

JB didn't talk nearly as much as Grant did, but he noticed things. He put an arm around her shoulder as they walked back to the dance.

"Sorry about that," Rose said, half turned into his broad chest.

"It doesn't matter. I'm happy to be here with you."

That's right. They were together at prom, and all of that *Gazette* nonsense was over. What did she need a stupid award for, anyway? That was the old Rose: grabby, ambitious, winning for the sake of winning, laughing with Grant over something that probably wasn't the least bit funny. This Rose would float above it, serenely letting the award (and Grant, and Northwestern, and the *Gazette*) drift out of her life.

Grant opened the bottom drawer of the editor in chief's desk, shifted aside a carefully placed file folder, and stared at the Midwest Regional Excellence in Journalism Award. If he shouted, he could probably stop Rosie and her date; if he ran, he could catch up with them before they reached the gym.

Here's your trophy, he'd say, and *Oh! Thank you so much!* she'd say back. And her eyes would light up, and she'd remember all the work that had gone into the paper that had led to the award, all the ways that Grant himself had helped her win it, and then she'd shake her head as if awakening from a highly realistic dream and say, *I didn't really quit the paper, did I?* And he'd say, *No, you didn't.*

Right. That's exactly what would happen.

He re-covered the award and closed the desk.

There was no reason for him to be at the *Gazette*. They were days away from graduating, and he had no official responsibilities at the paper. Still, he'd basically put together the entire grad issue himself—with Nick's help. It would be printed tomorrow, ready to be handed out at graduation on Monday.

Every closing for the past four years, he'd stayed late, obsessing over every headline, every punctuation mark. The new editor in chief had declared at 5:45 p.m that they were finished. If she wanted to settle for mediocrity and typos, well, it wasn't Grant's name at the top of the masthead anymore . . . but he couldn't help checking up on it.

He closed the *Gazette*-room door and felt in his pocket for the key. "Right," he said out loud, recalling that he'd had to turn it over to the new editor in chief last week. In a way it was lucky for him that she was so careless with her responsibilities, otherwise the door would've been locked and he never would've been able to get in. Not to mention that if she'd cared more, she certainly would've kicked Grant out of the room after her first story meeting a month ago, which he refused to allow her to lead.

He knew he was being a jerk, but she had a whole year more to lead the paper. He only had this last issue.

He didn't see Rosie or her date in the hall outside of the gym, so they must've sneaked back inside without any trouble. The pounding bass echoed through the empty hall. He held the door handle and took a long breath before swinging the door open and ducking into the light and music and sweat smell and humidity.

Strands of Chrismas lights hung on the folded-up bleachers. Large circular tables surrounded a makeshift dance floor, and the DJ had set up his table, speakers, and portable laser lighting rig on the stage.

Nick and Oliver sat at a table near the stage. Grant made a beeline for it.

"Everything's fine at the *Gazette*," he announced. Nick and Oliver looked up at him, surprised.

"What did you do?" Nick asked.

"Nothing," Grant said, and sat, then attempted to lean back in his chair casually. "I said everything's fine." He cleared his throat. "Ran into Rosie. She was looking for her award."

"Did you give it to her?"

"I . . . she decided she didn't want it."

"Her dress is adorable," Oliver said.

"Oliver, don't be a cliché," Grant said.

"Don't tell my boyfriend not to be a cliché," Nick said, and then turned to Oliver. "You can be as cliché as you want. Grant's not your boss."

"Okay," Oliver said, smiling sweetly at Nick. "Then I'd also like to say that Rose's boyfriend looks like Michael B. Jordan's long-lost twin, and it's really working for me."

Nick frowned. "All right, no need to lean into it."

Grant tried to straighten his cummerbund without making it look like he was straightening his cummerbund. It felt like it was riding up, but who the hell knew where a cummerbund was supposed to sit? He should've gone with a vest—every other guy at the prom seemed to have gone with a vest and tie—but he had thought the cummerbund and bow tie would be more classic. Classic, or out of date. Hard to tell the difference.

"She seems bored, doesn't she?" he asked.

Nick had his arm around the back of Oliver's chair, Oliver leaned his head on Nick's biceps, and Oliver's cane rested in the crook of his elbow. Canes as accessories were against the prom dress code, but that didn't apply to Oliver's cane, which helped him walk. It had even gotten dressed up for the occasion with green craft tape that matched Oliver's tie.

Nick and Oliver looked cozy. If Grant tried to put his arm around someone or something, he'd lose control of the cummerbund situation entirely.

"I don't know, Grant," Nick said.

"She must be bored. I don't see how she couldn't be. She has nothing in common with that guy."

"Maybe it's interesting for her to be around people not exactly like her."

"She'll be back."

Oliver glanced at Grant. "Back where? To you?" He raised one eyebrow, in a way Grant was sure he'd practiced in the mirror. Oliver was an actor. They all had their favorite faces.

"No, not to me," Grant said. Because Rose and Grant had never really been together—which Nick and Oliver knew perfectly well. "I mean the paper."

"Dude," Oliver said. "Didn't she quit months ago?"

Nick joined in the pileup. "And school is *over*. There's nothing to come back to."

"Yeah, but . . ." Grant gave the side of the cummerbund a yank. "Still. She'll be back."

Neither Nick nor Oliver deigned to respond to that. Grant was well aware that he was running out of time. There was only graduation left, and the blank months of summer, and then he'd go to Northwestern and Rosie would go to the University of Michigan, and if they didn't figure things out before then, they might never see each other again.

That was a future that did not make sense to Grant. He refused to accept it.

Oliver popped up his cane with the back of his elbow and went to talk to some of his theater friends, and Grant scooted his chair closer to Nick's. "We could tell Rose the printer's server crashed and we have to redo the entire grad issue in one night."

"Absolutely not," Nick said. "First of all, totally implausible, because I've never not had a backup in my life. And secondly, no way am I redoing three weeks of work so you can entrap your ex."

"We could plant some weed on JB," Grant said.

"Whoa, way to make a leap."

"I'm spitballing."

"Well, stop. It's not fair to JB. And where exactly did *you* plan on getting weed?"

"I heard that Owen Pettibone sells—"

Oliver shook his head. "You'd never dare."

"How about Mairead Callahan's stalker? She posted that she's afraid he's going to show up."

"No one cares about Mairead's probably imaginary stalker."

"Okay. We could phone in a bomb threat?"

"Grant. On the off chance you're serious: No."

Grant sighed and leaned his elbows on the table. "I don't appreciate having all my best ideas shot down. Why don't you come up with something?"

"How about we have a nice prom and let Rose have one, too?"

Grant narrowed his eyes at Nick. "Since when are you totally chill and unworried?"

Nick shifted in his seat. The shot had hit its target, but Grant didn't feel particularly satisfied. It wasn't fair to pick on Nick, who was at risk of worrying himself into a small, miserable life. As Nick's best friend, Grant should be building him up instead of cutting him down, because if Grant wasn't careful, Nick would have a nervous breakdown before the first day of college.

"Hey," Grant said, feigning jollity, "you two look like you're having a good time tonight. I like Oliver's tie."

Nick frowned. "Don't try to distract me. All I'm saying is let go for the night. Leave Rose alone. Have some fun. Dance with someone else, maybe, instead of moping around after her."

"I have never moped a minute in my life."

Nick patted Grant's shoulder. "Keep believing that."

"Something will happen," Grant said. "You'll see. Something always happens."

HOPEFUL JUNIOR TAKES A ROMANTIC LEAP

Grant patted Nick's shoulder. It was October of their junior year and they were sitting in Grant's driveway in Nick's father's car. "Don't worry," Grant said. "Nothing awful's going to happen. You're going on a date. It's, like, a thing people do."

"Oh god. Oh god. Oh god." Nick curled over the steering wheel. "I don't have time for this. I can't afford to spend every second of my life freaking out about a guy. I have *things* I need to *do*. The paper! SATs! College!"

"Well, that's a positive spin, then," Grant said. "If it's a total garbage fire, at least you won't have to worry about it anymore."

Nick moaned.

"Listen," Grant said. "That first date was fine, right? You guys had a good time?"

Two weeks earlier, Grant had assigned Nick to review the fall play. The lead was played by a sophomore named Oliver

Murdoch. Grant had heard from Rose, who had heard from Rose's best friend Jenna, that this Oliver Murdoch was a member of the LGBTQ and Allies Club, identifying G. Nick had never joined the LGBTQ & A because he was busy with the paper and he had a hard time warming to people, as a rule. Grant had always been the exception, but even between the two of them Nick wasn't exactly bubbly.

One week after the play, Nick and Oliver had met at the bookstore and then moved on to browse for comics at the comics shop. And now they were supposed to be going to a movie. Nick should have picked up Oliver ten minutes ago, but he was still sitting in Grant's driveway, frozen with panic.

"That first thing was fine, because it was barely even a date really, and I thought there was no chance he actually liked me, so I could relax." Nick sighed into the leather steering wheel. "Now he's going to want to talk to that cool, unworried guy who doesn't really care what people think of him, and he'll be stuck with me instead."

"Yikes," Grant said.

"I know. I suck."

"No, Nick, yikes for the epically low self-assessment. First of all, no one's 'stuck' with you. If he thinks he's 'stuck' with you, he can go fuck himself."

"Gaaaaaaahhhhhhh."

"And second of all, you're a couple of human beings getting to know each other. What do you want to bet he's really nervous, too? You've got nothing to lose by going for it."

Nick turned his head to glare up at Grant with bloodshot eyes. "Do you even believe the stuff you're saying? Live life to the fullest, grab the bull by the horns, all that crap—like, really?"

Grant thought about it. He stared up at his house, where his dad and stepmom and younger brothers were eating their dinner, and where he'd only been living as a permanent resident for the past two months. Across town his mom was eating dinner alone. If Grant had still been living with her, he would've had a hard time taking the question seriously. Of course all that stuff was bullshit, his mom would say. Those time-worn lines were comforting lies we told ourselves so that we could live through humiliation after humiliation. No amount of positive thinking meant anything against the forces of fate and the rotten core of most human nature.

She'd say it in a loving way, with a conspiratorial us-against-them grin, but yeah. Even though she taught yoga, his mom didn't really go for inspirational moments. And neither did Grant, usually.

But Grant lived with his dad now. His dad and stepmom were both lawyers, and they were intensely practical. They'd have no idea what to say if he asked them about believing he should seize the day. But he'd chosen to live here. Rosie had told him it was going to be okay and in general it was. He'd thought at the time that Rosie's saying it was going to be okay was a clichéd platitude, but it had turned out to be true. Maybe they're only clichés when you tell them to yourself, but when other people tell them to you they're real.

(His fingers twitched toward his phone so he could text Rosie. Lately he'd get anxious if he hadn't heard from her in a few hours. Not, like, Nick-level anxious. But he'd feel a tingling on his skin, like the touch of a mosquito a second after it takes off, as if he'd missed something important that was going to bother him later.)

"Yeah, I do believe in all that crap," Grant said. "All you have to do is show up and be you. If it doesn't work, that's not a judgment on who you are as a person. It only means it doesn't work. And if that's the worst thing that happens, that's nothing."

"Oh yeah? Is that why you're always going on so many dates?"

Grant shrugged off Nick's sarcarm. Nick wasn't wrong. Grant had been busy with the paper and getting decent enough grades for Northwestern and for his parents to relax and his mom's illness and everything else; he hadn't really had the time to think about girls in, like, a concrete way, that wasn't just thinking about how nice they looked in tank top weather. He certainly hadn't thought about asking one of them out in a long time. He'd thought about dating like Nick had: a distraction from what was really important. The *Gazette*. Getting into Northwestern. Taking over the world. But hearing his own excuses come out of Nick's mouth made it sound less like focused determination and more . . . Nick-like. Neurotic. (*Sorry, Nick.*)

If he did ask someone out, it would have to be a specific girl, not a Girl Walking By, or Girl Ringing Up His Order of Cheese Fries, or Girl on TV. A girl who would want to talk to him and if he was lucky kiss him and if he was really really lucky . . . more.

For a moment he thought he might catch Nick's wave of panic, and then he told himself to get a grip.

"Okay, dude," Grant said, smiling. "If you do this, I'll ask someone on a date."

Nick turned sharply. "For real?"

"Yeah. No problem."

Nick blinked slowly and took a deep breath. "Well. I need to see that. So I guess I'm going." He ran his hands through his hair and then smoothed it down. He looked in the mirror in the visor, made a face, and snapped the visor back to the ceiling. "Thanks, Grant."

"Not a problem. Maybe it'll be fun."

Nick rolled his eyes. "Yeah, this is a real barrel of laughs so far."

Grant got out of the car and gave Nick a cheesy thumbs-up as Nick backed out the driveway. Grant had his phone out and was texting by the time Nick turned the corner.

> Nick safely on his way. If this doesn't work, I think we all may need to change schools.

Rose's response appeared almost immediately.

> How'd you get him to go? Xanax, hypnosis, extortion?

> I said if he went through with it I would ask someone on a date.

There was a pause, and Rose's response, when it arrived, was shorter than he'd expected based on the typing time.

> You did what?

Yeah, I told him it was no big deal.

It's no big deal?

Am I typing in cyrillic? Yeah, no big deal. It's a date.

Idiots go on dates; I think I can handle it.

Rose didn't respond. Grant let himself into the house and heard his brothers screaming in the living room. It was comforting to come home to noise and chaos instead of waiting, watchful silence. He felt good. The paper was going well. He was getting the grades he needed. He had one best friend off safely on a date. He had another best friend on the other end of the phone. And soon he would have a girlfriend, too.

I'm thinking of asking Mer Montez, he typed.

Mer—Mercedes, technically, though no one called her that—had been smiling at him more than usual in the precalc class they shared. Since there was no other reason in the history of the world for anyone to smile in precalc, Grant felt pretty secure that she'd say yes. Now that Grant had finally grown six inches, he wouldn't feel like he was a child asking his babysitter to marry him. And everyone agreed Mer Montez was beautiful. It felt superficial to consider that, but by what other metric did people decide who they wanted to ask out? He didn't see the point in asking someone he thought was plain, simply out of principle.

Are you joking? Rose texted.

The table in the kitchen had been cleared, and his dad had left Grant a plate of mac and cheese, but it was cold. He sat in front of the dish and ignored it while he texted.

Rose couldn't have thought he meant to ask *her* out. That

would be entirely unnecessary, since they already spent every second together and were better together than boyfriend/girlfriend. She understood that. They transcended all that crap. And what if he asked and she said no? He couldn't even contemplate it.

Not joking. Mer + Grant = twu luv.

Pause for response.

I ship it. Grer forever. Or do you prefer Mant?

Grant relaxed. He knew she wouldn't have thought he meant to ask her out. All was well.

BTW I missed dinner. Pick me up in ten minutes for the diner?

Grant could practically hear her sigh through the phone. He could practically see the wry smile on her face.

Fine. But you're paying for my fries.

Rose hated to admit it, but she wished she'd gotten the trophy from the *Gazette* room. The Midwest Regional Excellence in Journalism Award was the one concrete thing she'd accomplished in her four years at the *Gazette*, and it had been given to her personally ("For Excellence in Feature Reporting and Writing"), not the *Gazette* as a whole or her-and-Grant as a team. So much of her time at the *Gazette* felt muddled or unsatisfying in retrospect, but the MREJ had been a pure victory. Even Grant couldn't ruin that.

And she wouldn't allow him to ruin prom. She was going to make herself happy no matter what. Prom would be awesome, and not another replay of Northwestern.

She had the thought and immediately tried to forget it. Thinking about how she wasn't going to go to Northwestern after years of planning for it would bring bad juju. Forget Northwestern, forget the MREJ. Relax. Have the time of her life.

"Rose!" Jenna Chen threw her arms around Rose's neck, and Rose turned to hug her best friend, who held her at arm's length to look her up and down. "Oh, you look amazing. Ugh. Not fair."

Rose was alarmed to notice that Jenna had started crying already, her mascara pooling underneath her eyes like a football player's face paint. "What's the matter?" Rose asked.

Jenna shook her head and tried to smile. They sat at the nearest empty table. "It's just . . . Marty's not here. I shouldn't have come."

"Don't say that. This could still be fun. Look—you get a keychain, and it lights up and everything."

Rose flashed the souvenir keychain at Jenna, who only blinked dolefully. "Marty would've loved that thing."

"You can bring him one. Here, take JB's."

Jenna gripped the extra keychain. Her lower lip started wobbling. "Thank you," she said. "I still can't believe they wouldn't let him in. So unfair."

"Mmmmmm."

"You agree that it's unfair, right?"

"Uh-huh."

"I wish you were still on the paper so you could've written an article telling Marty's side of things, instead of that totally biased article Grant wrote."

Grant's piece had been scrupulously balanced, actually, relaying the facts of Marty's one-man senior-prank fiasco without descending into furious name-calling, which was what everyone else in school (and the neighboring schools) had done. Rose declined to tell Jenna that when her boyfriend accidentally killed a rival high school's parrot mascot by letting it eat a Big Mac and milk shake that had been sitting in the back seat of his car for the better part of a week, he lost the right to get a "side" of his story. Rose and Jenna had been best friends since the sixth grade, and Rose had a small parcel of secrets and half-truths and lies that she kept from her best friend in order to remain best friends. She would add this one to the pile.

"He told me to come, you know? He made me *promise* I would be here, even knowing he couldn't go." Jenna wiped furiously at her eyes, making the mascara situation worse. "I'm glad you're here. I don't think I could handle this on my own."

"I'm here for you."

"Thanks, Rose." Jenna sniffled. She started to cry again for no obvious reason, tears dripping delicately down her cheeks. She saw Rose's expression, which made tears flow faster. "It's okay to admit you have a feeling, you know. It doesn't suddenly turn you into a damsel in distress."

"I would never say you were a damsel in distress," Rose said.

"I meant *you*. Are you okay?"

Rose thought of running into Grant at the *Gazette* room. She thought of JB, off getting her a drink. She thought of the *Gazette* and the MREJ and Northwestern. She reminded herself that in three months she'd be gone. "I'm great." Rose took Jenna's hand and tried to pull her up. "Come on, let's dance."

Jenna shook off Rose's grip and slumped deeper into her seat. "Do we have to?"

"I think it's what we're supposed to do."

"Since when do you care about what you're supposed to do?"

It was less of a rhetorical question than it seemed. It spoke to the foundation of Rose and Jenna's friendship. Jenna had been rebelling against her parents' expectations since she could walk, but Rose had been raised to think outside the box. People underestimated her mom for being a single mother and former 90s-rave drug addict with many interesting tattoos, and then by extension they judged Rose. She was aware that it was an insult to all that her mother had done for her, as well as her decade-long friendship with Jenna, to try to go with the flow and be a part of the crowd.

But caring about the paper hadn't gotten her what she wanted. So it was worth a shot.

LATE NIGHTS FOR FRESHMEN STAFFERS

On Rose's first day at the *Gazette*, one month into freshman year, she'd been given an assignment and a computer immediately. Only half of the computers were in use.

"We're a tad understaffed," the intensely glowering editor in chief had told her. "This is a growth opportunity for you. Lots of responsibility, if you can handle it."

Rose immediately knew she would handle it.

The boy at the computer next to her smiled as he continued to type. He was short and wore glasses and looked at Rose as if he actually saw her. "What he's trying to say is that no one reads the paper and no one wants to write for it except for résumé padders and nostalgic obsessives. Which one are you?"

"I don't know. I'm Rose," Rose said.

"Grant Leitch. If I had to guess, I'd say you were a résumé padder. You have the stink of good grades all over you."

She sniffed her underarm, earning another (different) smile. "Which are you?" she asked.

"Oh, I'm in a special category. Those who believe that the paper can actually matter."

Rose thought about it for a second. Grant bit the fingernails of his left hand while his right kept tapping on the keys. "I want to be in that group, too," she said.

Grant nodded. Rose turned to her computer and got to work on her first assignment. It had been so easy—not the writing itself, which she was still figuring out—but sitting there, doing her work, talking to Grant. It was the first thing in her life that had worked exactly as she'd imagined it would from the outside.

Ever since she'd seen the stacks of papers in the corner of homeroom in her first week of school, she'd wanted to be there, making the paper herself. That first paper had pictures from homecoming, profiles of a few new teachers, movie reviews, editorials about censorship in the library. Nothing revolutionary, but whoever wrote these articles seemed to know things, whereas Rose, with every passing day, felt like there was more and more evidence of all the things she didn't know. She enjoyed the feeling of having a paper wedged under her elbow. It made her feel old. Here was her paper. If only she could get a cup of coffee and bills and a bad hip and reading glasses, she'd be grown up.

"What do you mean, grown up?" her mom had asked.

"Like, a person who's got it figured out it."

"I don't think anyone's actually got it figured out," her mom said, but Rose assumed she only said that because she had taken so long to get her life in normal working order. Rose couldn't afford to have that mind-set. She couldn't make her mother's mistakes; she had to get it together *now.*

It wasn't until her first *Gazette* closing, a month into her tenure, that she realized what she'd gotten herself into. The editor in chief told Rose it would be a late night, so she informed her mom she'd be home by nine. She went to the *Gazette* right after school and settled at the desk next to Grant's, which, after only a couple of weeks, had become her seat.

Closing the issue meant they had to submit the final files of the month's paper to the printer, checking every word and picture. She'd written one sports story, one interview, and three event listings, all of which she checked obsessively until nine o'clock, when she started to pack up her bag.

"Where are you going?" Grant asked.

"I'm—" She stopped. Grant and his friend Nick Powell were still at their computers, as were the editor in chief and managing editor. "It's late."

"But the paper's not done yet," Grant said.

"I told my mom . . ."

Grant waved his hand in her direction. "No problem at all, Rosie," he said. "This isn't brain surgery. If we have to finish the last couple of layouts without you, I'm sure we can handle it."

That earned an eye roll from Nick.

"No one reads the physical paper anyway," Grant said, warming to the subject. "We should really forget about the whole thing, hit publish on the website, and go to a movie."

"All right, all right," Rose said. "I'm here. Let's work."

"As long as it's not too inconvenient for your busy schedule."

"I'm not listening. I'm editing."

"Eh, let spell-check flag it. I mean, who cares, right?"

Rose put her fingers in her ears and hummed loudly. When she glanced up at Grant, he was grinning at her. It was the type of smile that she couldn't help but return.

She called her mom, and then she tweaked layouts and proofread and rewrote copy. At around midnight she and Grant got into a fight with the editor in chief. She could tell that the point wasn't important, even as she heard her voice rising in volume. The placement of a story—a pun in a headline—a pie chart versus a bar graph. Whatever it was, without warning, became the most important question of all time, and the thin thread holding the entire issue together.

"You can't possibly believe—"

"You'd let our reputation be tarnished—"

"The only reasonable person in this room—"

"I won't do it—"

"I'll never agree—"

Etc.

It was Rose and Grant versus a senior, and her side won.

They finally finished up around three a.m., and the editor in chief and managing editor invited Grant and Rose and Nick to the diner with them.

As far as Rose could tell, Grant didn't even bother asking his parents if he could go. Rose's mom took a little more convincing.

"I've never heard of high schoolers staying out this late without any drugs or alcohol," her mom said, voice groggy from being woken up.

"Sorry. I guess I'm not as cool as you were."

Her mother snorted. "Send me a picture of these nerds."

Rose did, and her mom responded with the "crying-with-laughter" emoji, so she guessed she was allowed to go.

They piled into the editor in chief's beat-up car and sang along to the radio out the open windows onto the empty streets. The diner was at the edge of town among the tire shops and big-box stores, set back from the road. Rose had never seen it before, let alone eaten there. It had dark walls and booths, and the smoking section still smelled like smoke, even though it hadn't seen a lit cigarette since the turn of the century.

They squeezed into a booth and ordered—buttered toast for Rose and fries for Grant and a glazed doughnut for Nick and coffees all around. The seniors asked them questions about themselves and told stories about closings past. All five of them laughed the way you only laugh if you've been up for way too long. Rose's elbow touched Grant's, and then her arm and leg and side as they both scooted closer together by degrees. His face was so close to hers, her hair brushed his neck every time she turned her head. Once he even lifted a hand and held a piece of her hair, lightly wrapping it around his finger and then letting it go. Interspersed throughout the regular conversation he made jokes only for her, whispered out of the corner of his mouth, and not throwaway material, either, but solid zingers that would've killed the entire table but that he chose to give to her alone.

And she'd been so exhausted and happy, because it felt right.

JB brought Rose a drink just as a slow song started, so she put the cup of punch on the table and pulled him into the crush of the dance floor. When they found a spot, he smiled at her and opened his arms. She wrapped hers around his neck and leaned on his chest. The song wasn't that bad, and everyone looked beautiful and happy, the best version of themselves. She even saw Owen Pettibone, class skeeze, in a tux and swaying to the music just outside a clump of girls.

This was what prom was supposed to be. She closed her eyes.

Over the past four years, as promised by her first editor in chief, Rose's responsibilities on the *Gazette* had grown. (Grant grew nine inches, too.) And she had really believed that reporting on what was happening in their school provided a service to the other students—a voice to those who otherwise suffered at the whims of the administration and school board. Every time

Vice-Principal Hackenstrat pulled them out of class to complain about what they'd put on the front page or came by the *Gazette* room to harangue them about an editorial, that was proof that someone cared—that what their words said made a difference. When Rose tucked the paper under her arm, she still felt like she had stepped into a sophisticated world, outside of the usual high school bullshit. Even if no one read it and print was dead, and they might as well have been chiseling stories into stone tablets, it felt like it mattered. Like *she* mattered.

And then it didn't.

Rose opened her eyes and looked up at JB. He looked down at her seriously. "I'm glad you changed your mind about me," he said.

"I'm glad, too," she said, and willed herself to stop talking there.

If she'd gone on, she would've said that she hadn't changed her mind—she'd always thought he was hot and a good person. But in the past two months, everything else in her life had changed. Or, no—her life hadn't changed. It had always been this way, but she'd been looking at it backward, or through a heavily distorted filter that had finally gotten cleaned.

Jenna wanted Rose to admit that something terrible had happened that made her quit the paper and go out with JB. Grant kept digging around trying to figure it out, too. But it wasn't like that: the poles had reversed themselves, and what was wrong was right, and good was bad, and she didn't have to be sad and confused and upset about any of it because as soon as she'd noticed what was going on, she had taken the necessary steps to fix it.

No reason to keep dwelling on it. She'd moved on.

Grant sat at his table and stared up at the DJ, who had set up all his gear on a folding table on the stage. The prom's theme was vaguely nautical—ships and sailors and bon voyage-ing—but the DJ traveled in a theme bubble of his own, and that theme was tropical. The table was ringed with a grass skirt, he had on two brightly patterned shirts layered one over the other, and there were pineapples literally everywhere.

"All right, Hawks High, are you having a good time!" he shouted into a pineapple microphone.

Grant started counting the pineapples.

"Peace and love, my young friends," the DJ said. "Let's slow it down a little bit and see where the ocean breezes take us."

Grant was disappointed when the strains of an Ed Sheeran song started up. The DJ placed the pineapple microphone on top of a (pineapple-stickered) speaker and nodded along with the strumming guitar.

In the center of the dance floor, Mer Montez gestured angrily at Fisher Louis, who tried to grab her arms and hold them to her side. He was twice her size and pure muscle, but she must've been really mad, because she kept breaking free. She and Grant had never argued like that when they were a couple. Somehow the thought didn't make him feel any better.

"So long, Chief," Nick said as he stood to join Oliver on the dance floor, where they swayed together. That left Grant alone at the table. He leaned back, attempting to look bored. It had not occurred to Grant—literally never, until that moment—that he might've tried to find a date to the dance, at the very least because it would mean he'd have someone to talk to.

And without his even trying to look for her, there was Rose, dancing with her jock boyfriend. Why did he have to have so many muscles? It seemed excessive. And Rose . . .

He shouldn't have looked. He should've known better.

Because of course she wasn't looking around to see where Grant was. Of course she didn't care if his cummerbund was straight or if he posed in exactly the right way. Of course she was smiling up at her date. Of course the expression on her face was somewhere between pleased and utterly rapturous.

Grant turned back to the DJ. Fifteen pineapples. Sixteen. Two stickers on the laptop—eighteen.

Since he was looking up at the DJ table, Grant was the first person to see Marty Caulfield leap onstage wearing a white sheet, clumsily tied in an approximation of a toga. His hair was plastered down over his forehead, and he had a sad string of leaves wilting over one ear.

"Ha!" Grant said out loud, involuntarily.

Marty grabbed the pineapple mic from the top of the speaker. He shouted into it. It wasn't on. He turned it on and ducked the outstretched arms of the DJ, who had lunged for his mic.

"Friends! Romans! Countrymen!" he said into the mic, completely drowning out Ed Sheeran's soulful voice. "Lend me your ears, and stuff!"

"Booooo!"

"That's right, whooooo! Thank you!"

"Get off the stage, murderer!"

"I'm here for one thing only, and I will leave you all to your dancing. I'm here—" He ducked the DJ again, tripping over the hem of the sheet. "I'm here to tell you that time passes! Tempus fugit, my buddies! And so you've got to cling to the things that mean something to you. And for me, the thing I want to cling to so bad is my number one girl, Jenna Chen. Jenna! I love you!"

"I love you too!"

"Booooo!"

"How dare you boo love?" Marty stopped running from the DJ and allowed the microphone to be ripped from his hands. The Sheeran song had ended, so he only had to be louder than the crowd's heckling in order to be heard. "How dare you try to keep me from my beloved?"

"Booooooo!"

"You're making a big mistake! You'll all see!"

Vice-Principal Hackenstrat climbed the stairs to the stage deliberately, gesturing at Marty to come with him. But Marty seemed too fired up to stop and continued shouting. Perhaps he'd realized there could be no real consequences for anything he did. He'd already been banned from graduation and from prom itself, as Grant knew from writing his article about the parrot debacle. Marty had nothing left to lose.

Hackenstrat grabbed Marty's arm and pulled him toward the exit at the back of the stage. The DJ put on another song. "Sorry about that, my beautiful children of sound and light. Let's get back into the groove."

"I love you, Marty Caulfield!" Jenna screamed from the edge of the stage. Rose had her by the wrist, seemingly all that was keeping her from chasing after the VP and his charge.

"I love you, Jenna Chen!" Marty shouted back.

The whole thing was pointless and stupid and added yet another theme (Roman) to an already theme-stuffed evening, but Grant felt a little wistful as he watched Marty be dragged away. Marty and Jenna loved each other. Marty went up onstage and yelled it in front of everyone.

Grant could be bold about a lot of things—the *Gazette*, a story, school—but he'd never managed to be bold like that.

And now it was probably too late.

TWO

As soon as the door closed behind Hackenstrat and Marty, Jenna started moving, and as Rose's hand was still clamped to her wrist, Rose was dragged along.

"Hold up," Rose said, stumbling over the hem of Jenna's powder-blue dress. Jenna yanked the dress from under Rose's feet, ripping it along the side seam up to her knee, and kept walking. Rose apologized, but Jenna didn't seem to hear her or even notice the rip.

"We've got to catch up to them," Jenna said.

"We do?"

"Hackenstrat has it in for Marty."

Rose couldn't imagine Vice-Principal Hackenstrat having it in for anyone. He'd fought with Rose and Grant on occasion but usually gave up because he couldn't stay angry. Even when the school board had denied his plan to beef up the school's security, which he blamed on the *Gazette*'s editorial, he'd sniped at them for a week or two before drifting back into his usual attitude of beleaguered resignation.

"I don't think it counts as a vendetta when someone gets in trouble for crashing a prom he's been specifically banned from attending," Rose said as she hurried after Jenna.

Jenna waved away Rose's comment. "He came for me, Rose. The least I can do is be there for him, too."

"And I'm coming because . . . ?"

"Because I need you. And you said you were here for me. Was that bullshit?"

"No."

"Good."

They pushed through the gym's interior double crash doors, ignoring the chaperones on the other side of the gym calling for them to come back, and headed down the long dim hallway in the direction of the office.

"They won't get away with this," Jenna said. She kicked off her shoes, and they hit a locker with a bang. "It was harmless. He was only saying he loved me. Oh my god, can you believe he did that? It was so perfect, I can't believe it. Except for Hackenstrat's ridiculous interruption. What an ass. My poor Marty."

Jenna continued fuming and swooning as they walked, so Rose surreptitiously pulled out her phone and texted JB.

Sorry—Jenna's pretty upset. Be back soon!

As soon as she hit send, a text came in. But it wasn't from JB.

Told you something would happen.

Rose wasn't going to respond, except that she didn't want Grant to think even for a second that she was considering writing an article for him.

> Marty Caulfield's declaration of love is hardly big
> news.

A text came in from JB, but it was immediately bumped by another one from Grant.

> I mean, you're going to the VP's office already. It
> sort of seems like you've assigned yourself the
> story.

I'm helping my friend, **Rose wrote**. You've heard of friends, right? They're like staff only you can't tell them what to do every second of the day. And they actually like you.

> Ouch.

Rose jammed the phone back into her wristlet and was struggling with the zipper when another text came in.

> If he's still wearing the toga, try to get a picture.

Rose clenched her hand around the phone and purse and held them behind her back, where the texts wouldn't be visible.

"We only have three months until college, and I refuse to let Hackenstrat take any of that time away from us," Jenna was saying.

"What about after you go to college?" Rose asked. "Wellesley to Penn State. That's not exactly a short drive."

"Six hours and forty minutes, no traffic, no bathroom breaks."

"So you're going to pee in a diaper and go eighty on the turnpike every weekend?"

"We'll make it work," Jenna said. "That's not something I worry about."

The freedom to not worry about something—anything—seemed luxurious to Rose. She worried about everything.

SENIOR MAKES SURPRISING COLLEGE CHOICE

The night that Rose heard from Northwestern, she was working on a story for the *Gazette*. Because of course she was. That was all she did: gather the stories, write the stories, fight about the stories. It was April of senior year and she'd been doing exactly the same thing every day for three and a half years. The *Gazette* was her life.

When she saw the email pop up, her entire body went hot and then cold, and her hand shook too hard to click on the message.

Practically since the day they'd met, Rose and Grant had planned to go to Northwestern together. Northwestern had one of the best undergrad journalism programs in the country. They'd been going to the campus for concerts and to hang out in coffee shops, pretending to be twenty, since they were freshmen, and so it made sense. Of course she would go to Northwestern.

She could do whatever she wanted to do. "Imagine what you can do with your life if you don't waste two decades sleeping with heroin addicts," her mom always said, and Rose had always imagined along with her. (Besides, the thought of heroin addicts made her queasy. All those needles.)

Once she managed to open the email, she stared and stared at the screen, reading the letter again and again and waiting for the news to sink in.

Her phone blinked at her. A new text from Grant. He'd probably gotten the same email. She kept staring at her computer screen.

She'd done it. She'd gotten what she wanted. She was going to go to Northwestern, become a real journalist, and decorate her future home with a wall of Pulitzers.

She leaned back in her desk chair. If this was all she'd ever wanted, and she'd finally done it, why didn't she feel . . . happy?

Why didn't she feel anything at all?

It was three in the morning on a Monday—Tuesday morning, technically—and she hadn't had a full night of sleep in a week. She had six unanswered texts from Grant on her phone, some from right before the Northwestern email came through. The article she was writing wasn't finished, and she had two more to write before the closing on Friday—not to mention her homework to do.

So maybe she was simply too tired to appreciate her good news. She'd be happy in the morning, probably, after a cup of coffee.

She closed the computer, turned off her phone, and lay on her bed. But she couldn't fall asleep. She stared at the shadows in the darkest corner of her room.

The thought occurred to her, and it wouldn't leave her alone: *What if I wake up and I'm still not happy?*

She'd been working so hard for so long to get to this point. But if it didn't make her happy, maybe she didn't actually want to go to Northwestern.

If she didn't want to go to Northwestern, maybe she didn't actually want to be a reporter.

If she didn't want to be a reporter, maybe everything she'd done for the past four years had been wrong, and she didn't have to work so hard. Maybe the fact that it had been a struggle meant that it wasn't the right thing to do, and she had been swept along by Grant's enthusiasm.

Maybe she wasn't living her own life at all. Maybe she was living Grant's.

She pulled her phone out from underneath her pillow and swiped to Grant's texts. He'd gotten in, of course. He sent her GIFs of fireworks and a fox chasing its tail in the snow and a toddler setting off a glitter bomb. When she hadn't responded, he'd gotten more subdued, until his last text came through.

Rosie, you got in. Right?

Her thumbs hovered over the phone's keyboard. Her instinct was to reassure him: of course she'd gotten in, everything was fine, don't worry. Only everything wasn't fine. And why should her priority be reassuring Grant?

She could tell him the truth. She'd gotten in, but it felt wrong, and she was having doubts.

She shoved the phone back under her pillow and tucked her hands under her armpits. She could *not* tell Grant the truth. Picturing the words in a text window gave her heart palpitations; the acid of dread pooled in her stomach.

He would not understand, because he was Grant. He would try to convince her that she was wrong, and he might even succeed in confusing her enough that she would doubt her feelings.

Did Grant make her happy?

The question was so big and sad and inevitable, she almost groaned out loud. The answer came to her right away, the thoughts that she'd only sort of acknowledged but were suddenly spilling out, ready to drown her.

Grant wanted her to be his star reporter, nothing more. Grant kept her exactly where he wanted her: addicted to the paper, addicted to him. She'd thought a couple of months ago when Mer Montez had finally dumped him . . . But no. If he'd been interested in her, he never would've asked Mer out in the first place, or he would've dumped Mer when Rose and Grant had kissed last year. If he liked her at all, he would've agreed to go to prom with her right away instead of turning it into a fight. Grant knew if he stayed unavailable, she'd keep chasing him—or not him exactly, but the feeling she got when she was around him, the zinging of electric molecules as they crashed into each other. (Or whatever. She'd gotten a B– in physics.)

The point was, Grant was an illusion. He wouldn't know

how to deal with feelings that didn't line up with his own. He was the thing she could chase forever and never catch, like the perfect story.

She knew with a sudden certainty that this state of churning ambition, constant wanting with no *having*, would only be worse at Northwestern. She could see herself working and working forever for a feeling of satisfaction that would always be just out of reach.

She got up, opened her computer, and deleted the email from Northwestern. Then she fell asleep.

When the acceptance letter came in the mail, thick with forms and good cheer, she threw it in the garbage without opening it. She let Grant and everyone else believe that she hadn't gotten in—because it was less terrifying than telling them she'd been wrong for so long, or having to hear them tell her that her feelings were mistaken, or facing Grant's rejection when he could no longer understand her—and she told her mom she wanted to go to the University of Michigan–Ann Arbor. A great school. Nothing to feel sad about.

She'd been so, so wrong. No doubt there was more she'd been wrong about—all the little choices that had made up her high school experience. She didn't have much time left, but she could try to be happy without the struggle. Without Grant.

Grant checked his phone. No response from Rose.

She never used to leave him hanging, but that was the way things operated in this new, suboptimal reality. Even when something happened that was fun or interesting or newsworthy and he *knew* she'd have thoughts, she refused to share them with him. Well, fine. He'd have to find a story so compelling, she couldn't resist. Apparently Marty Caulfield crashing prom wasn't enough of a draw.

He looked around. Nick and Oliver were dancing. So were Fisher and Mer, though they didn't look at each other. Mairead Callahan, the class's social butterfly, was snapchatting the dance floor. And there was JB, wandering toward his table—also checking his phone, and frowning.

Grant smiled.

The DJ had started a string of fast songs, hoping to recapture the energy of the dance before Marty's interruption. Grant made his way across the dance floor, dodging elbows and pushing jumpers to the side.

A green-striped cane across his chest stopped him in his tracks.

"Oliver and I are going out for some air," Nick shouted, his arm supporting Oliver as Ollie kept Grant from reaching JB. "Don't do what you're thinking of doing."

Grant attempted to make his face look blank and innocent.

Nick nodded over at JB, who had put away his phone and was standing with his hands in his pockets. "I see where you're going. This isn't going to end well."

Grant lowered Oliver's cane and stepped out of its range. "What's the worst that could happen?"

"Death. Destruction. The end of the world."

Grant kept walking, waving over his shoulder at Nick and Oliver.

Nick worried too much, and he didn't understand. Grant wasn't trying to mess with JB. He didn't have nefarious plans, no matter what he'd brainstormed. The only thing driving him across the crowded dance floor was his pure journalistic curiosity.

If he was going to understand what had happened with Rosie—and a part of him still wanted to figure it out, to know why someone he knew better than anyone could seemingly change overnight into someone who didn't want to be in the same room as him—he was going to have to understand where she'd ended up and try to reverse-engineer how she got there.

He sidled up to JB and crossed his arms over his chest, which gave his hands something to do and also handily covered up whatever was going on cummerbund-wise. "Quite a shindig," Grant said.

JB nodded, but Grant could see his heart wasn't in it.

"Crazy about Marty, huh."

"I wouldn't call him crazy. He's a good guy."

Grant raised an eyebrow. "The parrot murderer?"

JB shrugged. "He didn't do that on purpose."

This was believing in the essential goodness of humanity on a scale that Grant had not anticipated. He wondered how far this goodness went. Was that what Rose wanted? Someone to draw smiley faces on her articles, tell her she was the greatest? She was the greatest, sure, but who actually goes around telling people how awesome they are all the time?

"JB, I can tell *you're* a good guy. And I don't want things to be weird between us."

"Why would things be weird between us?"

"Well, because of Rosie."

"What about her?"

"That we used to . . . That she and I . . . We were on the paper together. She didn't tell you?"

JB took his hands out of his pockets to cross his arms over his chest. It made him seem broader, and he was already as broad as a person could be without actually being two people standing next to each other. "No, she told me. But you and I don't have a problem."

"Well, good. We both have Rosie's best interest at heart, and that's—"

"No, I mean, we're not going to have a problem, because there's no reason for us to talk."

Grant stopped nodding along with the music for a moment and gave JB a closer look. "We're talking right now, aren't we?"

"Yeah, but I don't know why."

People often surprised Grant. They said or did things that he never would've said or done; they acted against their own self-interest in ways that made their lives complicated; they sacrificed for the greater good. He loved that about people—their constant unexpectedness.

But rarely did someone so surprise Grant that he lost the ability to speak.

"Right," Grant said, because he refused to submit to the silence. "Okay then."

SHAKEUP IN SENIOR *GAZETTE* STAFF

Grant had been stunned into silence when Rosie had quit the *Gazette*.

It had come out of nowhere. She'd been distracted ever since they got their college acceptances—she'd made excuses not to go to the diner and got rides home from Masha, the arts editor, instead of with Grant and Nick—but he'd thought she was processing her disappointment about not getting into Northwestern. He had given her space. He didn't want to be a walking reminder that he'd gotten the thing she'd been denied.

After only a few days, the slight amount of space he'd given her had started to feel like a huge canyon. He itched to call or text her. He wanted her opinion on absolutely everything he saw: the consistency of the french fries at lunch, the color of his shirt and if it matched his socks, the B he'd gotten on a history quiz.

Plus there was news. Owen Pettibone had gotten caught with

copies of six different essays written under six different names, which each of the students claimed had been given to him "as study aids," but everyone knew was an Owen Pettibone cheating sideline. He'd been lucky he'd only been caught with essays and not some of his more obviously illegal product. There had to be a way for them to write about Owen without pissing off Hackenstrat. He needed to talk to her about it—figure it out together, the way they always had.

One day Grant saw Rosie talking with Jason Baxter at her locker—smiling—and he almost walked into a wall. Since when did she know JB? When JB wasn't swimming, he volunteered as a counselor at sports camps for underprivileged kids, so basically, he had a reputation for being absurdly decent, which meant dull because nothing ever happened to him. He certainly wasn't heralded for his quick wit. Since when did Rosie smile so easily? She hadn't smiled at the *Gazette* in weeks. He made a resolution to craft some great material for that afternoon.

Even then, he wasn't prepared. She approached his desk, and he opened his mouth to bring up Owen Pettibone, but she didn't give him a chance. She said this would be her last day.

"Not funny," he'd said, Owen Pettibone forgotten.

"It's not a joke."

"But . . . why?"

"I want something different."

"It's April. There are only a couple of issues left." She shrugged, and Grant stood. "You can't leave. You love the *Gazette.*"

"I don't know if I do."

"You don't know . . ." Grant trailed off.

"I'm sorry, Grant," she said, but she didn't sound sorry. She sounded angry. "I'm done."

She turned to leave, and Grant's eyes widened. He practically climbed over the top of the desk to go after her. "Wait, Rosie— wait."

She stopped in the doorway to the *Gazette* room. The rest of the staff was watching; he could feel their eyes on his back. She couldn't actually leave. This was only a moment. A small moment of . . . something. Rebellion? Making a point? He had to get through this moment and everything would go back to normal.

"I'm sorry," he said, and for a moment it hung there in the room.

Rose turned her face into stone. "You should be."

"Yes, that's why I said it."

"Do you know what you're apologizing for?"

He gestured at himself, the room, the whole world. "You know. Everything."

"Goodbye, Grant."

"Okay, okay! I'm sorry you're mad at me. I'm sorry I got editor in chief and you didn't. And I'm sorry you didn't get into Northwestern. I'm sorry if you feel like I stole something from you."

She stared at him blankly. Grant considered himself good with words, able to shape them into anything he needed, but never had they felt so obviously inadequate and potentially painful.

"If you're upset," he said, treading more carefully, "I can help you. We can figure this out. You can always try to transfer to Northwestern at the end of freshman year—we can start thinking about that now. And you can finish this year, now, with the *Gazette*. It's where you belong."

"I don't belong to you. And I do not need your help."

He wasn't sure how she'd made that illogical leap. He switched tactics. "Are you dating that do-gooder guy? JB?"

"Jason Baxter. Maybe."

"Is that what this is about?"

"Why would who I date have anything to do with what club I'm in?"

Grant did not know how to answer that except with the truth, which usually would work but in this case was the only thing he couldn't say. So he went for an easy answer instead. "You have nothing in common with him."

She leaned toward him, and for a strange second he thought she was going to hug him. "No, he has nothing in common with you. That doesn't mean I won't like him."

He stared at Rose, momentarily speechless, and she stared back.

Something shifted between them. Grant's stomach flipped, and he said the first thing that came into his head to fill the endless silence, even though he knew it wasn't the right thing, not by a long shot.

"You can't really like him," Grant said, finally, voice empty of all teasing. "In order to like someone, you have to have a heart."

Her eyes had widened, and her features softened, and he saw all at once that not only had he failed to find the right thing to say, he'd actually said the wrong thing. The wrongest thing. Words that could pierce through soft tissue—words that might bash and break bones.

"Leave me alone, Grant," she whispered, and she left the *Gazette*.

Rose and Jenna were within sight of the administration office when the door opened and Vice-Principal Hackenstrat came out.

"Ah, ladies," Vice-Principal Hackenstrat said, closing the door behind him. "You should be enjoying your evening at the dance."

Jenna approached him, practically shaking. "We demand to see Marty. Is he okay?"

"He's perfectly fine. Why don't you go back?" Hackenstrat said, sweeping his arms in the direction of the gym. "Now, here's the officer—"

A rent-a-cop in a polo shirt strolled down the hallway from the bridge. Hackenstrat waved at him.

"Are you arresting Marty?" Jenna's voice went up several registers.

"This isn't your business. Marty Caulfield—"

"That's not a real cop, Jenna, it's security they hired for the—"

"You can't arrest him! He did nothing!"

"He broke into a private function, which is not—"

"Sir, miss, other miss, I'm only here to have a conversation."

"He's not a criminal!"

Hackenstrat sighed and gestured for the rent-a-cop to follow him. "He may not be a criminal, Jenna, but he has a loose interpretation of the rules."

"Maybe the rules are wrong."

"That's possible, but you're not going to change them by going around breaking every one you can find." Hackenstrat nodded at them, a dismissal. "Marty will be fine. You'll see him later, off school property. Have a wonderful evening."

The VP and the security guard stood outside the administration-office doors and chatted. The guard laughed. Neither of them seemed in any hurry to go into the office and get Marty. Hackenstrat looked at Jenna and Rose significantly and tilted his head. Clearly they weren't going to go get Marty until Rose and Jenna were out of sight.

Jenna and Rose looked at each other. Jenna took a breath and seemed to settle into herself.

"Thank you for coming with me," Jenna said. "I think . . . with Marty . . . sometimes I forget where am I or how I got there, you know? It's . . . consuming."

Rose thought she did know. To feel so completely engrossed that she forgot there was a *her* at all . . . That had happened occasionally when she was working on a story. When she finally blinked awake on the other side of it, it felt like someone else had written the words. And at the same time, the best version of herself. It was disorienting.

"I understand," she said.

They started walking back to the dance, more slowly now that the urgency had left them.

"Do you miss the paper?" Jenna asked.

"No. I'm not sure I ever liked it, actually."

"Really? It sure seemed like you did."

Rose couldn't explain. Was she on the *Gazette* because she enjoyed it, or because she was good at it? Or because Grant had convinced her it was her purpose in life? Did she work hard and write and write and write because she wanted to be a reporter, or because she knew it was expected of her? How much of her only wanted to be the girl who Grant saw when he looked at her, or the eventual adult her mom so badly wanted her to be?

Jenna's parents had put pressure on Jenna to succeed, like Rose's mom had, but somehow it felt different coming from them. Rose figured it was partly cultural. Jenna's parents were born in the United States, but they'd done everything they were "supposed" to do as good first-generation Chinese children. Whatever doubts or dreams they might've had when they were younger, they had not deviated from the path that had been laid out for them. Jenna's older brother, Michael, had been the same and was now studying premed at Harvard. When Jenna came along, they had no idea what to do with her.

"Do you ever wonder what the difference is between me and Michael?" Rose asked.

Jenna snorted. "Michael's only dream in life is to one day own a boat. There are too many differences to list."

"But I mean . . . there's this person I'm expected to be. And I was going along with it. No matter what I really wanted."

"Okay, so, what *do* you really want?"

Rose shrugged. She had always known she wanted to do something big and important—"make an impact," her mother would say. But until she joined the paper freshman year, the specifics of how she was supposed to change the world had stayed hazy. She could imagine herself giving speeches and getting awards and carrying a briefcase, but she never quite knew what the speeches were about or what the briefcase held.

Rose laughed a little, pretending to be fine. "Forget about it. I'm okay, honestly. Better than okay. Great."

"You'd tell me, though, right?" Jenna asked. "If something was really wrong. Right?"

"Sure," Rose lied. "Of course."

Rose thought of sweet, handsome JB waiting for her in the gym. He wouldn't mind that she'd been gone, even though it meant that so far they'd only danced once the entire time they'd been there. He would want her to be happy, whatever that meant.

If that was even possible.

She hadn't been back to the *Gazette* room in two months. She couldn't go in if Grant was there, but maybe now that he was gone . . .

"Can we make a stop?" Rose asked. "I have something I need to pick up."

BEST FRIEND KEEPS SECRETS

Jenna Chen was not an easy person to lie to, and yet Rose had managed, over the years, to amass a significant hoard of secrets from her best friend. Five big ones, to be exact.

Their friendship hadn't always been like this. Rose used to tell Jenna everything, because the way that Jenna asked questions made it impossible for Rose to weasel out of answering. It was a skill Rose tried to cultivate in her interviewing, but Jenna came by it naturally. Nosy, a person might say. Not Rose, of course. But someone.

Rose and her mom moved to town the summer before sixth grade. On the first day of school, when Rose joined Jenna's class, Jenna sat right next to her and examined her curiously while everyone else scrambled for their seats.

"You're new," Jenna said.

"Yes," Rose said.

"I'm Jenna. What's your name?"

"Rose."

"Where did you live before?"

"The south side."

"What ethnicity are you?"

"Um. My mom's Italian. My dad's family was Cuban."

"Do you like it here?"

"I don't know," Rose said. Jenna pursed her lips at that answer and leaned back in her chair.

Rose couldn't imagine asking Jenna what her ethnicity was— she almost never brought up race. Rose had very little contact with the Cuban side of her family, so sometimes she felt like other kids of color expected something from her that she had no idea how to give. Besides, she couldn't even dredge up the courage to ask where Jenna lived or if she liked it here, let alone anything more personal. She resigned herself to never speaking to this girl ever again, and turned to face the front of the class.

As soon as the teacher's back was turned, Jenna leaned over the aisle.

"Is your dad dead?"

Rose looked at her, alarmed.

"I'm sorry if he is, but I was wondering because you said his family *was*, not that he *is*."

"He's alive. He doesn't live with us."

Jenna nodded as if that answer satisfied her, and Rose continued to try to listen to the teacher. She kept expecting Jenna to interrupt her again, but she didn't, which was almost more distracting than if she'd talked the whole time.

When the bell rang for lunch, Jenna started up again as if they'd been talking nonstop the entire time.

"My parents are together, but that's only because it would never occur to them to get divorced. How old were you when your parents split up?"

"They were never married."

Jenna's eyes lit up. "That's awesome. I bet you're the only kid in school with a random deadbeat dad."

"He's not a deadbeat," Rose said, although she hadn't seen him since she was a toddler and that probably fulfilled the technical definition of deadbeat. "My mom didn't need him."

Jenna sat down at a round lunch table and expected Rose to sit next to her. "Everyone in this school is the worst," she declared. "You probably shouldn't have moved here."

"My mom thought the schools were better."

Jenna snorted. "They're only good if you're some sort of homework robot."

Rose thought of her neatly organized desk, her collection of Post-it notes, and her carefully highlighted day planner. "That's kinda what I am," she said.

Jenna shrugged. "Well, I sort of am, too. Not by choice, but still. We should probably be friends, otherwise you'll end up friends with the rest of them and hate them and yourself. Trust me on this."

The two of them started spending hours in the library laughing at each other's stupid jokes, reading each other the best scenes from their favorite books, plotting ways to appall and outrage Jenna's parents, and generally being antisocial weirdos together. They drew matching tattoos with a Sharpie on their inner wrists: a girl with knives for hands, glaring out at the world.

They told each other everything. Rose told Jenna every time her mom snapped at her, the first day she got her period, and when Ashley Albertson said she should cut her long hair or lose weight because "both at the same time makes you look even bigger than you are." Jenna told Rose about her parents' obvious preference for her older and less obstinate brother, whatever girl or guy she had a crush on, and the time that her uncle's work friend tried to kiss her in her garage during a family barbecue.

Then high school started. Rose joined the paper. She got better at asking people questions. And things between Rose and Jenna changed, little by little.

When it came to Grant, Rose still answered Jenna's questions with the truth—but only part of it.

"Do you like him?" Jenna asked after meeting Grant freshman year.

"He's on the paper with me," Rose said, as if that explained anything.

She didn't want her friendship with Grant to get turned into something silly, like a crush she'd have on some guy who sat next to her in English, passing notes back and forth and waiting for a sign that he liked her. The things she thought about Grant were much more complicated, so she didn't explain. Secret number one.

With sophomore year came secret number two: she never told Jenna about going to talk to her dad. There hadn't been any point. It was over and done, immediately in the past.

Junior year and secret three: the incident with Fisher. Rose didn't mention it, and since Jenna didn't know to ask, Rose didn't have to lie to her face.

Secret four, kissing Grant, was different from the thing with Fisher or finding her dad. It had been exciting. She liked remembering bits and pieces of it—holding his hand, the look in his eye right before he leaned in, as if he was really seeing her and not spinning ten different schemes through the back of her head, her head on his chest as she fell asleep.

But it hadn't been perfect, because Grant was still dating Mer, and then Grant didn't break up with Mer, and so the memory went from one that Rose treasured to something she felt a little queasy recalling. She had made a mistake. No need to increase the embarrassment and self-pity and tell Jenna about it. Secret number four.

Secret five was rejecting Northwestern, and at that point, she really didn't have a good reason for not telling Jenna the truth, but by then she'd gotten into the habit of not talking about certain things, and besides, she didn't tell anyone about getting into Northwestern, so it wasn't like she was singling out Jenna for exclusion.

Telling anyone about the things that made her cringe—the

regrets, the mistakes—wouldn't ease any psychic burdens. It would only make her feel worse.

She didn't think about those things, and they had no effect on her day-to-day life. So it wasn't even fair to call them secrets, really. Looking at it that way, she didn't keep any secrets from Jenna at all.

"Hi, Grant."

At the sound of the voice, Grant felt himself wither. He took a deep breath before turning, but he couldn't summon a proper breezy nod. "Hi, Mer."

Mer Montez stood in front of him, statuesque and sparkling in a purple dress. "You look nice," she said. "I like the cummerbund."

"No, you look nice. I was going to say—you interrupted me, but yeah, I was going to say that you look nice, that was my first thought."

Mer smiled sadly. "Who are you here with?"

"Um. No one." Mer's smile got even sadder. Grant's cheeks flushed. Mer had broken up with him—so why did he feel like the one who'd been the jerk? "How's Fisher?"

"He's good." She nodded over to where Fisher Louis, her

boyfriend, the one she'd dumped Grant for, had gathered a group of swimmers and assorted jocks to listen to one of his stories and laugh at the appropriate places.

"Really? I thought I saw you fighting before."

Mer tilted her head. "Oh? Maybe we were talking loudly. It's hard to hear, you know, with the music. . . ."

Grant couldn't interrogate Mer. She'd never admit there was anything wrong between her and Fisher anyway. Not to him. "Sure," he said.

"We were in the limo with Rose and JB. I didn't know they were a thing."

"Uh-huh," Grant said.

"You know, I always thought you and Rose would end up together."

"Oh, hmmmm," Grant said.

"It seemed kind of obvious, actually."

"Aaaaaaah?"

"But if it didn't happen, I guess I was wrong to be jealous of her." Mer laughed lightly, as if it were frankly ridiculous that anyone like her would ever be jealous of any other girl in the world.

"Ha," Grant said, then attempted to find an actual word to follow it and failed. He didn't understand how it could be so difficult to have a conversation with Mer, when at one point he'd talked to her for hours a day. He couldn't recall any of those conversations in any sort of detail. Even if he'd been taking notes and recording them, he doubted he'd be able to come up with a single shared anecdote. How could a year of his life, all those hours and hours, simply vanish?

He was spared from having to come up with anything else by the senior class president tapping on a pineapple-shaped microphone. She stood next to the DJ's table clutching the mic in one hand and an envelope in the other.

"It's time to announce prom king and queen," she said, and the room broke out into applause. "On behalf of the senior class, I'd like to congratulate our new prom king, Fisher Louis!"

More clapping from the audience. Fisher jumped up onstage, skipping the stairs. He threw his long arms into the air and hooted. Grant turned to say something to Mer, but she wasn't looking at him—she was watching Fisher, biting her ruby lipstick in worry.

"And congratulations to your prom queen, Mercedes Montez!"

Mer's frown disappeared and she glided toward the stage as the crowd cheered. Grant joined in. Mer deserved this honor (if that's what it was). She was a genuinely kind person who had always seen the best in him. He wanted her to be happy, and he was relieved that she had realized Fisher could make her happy much better than he could.

At first Grant couldn't hear the alarm over the cheering. Then, once Mer had reached the stage and accepted her crown, and the clapping started to die down, he couldn't believe that it was real. Grant became suddenly aware of the pounding of his heart in his fingertips. He didn't move.

As the silence spread, everyone stood in clumps staring up at the speakers above the gym doors. The class president let the mic and the envelope drop to the floor.

"Lockdown procedure in effect. I repeat, lockdown procedure in effect."

Vice-Principal Hackenstrat's voice came in over the loudspeaker. He had a hitch in his breath but was otherwise calm.

The chaperones went to the doors and locked them. The noise of bolts slamming into place echoed through the suddenly silent gym. Grant swallowed hard. No one was moving—no stampede or crush. Where would they go? This was a lockdown.

The class president ran off the stage. Someone came up and whispered to the DJ, and he turned off his rotating colorful lights.

Grant noted it all, filing each detail away.

When the silence was complete, the entire gymful of students seemed to take a breath. A lockdown procedure could mean many things. All through high school, they'd had regular drills—but they wouldn't have a drill during prom. So whatever it was, it was real.

They'd seen the news. They knew what was most common, the danger that was always out there. All too common, all too frequent. Grant, queasy, tried to think of another explanation, but there was only one that made sense. He knew it in his bones.

There had to be someone in the building with a gun, trying to kill them.

THREE

Rose and Jenna held each other's hands.

"Holy shit holy shit," Jenna said, an incantation.

The emergency light flashed over their heads. The gym was still around the corner and all the way down the hall; the administration office was the same distance away in the other direction. They were surrounded by empty classrooms and cavernous hallways that suddenly seemed ominous instead of peaceful. Any second someone could appear from the dark, materializing like a bad dream.

"Here," Rose said, and pulled Jenna into the closest open classroom. It was a lab, with rows of high tables and stools, across the hall from the *Gazette*. Rose let go of Jenna to close the door behind them. She locked it and then attempted to wedge a stool underneath the handle. The stool kept falling over, and eventually Jenna grabbed Rose's arm and pulled her away from the door.

They ran to the back of the classroom and ducked behind the bench.

"Holy shit holy shit holy shit," Jenna repeated.

"It couldn't be a drill—"

"Not during prom, oh shit oh shit."

"It has to be—"

"Yeah. Has to be."

Jenna held Rose's arm so hard her nails bit into the skin, but Rose barely felt it. "It's okay. No one knows we're here."

"No one knows we're here!" Jenna whisper-shouted.

"If someone's out there, they won't go through every empty classroom. We're fine. It's probably a false alarm anyway."

Jenna turned to her, wild-eyed. "Probably?"

Rose couldn't reply. There had never been a false-alarm lockdown before. They always scheduled the drills a month in advance, and sent home letters saying it would happen on such and such a date. They never happened otherwise.

This was real. Something had happened.

God, had Hackenstrat been right all along? They were vulnerable. They should have been more vigilant. More prepared.

"It's okay," Rose said. "Everything's going to be okay."

"You don't know that." Jenna let go of Rose's arm so she could squeeze her hand. "Everyone dancing—Rose, what if someone's in the gym?"

Rose thought of Grant and JB and Nick and everyone else she'd been in school with forever. They were all there. Down the hall, but very far away.

There could be someone out there taking aim at people she loved. People she loved could already be dead.

Rose could feel all the bones in Jenna's hand. "We're here. We'll—oh!"

Her phone made the text noise. She let go of Jenna and hurried to turn it silent. The text was from Grant.

Where are you?

And then one appeared from JB.

Are you okay?

JB first, for asking how she was: Fine. We're in a classroom. What's going on?

And then Grant, because if anyone knew, he would: In a lab. What's happening?

Jenna had gotten out her phone and was texting furiously.

"Anything?" Rose asked.

Jenna shook her head. "Marty's phone is always dead. He probably didn't even bring it."

Rose opened Twitter, then Snapchat and Facebook and Instagram. Nothing except more questions, more panic.

Grant's reply came first: No one knows. Doors are barred. They're taking roll.

Rose didn't answer and kept searching. She heard sirens outside; the police were automatically called during lockdowns.

JB texted back: Everyone's okay here. They stopped the music and we're sitting in the dark. Stay safe.

Stay safe. She hadn't even asked how he was. She was as bad as Grant.

You stay safe too—

Delete.

I'm glad you're okay—

Delete.

Please tell me if anything—

Delete.

Rose texted her mom, one quick one to say she was fine and let her know what was happening, and then a longer one. More personal. She didn't say "if I don't get out of here" but her mom wasn't stupid; she would see it between the words. She had to send something, though.

She couldn't do nothing and wait for something to happen to her.

Grant held his phone tightly, with both hands, close to his chest.

Rosie had texted. She was with Jenna.

Nick had texted. He and Ollie had sneaked into the library for some privacy, and as far as they could tell, they were the only ones there.

He told his mom and dad and stepmom that he was okay.

The phone buzzed with messages but Grant let it buzz. Everyone left in the gym gathered in tense little clusters along the walls, whispering and typing on their phones. Grant mindlessly followed the person next to him, and he ended up standing in a group near JB. Of course Mer was there with Fisher Louis, who stuck out in his purple tuxedo and bleached hair. Mer hugged JB, then Grant. It wasn't even that awkward.

Everyone had decided, without any discussion, that the lockdown was due to a kid with a gun. They had no actual facts to go on—maybe it wasn't, a hopeful voice in the back of Grant's head insisted, maybe this was all for nothing, a false alarm—but in the absence of information, the worst-case scenario took over.

They were in danger. Something awful had happened.

Grant couldn't look at his phone. He stared blankly at the dark gym, the other students, dark shapes in the darkness, murmuring to each other.

"I hope they kill the motherfucker," Fisher Louis said.

Grant didn't say anything, but he knew—because he knew these types of things, because he read the news, because he wanted to see how events like this were covered—he knew that they most likely *would* kill the motherfucker. The gunman almost always died. (And he was almost always a man. A boy.) A person who would do this had already accepted and embraced death. He wanted to go out in a hail of bullets, and the cops obliged. When he didn't die, like the asshole who shot up a movie theater in Colorado, nothing became any clearer. The idea of justice for someone who could do something like that . . .

(Goddammit, Grant. *Events like this. A person who would do this.* He had read about these tragedies for the *coverage*, to watch reporters and news outlets doing their jobs. Whether to name the killer, how deep to get into his personal history. How to talk about the victims, when to quote the police or homeland security. All things that felt extraordinarily and almost offensively unimportant while he was in the school where the *event* was happening. Everything he'd ever done had been playing pretend. That was all he knew.)

"Hey, man," JB said, putting a hand on his shoulder. "You okay?"

"Yeah, I—I'm fine." Grant looked around the gym, which a few minutes earlier had been lit up with flashing lights. At his classmates, who had been bright and dancing. Mer was hugging her chest, flinching as Fisher described what he would do to the gunman.

Grant saw the DJ sitting on the edge of the stage in his Hawaiian shirts, holding an inflatable pineapple. Strange—or, he supposed, not really strange at all—how something could lose all humor when any of them could die at any moment. Hell, Pineapple DJ could've had a heart attack and died while spinning—death was only a light step away for everyone. Grant had been too hard on him, even without the wakeup call of the sudden lockdown.

"I'm sorry," he said.

JB looked at him. "Sorry?"

"Before. I wasn't really thinking of you as a person, but as a construct keeping Rosie from me. But you've been a person the entire time. A good person. A better person than me, for sure."

"Um. Thanks, I guess."

Grant nodded, but he didn't feel any better. He'd been chickenshit before, he knew that, but that was nothing compared to now. Now he was fucking terrified.

CONFUSED JUNIOR OPTS FOR STATUS QUO

The morning after Grant and Rose had kissed for the first and only time, exactly one year ago, Rose had opened her eyes and smiled at Grant. He thought about leaning his head down and kissing her again, his morning breath be damned, but then her eyes widened and she scrambled away from him, to the other side of the back seat of Rose's mother's Subaru.

"Shit! What time is it?" Rose asked.

"Six, I think?"

"My mom's going to kill me."

Grant smiled and scooted closer to her. "But it's the closing. She knows it goes late. She's never had a problem with it before."

Rose looked at him and flushed. "Oh. Yeah. Right."

Grant wanted to pick up her hand, but she pulled both of them into her lap and cleared her throat. Embarrassed? But why would she . . . Because of her mom, maybe?

"I think I get it," Grant said. "Are you worried your mom will be able to tell you weren't working all night? That something else happened?"

"I'm not worried," Rose said.

"Well, good thing, Rosie—" He leaned toward her, and she opened her door and moved into the driver's seat.

Grant took a second to sit up straight and tell himself not to be disappointed. Then he climbed over the middle into the passenger seat.

"You want to get some breakfast?" she asked, and he nodded. She drove them to the diner, talking about their plans for the upcoming issue nonstop.

He was a little confused but mostly relieved that they were talking normally. Something was off, but it could've been worse. The fact that they were the same human beings they had been before made him feel like the entire world made sense. He'd been so relieved, he chose to coast on that feeling for a while.

He chose not to think about Mer.

Neither of them said anything about it—the kiss, Mer, what it all meant—the whole breakfast. They had plenty of other things to talk about; they could always talk about *something*. They didn't say anything on the drive home. They didn't say anything Saturday night.

It wasn't only that Grant didn't say anything; every time he tried to even think about it, his brain zipped from one overwhelmingly strong feeling to another equally strong but diametrically opposed feeling. Elation, relief, want—zip—guilt, doubt, confusion—zip—regret—zip—hope—zip—panic—zip—satisfaction—zip—zip—zip—

Anything that would've come out of his mouth would've been a horrible unfiltered mess. He wasn't used to being unable to get a handle on what he wanted to say—especially to Rosie. That added another confusing ingredient to the unappetizing stew of his emotions: anger, that the one person who could reliably understand him had been taken away from him, via his own actions.

Then it was Sunday, and Nick and Oliver wanted to go to a movie to celebrate the fact that they didn't have school on Monday, but Grant had a date with Mer. So he had to think about her. He had to think about what had happened with Rosie, and what he was going to do about it. He sat across from Mer at the ice-cream place and looked straight into her dark-brown eyes and thought.

He thought: *I have to break up with Mer.*

He thought: *I can't.*

He thought: *I don't even know if Rose wants to be with me or if she regrets the whole thing.*

He thought: *Or maybe she wants someone like Taj, to hang out with sometimes.*

He thought: *Mer does not deserve this.*

He thought: *And what do I say, exactly?*

He thought: *This is too hard.*

He thought: *Maybe that means I made a mistake.*

He thought: *I wouldn't be thinking about any of this if what happened with Rosie never happened.*

He thought: *If it was a mistake, I don't have to tell Mer anything, because it won't happen again.*

He thought: *I'm glad that's settled.*

"This is the best mint chocolate chip I've ever eaten," he said, and Mer said, "If you say so," and the moment was over.

Grant didn't make the conscious decision not to talk to Rosie about the kiss. It just sort of happened, as a result of not saying anything to Mer.

They started their summer jobs (his filing papers at his dad's office, Rose's at a writing tutoring company), and Mer went to her summer service program in South America, and Grant and Rose met up for dinner almost every day, and neither of them said anything about it.

Two weeks after, when Grant and Rose were in her mother's car on their way to the pool on one of their mutual days off, Rose looked like she was going to say something. She had a furrow between her eyebrows and stopped at a stop sign for much longer than it would take to check the traffic. Grant could see the subject like a cloud, stormy and sparking with stored-up lightning.

"Grant," she said.

"Rosie," he said.

And then she didn't say anything else. The cloud hovered between them. With every breath, he felt like he was accidentally inhaling it, this radioactive substance chewing up his guts. He pressed his back against the door of the car. Maybe he could make a smooth exit by opening the door and rolling away into some shrubbery, and she'd forget about him and drive away.

"Are you still with Mer?" she asked.

He exhaled as much of the poison as he could. "Yes," he said with his remaining puff of breath.

She considered that answer, examining him. The whole thing would've been less painful if they hadn't been going to the pool, because then she wouldn't have been wearing a red polka-dot bikini under a white tank dress, which is basically wearing underwear out in public. But he couldn't exactly ask her to go home and change so that he'd be able to answer her actually very simple question more thoroughly, and in a manner satisfying to both parties.

Instead he'd said yes. No explanation. No apology. No follow-up questions.

Rose took her foot off the brake and drove the rest of the way to the pool in silence.

There was nothing to do in the gym during a lockdown, when people might be dead and you might be next, but relive your stupidest moments.

Since that time in the car on the way to the pool, Grant had thought of a thousand better things to say than yes. *Are you still with Mer?* "For now, but I would like to kiss you again." "I broke up with her immediately, because I am not a cad." "I am an idiot made of garbage brains for dating her at all and never kissing you before." "I am free and clear and available for kissing, if you should care to return to such activity, and if you would not, I would appreciate it if you never say a single word about this ever again."

He knew he could've made the moment reappear anytime over the past year by *simply fucking saying something at literally any time,* but there had been the *Gazette,* and he was the editor in chief and she was the news editor. And they were best friends besides, and everyone seemed happy—so it didn't seem necessary to rock the boat, potentially overturning it entirely.

Then a year later she'd quit and gone silent and he couldn't say anything to her, not when she was so mad at him for no discernible reason. He had to get things back the way they were first, and then he could think about rewriting that embarrassing scene.

And now she was out in the school during a lockdown, and he was stuck in the gym and he couldn't talk to her, even if he managed not to be chickenshit and she miraculously stopped being mad.

He left Fisher and JB and Mer and paced around the gym, cycling between listening to the panicked whispers of his classmates and worrying and replaying the moment in the car. *Are you still with Mer?* "No." *Do you want to be with me?* "Yes, if I ever see you again."

Oh, that's dark, Grant. Too dark. Too real.

He had to snap out of this.

He had to do *something*.

He couldn't stay in shock forever.

Something terrible had happened, yes. Probably. Everyone had jumped to the conclusion that it was the worst of the worst, a school shooting like they'd all heard of for years, because what else could it be?

But they didn't know anything for sure. What had happened? Not the fear and panic and confusion, but the facts. Somewhere out there someone had to know the truth, and if Grant could find out who that was, he could tell everyone else, and knowing what had actually happened couldn't be any worse than imagining their own conspiracy theories.

He had a million questions, once he stopped panicking and allowed himself to think of them. Where was the gunman? How had he gotten in? Who was it? Why was he doing it? Had anyone been hurt? What were the police going to do to stop him?

Grant was in a unique position to answer these questions. And it was his responsibility to share what he learned with the world.

He didn't have to stand here and wait for every horrible thing he'd ever thought or done to catch up to him. He couldn't stop what was going to happen, but he wasn't helpless: he could use everything he'd ever learned or practiced or imagined to find answers people needed.

Rose had been right about him and prom. He didn't belong here: the cheesy dancing, the hullabaloo over photos, the pre-baked high-flying emotion in every second. It had been stupid to try to fit in. He'd always known that high school stuff was a waste of time—it didn't need to add motherfuckers with guns to be deadly.

He needed to get to the *Gazette* room and do what he was best at instead.

Rose scrolled and scrolled and scrolled, but she couldn't find what she was looking for.

There was no explanation of what happened. No police bulletin explaining that there had been a disturbance. No reassuring lines of text telling her the who, what, where, and why.

Why didn't anyone know? Why weren't they being told?

It wouldn't be so bad waiting in an empty classroom if she knew what they were up against. At least she had Jenna.

"Jenna?" she whispered, but Jenna shook her head. Jenna's breathing came out jerky, as if she'd forget how to exhale until the last possible moment. "Marty's probably hiding, like we are."

"You don't know that." Jenna put her head in her hands. "Please don't lie to me."

Any words of comfort would be lies, so Rose bit her lip and went back to her scrolling.

It felt like only seconds had passed, but soon people out-side the school picked up on the lockdown on Twitter. Lots of fear, but even less information—more wild theories. Someone had found a pipe bomb. A hated gym teacher had brought in an AK-47. A gas leak had killed two seniors hooking up in the cafeteria kitchen.

Rose checked her favorite local reporter's feed—Frances Haddad from the Chicago *Sentinel Journal*—but her latest tweet was from the mayor's press conference that afternoon. Rose tweeted at her, asking if she'd heard about the lockdown at Hawks High's prom, and if she could find anything out.

She opened up the texts with Grant. Who do you think it is?

His answer came right away. No idea. The only people I can rule out are here in the gym with me.

There was a pause. Rose could see that Grant was still typing, and waited for his text to come through.

Bigger question: If he's not in here, where is he?

Rose reached for Jenna's hand again, and they held on tight.

Rose was listening so intently, Jenna's breathing felt as loud as the DJ's speakers on full blast. If someone started walking down the hallway, Rose needed to know about it. She needed to know how this had happened, who was responsible, and what he might do next. Not that there was anything she could do if a maniac crashed down their door. But she needed to know, so it wouldn't take her by surprise.

Grant walked the perimeter of the gym, checking out each of the exits. There were two to the parking lot, one to the locker and equipment rooms, and one that led back into the rest of the school. He'd sneaked out of the exit into the school earlier in the evening, but there were four chaperones congregated around it now, eyeing it nervously. He'd never get past them.

Grant looked up on the stage, where the DJ sat with his pineapples. He had an idea.

Grant strolled up to the DJ. "Hey, man," he said.

The DJ, robbed by the crisis of his verbal enthusiasm, merely nodded.

"This sucks," Grant said, attempting to find common ground.

The DJ nodded. Grant hopped up onto the stage and leaned over the DJ's folding table. "What sort of board you got there?

Oh, a MacBook? Cool, cool. I use one of those myself. Can't beat the speed, right?"

The DJ briefly roused himself from his sulk. "You spin?"

"Uh, no. I meant I use one for writing."

The DJ sank back into himself.

"I write for the school paper," Grant said. "The *Hawks High Gazette*."

The DJ frowned. "They still do that?"

"What, the paper? Oh sure. I mean, it's not the major journalistic event it used to be, but it's a going concern."

"Huh."

"Yeah, I write for the paper. So I was thinking of doing a story on the behind-the-scenes stuff. You know, the lives of the people who make the prom such a magical place."

The DJ looked around. "Magical?"

"Well, you know. Usually."

The DJ grunted.

"If you don't mind, I'm going to get a sense of what the festivities look from your perspective, way up here."

The DJ rested his head on the top of his laptop and closed his eyes.

Grant walked around the table and pretended to gaze out on the party. "Hmmm," he said for effect, but the DJ completely ignored him. Grant kept backing up—slowly, slowly—toward the glowing red exit sign at the back of the stage. This was the door through which Vice-Principal Hackenstrat and Marty Caulfield had made their exit, and it was the only door without a group of kids or a teacher around it.

Grant continued nodding thoughtfully, occasionally framing the view with his hands in the shape of a rectangle, and creeping ever closer to the door.

It occurred to him that if he opened that door, he could be letting someone *in* as well as letting himself out.

When he reached it, he leaned for a moment against it as if he were resting. The stage was pitch-black except for the exit sign. Out in the gym, little flashes of light from the keychain flashlights popped up like fireflies, but he doubted anyone could see him way up on the stage.

He leaned his weight into the door.

A crack of light—mostly dark, but a different shade of dark—spilled through the door.

He would have to make a run for it.

Grant took a deep breath and leaned more of his weight out the door.

Someone grabbed his arm, making him stumble back into the gym. The door clicked shut, and whoever had grabbed him turned the emergency lock.

"Nice try," Ms. Davis said. "No one's running out to their death on my watch. Not even you."

"Oh, Ms. Davis. I didn't know you cared."

Ms. Davis dragged him back to the gym floor. "Stay," she said, and by then he had recovered himself enough to smile. "As you wish," he said.

He waited until she disappeared into the dark, and then he got out his phone.

Only 25% battery left. Shit.

He would have to make the next few minutes count.

Can you get to the Gazette room?

Rose stared at the text for a few seconds.

They weren't safe. They didn't even know what was happening. And he wanted her to go to the *Gazette room*?

She let go of Jenna's hand in order to type a response.

Are you out of your mind?

If we're lucky the new kids left us logged in to
the site. You could post a story online without
waiting to get Hack's approval or the password
from Nick. On-the-spot news!

IF WE'RE LUCKY?

You didn't say where you were exactly. Maybe the
Gazette's right down the hall.

It was right across the hall, actually, but that wasn't the point.

You want me to WALK INTO MY POSSIBLE DEATH
so I can WRITE ABOUT IT FOR YOUR PAPER?
Well, obviously not.

Rose leaned against the wall. Jenna stared at her phone, though she hadn't typed anything in minutes. It was unnerving to realize that time was passing, minutes ticking by like always, and yet nothing was happening. Rose felt stuck in that first moment of hearing the alarm and not knowing what to do. *Holy shit holy shit holy shit.*

"What was that?" Jenna whispered.

Footsteps slapped on the linoleum floor. Rose started shivering and couldn't stop. They strained their ears toward the noise—a door opened and closed somewhere nearby, and they jumped.

"It's okay," Rose said. "It was probably someone else who sneaked out. Like us."

Jenna grimaced at Rose, looking right through her.

Rose was sick of her own reassurances. The air felt charged; Jenna's breathing sped up and Rose's matched it.

This is what adrenaline does, a part of her mind told her. *You could probably lift a car right now if you needed to.*

It wasn't a comforting thought.

She looked down at her phone because if she looked at her phone her hands stopped shaking. There were lots of scared tweets, some hysterical snapchats from Mairead Callahan about her supposed stalker finally making his move, but no new texts. Frances Haddad had asked her a few follow-up questions and was posting the scant updates from the police.

Grant had backed down from his request, but Rose knew he hadn't changed his mind. He was gathering his resources and strategizing. He'd be back, to chip away at what she knew was safe and right, until she convinced herself that whatever he wanted to do was what she wanted to do after all. That was what he did. He'd done it every closing of the paper, and he'd do it now.

She only had to wait another couple of seconds, and there it was: a text from Grant. Because he'd never let it go that easily.

> It's just, I talked to Ms. Davis who's in charge here, and she says no one's been hurt. Which checks out with what the local news is saying. Whatever's happening, whoever it is out there, you wouldn't be walking into a hailstorm of bullets.

She wouldn't be taking a walk down a country lane, either.

> The local news has started to pick it up, but wouldn't it be great if they could link to a story from someone who's there? And not a bunch of tearful snapchats but something someone's actually written? Someone with talent?

The local news. He wanted to use this lockdown—the threat of violence in their halls, from one of their classmates—to get attention for the *Gazette*.

(She'd tweeted at Frances Haddad and was quoted in Frances's breaking news reports. Frances kept asking her things, like she was an authority. A source. She'd asked for this—so was she as bad as Grant?)

Write it yourself, she wrote.

You know Nick's the only one with the site
password.

She did know. When Grant, as editor in chief, had been given the password to post and make changes to the *Gazette's* website, he had immediately started posting whatever he wanted whenever he felt like it without permission. Hackenstrat might not have even noticed—he wasn't exactly a hands-on adviser— but Grant also made constant changes to stories that had already been published, without getting them checked out by Nick for grammar and formatting—Nick's pet peeves. So Nick had ratted him out to Hackenstrat, and now Nick was the only one of them with the password, which he guarded jealously.

I'd ask Nick for it and try to write a story on my
phone, but Nick's not actually here.

Where did he go?

With Ollie. The library.

Her heart spasmed from fear for Nick, caught outside the gym, but at least, like her, he wasn't alone.

She typed a final and definitive "no" and was about to send it when Jenna stood up.

Rose reached for her, but she stepped away. "Jenna, get down!" she whispered.

"Marty," Jenna said.

"Marty's fine."

"I have to know—"

"Don't be *stupid*! You can't go out there!"

"I have to find him, Rose—"

"You're going to leave me here?"

Jenna hesitated. "You don't really need me. You haven't needed me for a while."

"Jenna, please—you're going to die," Rose said, and tried to lunge at Jenna without getting up from her crouch. Jenna stepped away easily and backed toward the door.

"I'm sorry, Rose."

She unlocked the door and left.

PAINT PARTY SURPRISES WITH NEW CONNECTIONS

Rose didn't know anything about the paint party except that it was called the paint party and she and Jenna were going. It was halfway through junior year, a month or two after Grant asked out Mer Montez and she shockingly said yes, and Nick and Oliver started spending every spare second of their lives together. Suddenly everyone was pairing off, fitting neatly into matched sets, all except for Rose.

She still had Jenna—she always had Jenna—but Jenna wasn't on the paper and had joined the art club instead. Jenna loved drawing and had thought that an art club would be immune to the robotic tendencies of everyone else in school, "but it's all politics and cool hair and who can be the most broody," she'd complained. (Which meant she'd fought with them over something silly and couldn't show her face for a while until they cooled off.) So Jenna had managed to meet and infiltrate the arty kids at the neighboring high school.

They were a competitive group, especially when it came to their parties. The paint party was only one example. They'd had foam parties, silent parties, dress-like-your-favorite-Supreme Court-justice parties. Jenna never seemed to enjoy herself at these events, but she kept going and brought Rose along to keep her company.

"Why do you keep doing this?" Rose had asked on the drive to the paint party. "It's exhausting."

Jenna grinned then, a big, satisfied smile. "You should've seen the look on my parents' face when I explained what a paint party was."

"You haven't explained to me," Rose complained, but Jenna only said, "You'll see," and kept driving.

Jenna's parents had moved to a new phase of disapproval, in which they tried to pretend that everything Jenna did was totally normal. Dyed her hair purple? Nodded pleasantly. Ripped holes in all her clothes? Said nothing. Quit math entirely? Barely blinked. In some ways this was preferable to grounding her and trying to persuade and cajole her into acting more like her brother, but in another, more real way, it was much worse, and it ended up making Jenna attempt bigger and bigger rebellions in order to elicit any sort of reaction from them.

It made Rose very grateful for her own mom, who had her flaws but who saw Rose clearly for who she was, and encouraged her to be the best version of that instead of some abstract idea of what she was supposed to be.

"Where are we?" Rose asked Jenna.

"The paint party. I told you already," Jenna said. Rose could hear the scowl in her voice, which was all she had to go on because they were in a windowless room with no lights. They had been instructed to wear all white and had been admitted to the black box by a pair of ticket takers in masks. Rose shuffled her feet against the plastic wrap on the floor. This seemed exactly how an organized serial killer would gather a bunch of gullible high schoolers for a massacre.

Rose pulled at her white V-neck T-shirt, which had come in a pack of five. Jenna had purchased them so the shirt was uncomfortably clingy on Rose, who had several inches in all directions on her best friend. At least with the lights out, no one could see the shirt ride up her tummy. At least they were in an entirely different school district, so no one she knew would see her at all.

Loud EDM pounded through the speakers, and someone switched on a black light. Rose could suddenly see dozens of white shirts and flashing teeth packed into a small, square room. Jenna laughed, and Rose saw her molars and the whites of her eyes glowing but couldn't tell if she was making eye contact. It was disconcerting.

All the white shirts stood around, some half-heartedly rocking their shoulders to the beat.

Then someone screamed. There was a commotion and everyone spun and ran, immediately losing track of whoever they came with.

"Jenna!" Rose called out, but she didn't get a response. People ran past Rose as if she were invisible. She pulled down the bottom edge of her shirt and wished she were home with her laptop and a movie. That couldn't possibly feel as lonely as this did.

Rose felt something hit her stomach. She put her hand on it and it was sticky and wet and smelled like nail polish.

Paint. This was paint. A paint party.

Another balloon hit her back and exploded, paint running down her neck under her shirt. Someone slipped on the plastic floor, and when another person reached down to give her a hand, he fell, too. Then everyone was running and sliding on their knees and stomachs, paint lubricating the way.

Rose tried to slide from foot to foot like she was ice skating, but she kept running into people and falling. Everyone was running into everyone else all the time, holding on to someone's arm so as not to fall, accidentally-on-purpose leaning on someone so they slid with you. Someone rubbed their hand across Rose's back and then smeared the paint on the front of her own shirt. Someone else grabbed her shoulder, missed the sleeve, and slid down her paint-slicked arm to the floor.

She spun, trying to catch a glimpse of Jenna, and walked straight into someone's chest. He was skinny and tall but he didn't topple over; he grabbed both of her shoulders so that she didn't fall, either. Even when she had steadied herself, he didn't let go.

Other than the fact that he was taller than her and had a full set of reasonably straight teeth, she could not tell what he looked like. He seemed to be staring at her, though. Out of some sort of instinct, she put her hands out and rested them on his chest. She felt him take a breath.

The music was still pounding, the paint flying. But no one touched them. He leaned down and kissed her.

She kissed him back.

Some time later the lights came on. Rose and the mystery boy broke apart. He had dark-brown eyes and thick eyelashes, the only thing Rose could see when he blinked lazily. He nodded at her. "Hey," he said.

"Hey," she said.

Everyone at the party was coated top to bottom with paint, sometimes in interesting smears but mostly mixed up into a purplish-brown goop. The boy wiped his (very cute) face, leaving a Bowie-like red stripe diagonally across his dark skin. Rose noticed two red handprints on his shirt where she'd been resting her hands. Her mind churned with possible things to say, but before she could land on one, he nodded again, said "See you," and walked away.

"Rose!" Jenna shouted, crashing into her. "Was that Taj?"

"I don't know. Who's Taj?"

"The guy you were making out with, I think."

"Oh. What's his deal?"

Jenna handed her a towel with a calculating look. "He doesn't seem like your type."

"What's my type?"

"Brainy, miniature, motormouth know-it-alls."

Well, they both knew who that described. "You can't call Grant miniature anymore. He's like a foot taller than you now."

"Oh, he'll always be miniature to me."

"So what does that make Taj? A brawny, tall, silent, idiot?"

Jenna wrapped her hair in a towel like a turban and pulled Rose to the door to pick up their shoes. "The things I hear, he's, like . . . hard to reach."

He'd left without telling Rose his name, or getting her name in return, let alone her number or any way to contact her again. That was pretty hard to reach.

But in Rose's experience, you could be chatty and always around and a motormouth know-it-all and still be hard to reach, when it came down to it. At least with someone like Taj you might get what you expect. You wouldn't get your hopes up.

Since Ms. Davis had kept such a close eye on Grant, he decided to return the favor. She seemed like the only person in the gym who knew anything, even though she didn't know much. So he followed her as she circled the gym. He followed so closely that when she turned, she ran straight into him.

"Grant!" Ms. Davis said.

"Any word on when we're going to get out of here?"

"Not since the last time you asked, two minutes ago."

"Did you finish the roll call?"

"You saw me finish it, Grant."

"So—who's missing?" Grant reached for the clipboard in Ms. Davis's hand, but she pulled it away.

"Everyone who purchased a ticket is safely accounted for."

"Including Rose and Jenna? And Nick and Oliver?"

"Everyone who purchased a ticket is safely accounted for."

"Has anyone laid eyes on Owen Pettibone? He's a classic dirtbag."

Grant made another grab for the clipboard, but Ms. Davis dodged. "Owen Pettibone is fine, Grant. Don't go accusing people without proof. That's probably against your precious journalistic ethics."

"So who's the shooter, then?" Grant asked. "If we're all safely tallied?"

"I don't know, Grant. You've been following me. You know exactly as much as I do."

Grant thought maybe he knew even more than Ms. Davis, since he had been the one to tell her where Rose and Jenna and Nick and Oliver were. But she was the one with the clipboard. How frustrating.

Ms. Davis left him to check in with a group of crying prom-goers. Grant shifted his weight from foot to foot, trying to decide where to go next.

The mood in the gym had turned from shock and fear to something less pure—Grant sensed that at least some of his classmates were enjoying the feeling of being under siege. There was Fisher, of course, fleecing everyone out of their cash at poker and still demanding the shooter's bloody body on a spike. There was Mairead Callahan snapchatting, directing a tearful mono-logue directly to her stalker, begging him to give himself up to the police. She had collected a crowd, thanks to her loud crying, and her best friend held the phone as Mairead accepted hugs from a long line of sympathizers.

Her videos would be horribly sad, if indeed there was a live shooter in the building and he made it to the gym after all, and especially if he ended up being her legendary (probably fictional) stalker, but the longer the lockdown went on, the less likely that scenario seemed to Grant. Either the safety precautions were enough and all they had to do was stay put behind the reinforced doors until it was over, or there never was a shooter to begin with.

Grant was trying to be impartial and base his impressions on the facts, but he really, really wanted there not to have been a shooter at all. He approached Ms. Davis again. She sighed when she looked up and saw him.

"Who saw this person with a gun anyway?" he asked. "You said everyone's safe. So what about the person who set off the lockdown procedure in the first place? The one who saw the threat? He or she ducked, or what?"

Ms. Davis rubbed her temple. She had been Grant's sophomore English teacher, so she was both exasperated with and resigned to Grant pretty much permanently. "I can keep saying I don't know anything, but I'm getting the sense you aren't even listening."

"Who are you getting your instructions from?" he asked Ms. Davis as she moved to the next group. "Can I talk to them?"

"Mr. Hackenstrat is in communication with police. The police will let us know when it's safe to leave."

"So can I talk to Hackenstrat?"

"He's busy, Grant."

"With what? Isn't he trapped somewhere, like the rest of us?" Ms. Davis attempted to walk away faster, but Grant stayed at her elbow. "Why isn't he here, anyway? Oh—he took Marty to the office. So he's in the office still?"

Ms. Davis sighed for what felt like the hundredth time.

"Wait—is Hackenstrat the one who saw the shooter? Did he call the lockdown?"

"I don't know."

Grant slowed down, letting Ms. Davis get a couple of steps ahead of him.

"Marty—Marty Caulfield. He didn't have a ticket. You said everyone with a ticket was accounted for and safe. What about Marty?"

As soon as the classroom door shut behind Jenna, Rose scrambled to it in a crouch, locked it, and then went back to her corner. She huddled over her phone, trying to block the screen's light.

She had more messages from Frances Haddad. There were SWAT teams around the school. The police chief said he was in touch with an administrator in the building, who'd said only that there was a single person—a student—with a gun, somewhere in the building.

She couldn't believe Jenna had left her here alone. And that meant Jenna was alone, too, at least until she found her precious Marty.

Rose wondered if Jenna thought Rose's thing with Grant was as inexplicable as Rose found Jenna's thing with Marty.

Would Rose leave the safety of this room if she thought Grant was in danger? Not now, of course. But back when she was in the thick of it with him? Junior year, maybe. Rose scowled. She would have, wouldn't she? She'd've walked through fire if he'd asked. If she thought there'd be a story at the other end.

Would she leave the room for JB?

He'd never ask her to, so she didn't have to have an answer.

Rose turned off her phone's screen and sat in the dark, listening to the squawk of walkie-talkies and the polite brief beeps of police sirens.

So there was someone in the building with a gun. It was a large building. She hadn't heard any shots. She hadn't heard much of anything since the footsteps a few minutes ago.

Sitting alone in an empty classroom felt very different from sitting in the same empty classroom with Jenna. It wasn't her home base; it didn't feel safe at all.

And if it wasn't safe, what was she doing there?

Why stay in one place versus another, all things being equal, and all places being equally unsafe?

And if all things were equal, where did she want to be?

If she was going to face death, why not do it from a place she knew?

And then why not find a way to say something to the world before the end, while she was at it?

"Damn it, Grant," she said, and crept for the door.

"Marty Caulfield—is he okay?"

Grant felt the gym wobble, as if rearranging itself into a new reality.

Ms. Davis shook her head. "I keep telling you, I don't know—" Her cell phone rang, and she turned from Grant to answer it.

"Ask him if Marty's okay," Grant said.

Ms. Davis held up her hand. "Uh-huh. Uh-huh. Okay, thanks. Listen, I have to ask. Is Marty Caulfield—" She stopped as the voice on the other end of the line spoke at length. Her eyes snapped to Grant as her mouth dropped into an O. "I see. Thank you." She hung up and turned back to Grant.

"What? Is he hurt? What's happening?"

"The SWAT teams have entered and they're searching the building, starting on the other end. When they clear it, we should be able to go."

"But . . . what are they looking for?" Grant ran a hand through his hair, standing it on end. When she'd asked whoever was on the other end of the phone about Marty, she hadn't looked sad at the response. She'd looked shocked—and scared. "Oh," Grant said, putting it together as the words left his mouth. "They're saying Marty— No, not Marty. Really? Oh no. No no no."

Rose peered through the window in the door out at the hallway. It was empty, as far as she could tell.

She counted to one hundred.

Still empty.

She could see the *Gazette* door across the way—closed, but unlikely to be locked. Grant had been in there earlier, and he shouldn't have a copy of the keys anymore, now that he'd passed along the editor-in-chief title.

Very slowly, she turned the lock on her door. The click seemed to reverberate through the classroom, and Rose held her breath. She counted to one hundred again, breathing as silently as possible.

When nothing happened at the end of the hundred, she stood and shifted her phone to her left hand. Her hands started to shake almost immediately—the part of her head and neck that stood in full view of the door's glass pane felt exposed.

"Screw it," she said out loud, and grabbed the door handle.

She swung the door open and ran for the *Gazette* room. Her feet slipped in her fancy shoes and she gasped. Every second she spent in the hall she expected to feel the pain of a bullet in her arm or leg or stomach. At least if she got shot in the head, she figured, she wouldn't have to feel too much or have time to call herself an idiot.

She grabbed the *Gazette* room's door handle. Twisted it. Pushed.

She half fell, then spun and shoved, and finally she was in the *Gazette* room and the door was closed and locked behind her.

She rested her head on the wall, out of sight of the window in the door, and tried to calm her breathing. When she stopped gasping, she very carefully turned her back on the door and stepped into the darkened room. She didn't have to turn on the lights to know exactly where to walk to avoid bumping into any desks. She'd spent every day after school here for most of the past four years, and often during school, too, when she could find a reason to leave one of her other classes.

She breathed in. It smelled the way it always had, which was ridiculous, because it couldn't actually smell different from the rest of school—only it did. Maybe it was the paper itself, old issues stacked all along the back wall, cheap newsprint probably getting damp and decaying.

Her heartbeat slowed. The adrenaline she'd been coasting on since the alarm went off started to drain away.

Nostalgia rushed to fill its place.

She hadn't been inside the *Gazette* room in two months, and now that she was here, yes, she felt safe. She felt like nothing could possibly go wrong here, because it was a place that had gotten unstuck from time, and only existed in some strange past where she cared about the paper and this was her home.

She passed a row of computers and stood in front of Grant's desk. The editor in chief's desk.

She'd been so mad when Grant had gotten editor in chief instead of her. Hadn't they spent almost exactly the same amount of time on the paper? Hadn't they slaved away together on every aspect of every issue? What, was Grant a better *leader* because he was a *guy*? Why else would he get the role over her?

She'd actually written more articles than he had, so statistically, her contributions were greater. She'd pointed that out to Vice-Principal Hackenstrat, along with her suspicions of misogyny, and Hackenstrat had blinked at her.

"Well, that's exactly why you can't be editor in chief," he said. "Who would write all the articles if you're busy managing the staff?"

The unfairness of this had made her speechless with rage. She could still get pretty worked up about it, even though it had turned out that Grant made a pretty good editor in chief, cajoling and inspiring the younger staff members to actually turn in their work, pushing juniors and seniors to find better, more interesting stories, keeping the schedule—all without losing his good humor. Ugh.

Rose suspected that she would have been a different kind of editor in chief. A scarier one, maybe. Feared more than loved. Not that she'd ever find out now.

She'd declined the managing-editor position—traditionally an editor in chief's number two—partly because she didn't want to be Grant's lackey and partly because what she really wanted to do was keep writing as much as she could. She knew Nick would make a better managing editor anyway, with his eye for schedules and discipline and order. So she spent senior year (up until two months ago) in her second year as news editor.

It had been a wildly successful tenure. She'd proved it by winning the Midwest Regional Excellence in Journalism Award—which was where, exactly? She glanced around Grant's desk and along the windowsills and bookshelves. It was dark, but she knew the shape of the trophy, knew how it looked in the dark. It wasn't out in the open.

She was about to sit in Grant's chair and look through his file drawers when she heard a noise from the back of the room, past the rows of computers on desks, where there was a conference room table surrounded by rolling chairs. The noise was instantly familiar to Rose. It was the sound of someone in one of the chairs, standing up.

FOUR

Grant texted so hard, his thumbs started to go numb. He dropped the phone on the hard wood of the gym floor and swore.

If he broke the phone. If he had no way of reaching Rosie. If he never spoke to or saw her again—

"Grant?" Mer said, her voice soft. "Did you find out what's happening?"

Grant grabbed the phone and felt the screen for cracks. None. He looked up at Mer, but his mind was racing too fast to really see her. He had a scoop, but what the hell did it matter when Rosie was out there on her own? "Marty Caulfield," he said. "He's the guy."

"M-marty?" Mer's voice faltered. "That doesn't make sense."

Grant was already typing again. He didn't have time for Mer's commentary. He didn't have time to hold Mer's hand through the revelation. *Euuuhhhhhhgggghh, Grant, use a better metaphor than holding her hand! Remember what happened, you ass.* He had to think and wait and listen and hope and concentrate harder than he'd ever concentrated before, because Rosie was out there and he was not, and if anything happened to her or had already happened—

"Grant, listen—that doesn't make sense," Mer repeated.

"Sometimes people crack," Grant said, not looking up from his phone. Text. Send. Text. Send. "Sometimes they do things they know are a bad idea. You never really know people."

"Yeah, but—Marty?" Mer worried at the seam of her dress by her hip. "Grant, I really think you should—"

"What's up, Mer?" Fisher said, coming up to Mer and Grant. "Did you learn something?"

"Apparently it's Marty Caulfield," Mer said.

"Bullshit," Fisher said. "No way Marty—" He stopped suddenly, thinking. "That asshole. That little punk."

Grant nearly screamed. "Can you two—just—not be here right now?"

Fisher and Mer looked at Grant with pity. "We're in a lockdown, dude," Fisher said.

Grant whispered-yelled, "I know!" and then went to walk repeatedly into a wall.

Sometimes people cracked. And then sometimes they wished for a disaster to crash into them, and the universe obliged.

FLIRTING JUNIORS GO BEYOND TALK

On the night of their junior-year grad issue, Grant and Rose sat in the *Gazette* room in the dark. Out of habit, Nick had turned the overhead lights off when he left, and they were too tired to get up and flip the switch. Besides, Grant liked the way the room looked in the dark: the white glow of Rose's computer screen, the swirl of the screen savers on the other computers, the shadows climbing the walls covered with old issues of the paper and framed front pages and leftover crap from decades of people making a paper, exactly like he was doing.

Well, maybe not *exactly* like Grant did. If his so-far-limited experience of the rest of the world told him anything, it was that very few people cared as much as he did. About anything.

He changed a verb in the third paragraph of the editorial against Hackenstrat's privacy-invading security plans.

He changed it back. He stretched his arms over his head and looked over at Rose.

It struck him, as it occasionally did, how beautiful she was, with the look of intense concentration on her face. The facts of her thick brown hair and dimples and long, graceful arms were as invisible to him as the decor in the *Gazette* room. But when she was absorbed in work, he saw her fresh. Her entire being bent to a purpose—to write the article, to fix the problem, to make the world make sense, briefly.

What made her even more beautiful was that she was there for him. It had been a year and change since his mom got sick, and he had only just started to be able to think about that time without having his brain overload and shut down. So it had only recently become possible for him to appreciate that he'd had Rosie in his life this whole time. That she hadn't gotten freaked out and left him alone. That she made it possible for him to remember who he was. That she'd been beautiful the entire time, and he'd been too distracted to notice.

He must've been more tired than he thought, because he snapped to attention after who knows how long when she caught his eye.

"Where's Mer?" Rose asked.

"Prom," Grant said.

Rose's eyebrows lifted. "What?"

"Yeah, she and Henry Abragale are going as friends."

"That doesn't bother you?"

Grant shrugged. "Prom isn't really my scene. The dressing up, the weepy reminiscing, the overpriced party favors—"

"I mean, it doesn't bother you that Mer's going with someone else?"

Not much bothered him when it came to Mer. She was so easy to get along with. She agreed to any plans, she kept all her promises, she remembered everything they said to each other. Not that their conversations were all that much to remember—

Grant thought it and felt guilty immediately. Even thinking something mildly uncharitable about Mer cut like cruelty.

"Where's that guy? Taj?" he asked Rose.

"That is his name. And I have no idea." Rose frowned at her computer screen. "It's not like we're dating."

Grant didn't know what to make of that statement. He'd seen them out together. He knew she talked about him with Jenna. He'd assumed they were together. He'd assumed—but had been afraid of asking. Now he had the answer and he wished he didn't.

Grant shifted in his chair, uncomfortably conscious of something big and unavoidable bearing down on him. Whatever was about to happen would require something from him, but he didn't know what, and he didn't know if he'd be ready to part with it when it came down to the crucial moment. At the same time, he wanted to run straight into the oncoming disaster, let himself be crushed, forget about the past and the future and everything else he cared about.

"I think we're done," Grant said.

She looked up from her screen. "Really?"

"Yeah. We're not going to suddenly discover we forgot how to spell 'sophomore.' Let's send it and go to the diner. I'm starving."

Rose grinned, deepening her dimples. "Let me check one more thing—"

"No," Grant said, standing. He leaned over her shoulder and saved and exported everything he needed from her computer. He could format the files in his sleep. He set it to upload to the printer's server and pulled Rose out of her chair. "There. All done."

"Your first issue as editor in chief."

"Our first issue." He was still holding on to her wrists, but instead of dropping them, he turned over her hands and looked down at her palms. "You have pen calluses."

She closed her fists. "I like taking notes on paper."

"That's so . . . ," he said, but he didn't finish the thought. He might have said "adorable," if he hadn't chickened out.

When he started to walk to the door, he let go of one of her wrists and shifted his other hand to hold hers. It happened naturally, smoothly. She didn't break away.

They held hands all the way to Rose's mom's car.

At the passenger door, they stopped. Grant stopped because if they got into the car, he would have to let go of her hand, and he didn't think his hand would let him do that.

"Hands," Grant said.

"Cogent observation."

"I've always thought holding hands was something quaint, like in a commercial for heartburn medication."

"It isn't, though, is it?"

"No, it's not." He felt the big and unavoidable thing close by, pushing him an inch or two closer to Rose, so that they were in each other's space, so that they only had to whisper to be heard. "Did you know that you're most beautiful when you're concentrating really hard on something?"

She turned to face him, leaning her back against the car door. "What makes you say that?"

"It's true. I think we should all say true things."

"Well, then I should say I don't think you're physically repulsive," Rose said.

"I'm flattered."

"You can quote me on that. Not physically repulsive. Not at all."

He raised the hand that was holding hers to brace his arm on one side of her, and the other hand fit easily at her waist. Her free hand brushed the front of his shirt.

"You still want to go to the diner?" she asked.

"We don't always have to do the same thing we always do, Rosie."

"Whatever you say, Editor in Chief—"

He kissed her.

She kissed him back. She pushed his glasses away from his face and tangled her hands in his hair.

He smiled and kept kissing her.

Without turning away or letting go of his hand, Rose unlocked the car with her key fob and opened the back door. She ducked in backward and Grant followed, tired and giddy and relieved and happy and not ready to stop kissing her.

Eventually Rose fell asleep with her head nestled against his neck and he held her for four hours, completely wide awake himself, simply smelling her hair and feeling her breath on his chest. This was the crisis, come at last, and all he wanted was to stay forever in the moment. If he closed his eyes as tightly as possible, ignored everything else, maybe he would.

"Rose?"

"Holy shit. Marty. You scared the crap out of me."

Marty didn't say anything. Out the windows, police lights flashed. In the moments she could see Marty's face illuminated, it looked different. Older. As if some spark in him had died.

"Marty? Are you okay? Does Jenna know you're here?"

Marty shook his head and made a horrible high-pitched noise in the back of his throat. Rose's phone buzzed with many texts all arriving at once.

"Marty, you're scaring me. Are you okay?"

A police light flashed through the windows and Rose saw it.

Black. Easy to miss, but once you noticed it, impossible to look away from. Marty's hand gripped around its handle. It pulled down his arm. Pulled down the whole gravity of the room.

"It's me," Marty said. He sounded hollow. Rose wanted to take a step back but found that her feet were frozen in place. "I'm the one they're looking for. I'm the reason they ordered the lockdown."

Rosie—Marty's the shooter. I'm sorry I told you to go
to the Gazette room. You should STAY WHERE
YOU ARE and if you see Marty RUN.

DID YOU GET MY MESSAGE? MARTY CAULFIELD
HAS A GUN.

YES, THAT MARTY CAULFIELD. I KNOW. I KNOW.

ROSIE!!

Okay. It's okay. You're not responding. Fine. The
SWAT teams are clearing every classroom one
by one so they'll find him or they'll find you and
everything will be fine.

Rosie, please text back.

Rosie.

Rosie.

Rosie.

Please, Rosie.

Oh god I thought I heard something. Oh god what
was that noise?

Rosie?

Okay. Okay. Okay.

I'm going to keep texting you as if everything's fine
because if I don't I'm going to go insane and use
one of the DJ's pineapple speakers to break a
window and run to Canada.

Everything's fine. So. We're writing a story.

How to begin? What to include? I only have the one
source saying it's Marty, would prefer a second
for confirmation, even though I know it has to be
true. Doesn't look like the police have made a
statement naming him yet.

I did a bunch of background on him for the parrot
article. When this is over and we get to the
Gazette, the notes are in a folder on my laptop
marked "Norwegian Blue."

Why would Marty do this? He's generally the
embodiment of chaotic good. What does Jenna
say?

Rosie?

Hi.

Text anything back.

Maybe your phone died.

Maybe you're not getting these.

Or maybe you are and you can't answer.

I'm sorry, Rosie.

The past two months have been torture.

Rosie?

Rose took a deep breath. She told herself not to move, which was unnecessary, because she couldn't feel her legs. The only thing she could feel was her phone buzzing in her hand, but she didn't look at it. She was afraid that if she peeled her eyes away from Marty and the pistol, she would not see her death coming for her. To miss the moment of her own death to check her *phone*. No.

When she started to exhale, she realized Marty had been speaking the entire time in an urgent whisper.

"—dead! Even though I didn't do anything, I only put him back there for a little while when I went to class. Where else was I supposed to put a parrot, my locker? And that's why they're going to kill me, Rose. I promise you. I won't be able to get out of here alive."

"Don't say that," she whispered back, surprised to find herself comforting him.

"You know it's true. They'll kill me as soon as they see me."

"Not if you surrender."

Marty started laughing. A high-pitched, hysterical laugh, like something out of a Batman comic, then seemed to remember that he was supposed to be quiet and spoke in a tense falsetto. "Oh sure. You got a white flag around? No no no, I'll use this." With his free hand, he pulled the white sheet he was wearing over his head, but it got caught halfway and covered his face. Underneath, he had on a pair of oversized cargo shorts and no shirt, and he was surprisingly hairy. "Don't shoot! I'm innocent!"

When he managed to free his head from the sheet and toss it on the floor, Rose fixed Marty with a hard stare, trying to ignore the weapon and his seminaked body. "What happened, Marty?"

Marty threw up his hands and Rose flinched. He noticed. "This?" he whispered hoarsely, brandishing the gun. "This isn't mine! I found this in Hackenstrat's office."

Rose blinked. "What?"

"Yeah. Hackenstrat's *framing* me, Rose. He left the gun there for me to find, and now he's going to kill me."

"Hackenstrat framed you?" Rose repeated, trying to make sense of the words.

Marty brandished the gun awkwardly. "Well, I sure didn't bring this here myself. Come on. You know me. Would I take a gun to prom? Where would I even *get* a gun?"

Rose frowned. "What are you saying? That Hackenstrat forced this gun on you?"

"Not exactly."

"Exactly what happened, then?"

Marty put the gun on the conference table. It clanked heavily, and both Marty and Rose flinched. "I'll tell you everything. That's why I came here. You have to help me, Rose. You have to tell people it wasn't me."

She hesitated.

She knew Marty. She understood Marty—or at least she'd thought she did. Jenna certainly felt like she knew him, and Rose trusted Jenna with her life.

(Isn't that what the shocked neighbors and friends always said? "We never thought he could be capable of something like this." "He was so mild-mannered." "He seemed totally normal." So was Rose being open-minded, or a fool?)

She grabbed Grant's laptop from his desk, marched to the conference table, and sat next to Marty, pulling on his wrist to sit him down, too. "Start at the beginning. Don't leave anything out."

SURPRISING REVELATION SHIFTS RELATIONSHIP

Junior year had been both very confusing and very clarifying. Rose kept seeing Taj, the guy from the paint party, at other parties and coffee shops and plays and concerts. Eventually she managed to get her number into his phone, and he would occasionally text her. They would go out, they would make out, and then she wouldn't hear from him for three weeks.

He was most decidedly not her boyfriend. It wasn't the type of thing she needed to have a whole conversation with him over; it was obvious to anyone who paid even the tiniest amount of attention.

Her relationship with Taj, such as it was, was perfectly clear. And yet, she never knew when she'd see him again. They barely talked, so it was hard to tell if she actually liked him or vice versa. Jenna informed Rose that he had other girls like her at other schools across the Chicagoland area, and Rose didn't mind. Confusing!

Then there was Grant. He was going out with Mer, a development that no one could've predicted. Grant's mother had finished with chemo and radiation, and Grant had moved into his dad's. He seemed simultaneously more relaxed and more intensely into the *Gazette* than he'd ever been before.

"This is a key year, Rosie," he'd told her. "It's the year we'll talk about on our college apps. And all this time Hackenstrat will be deciding who's going to be editor in chief. We've got to be better than good."

No one on the *Gazette* staff other than the two of them was even in the running for editor in chief, but Rose didn't argue with him. It felt important. The whole year felt different.

One big difference—which she only really started to notice around January—was the way she looked at Grant. He'd finished his late growth spurt and gotten a better haircut, but that wasn't it, at least not entirely. A chemical change had occurred. Something in the way he smelled, or the way her skin responded to the molecules coming off his skin.

She and Grant had always flirted—it was how they communicated, their common language. But it was only words. She shouldn't say "only": words were what brought them together, words were malleable and surprising, and if they found the right combination, words would click into place like the tumblers in the lock of a safe. She meant words only, compared to words with a promise of a body to follow. Then there was the specific moment she realized this had changed, and words weren't the only thing between them.

They were working on a story about the spring play, which due to budget cuts was going to be a fully improvised modern version of *Macbeth*. The senior who was directing it was panicked that no one was going to audition and had sent Rose a dozen increasingly frantic emails overexplaining her methods and training, thematic choices, and finally a link to a series of grainy videos of famous comedians improvising at legendary Chicago improv theaters and the text "See?????"

Rose had been typing with Grant literally breathing down her neck—one arm leaning on the desk and one on the back of her chair, hunched over, glasses falling down his nose—when he'd made one too many suggestions and she pushed her chair away from the desk.

"Do it yourself," she said, and he took the seat immediately.

"It isn't that complicated. Starting with the budget cuts makes it sound like a story about money, but really it's about Allie Lang losing her grip on reality."

Rose stood behind him and watched him reordering paragraphs and combining sentences rapidly. He paused for a couple of seconds on a tricky transition, fingers tapping the keys lightly. He hummed, very faintly.

Rose didn't breathe. She was the one who usually typed. She wasn't used to standing behind him, wasn't used to being the one leaning over his shoulder. If she moved her face three inches to the right, their cheeks would be touching.

She turned her head very, very slightly and looked at his mouth. She couldn't turn any more without giving up all pretense of looking at the screen, but her eyes continued to drift up his jawline (some stubble, that was new) to the corner of his eye (laugh creases, not yet wrinkles but not far off) to his ear.

It struck her thunderously. She wanted to lick Grant's ear.

She wanted to lick his ear *right now*, as strongly as she'd ever wanted to do anything in her life. She had never wanted to lick the body part of another human before. She didn't even know if that was something either one of them would enjoy.

Ear licking. Where did it come from? Had she seen it in a movie once? No. This was a thought that had sprung fully formed into her head. A strong desire. *Desire.* She thought she might understand what that word meant now.

She couldn't move. She wasn't sure she wanted to.

It took her a couple of seconds before she realized Grant had stopped humming, and his hands had ceased moving on the keyboard. She pulled her gaze from his ear to his eyes.

He had turned and was looking right at her. Unmoving. The smile lines in the corners of his eyes were gone, because he looked, for once, completely serious.

Rose didn't know what to do with her hands. Or her eyes, or her head, or especially her mouth.

Now that she'd had the ear-licking thought, everything felt different. Not only Grant, who had turned into this lickable person, but herself, who had become someone who might, one day, lick someone.

She wondered if he could see the thought on her face. She knew she would have to wait for him to say something because the only topics circling her mind were mouth- and tongue- and skin- and ear-based.

"Bad luck," he said, and they both snapped back a couple of inches. "Bad luck. 'Macbeth.' In a theater."

"Right," Rose said.

"It's supposed to be bad luck to say 'Macbeth' in a theater," Grant repeated. "So how do theater people do the play at all?"

"Right," Rose said again.

"Sorry, Rosie," he said, standing. "I've been hogging the controls. You work your magic."

"Right," she said a third time.

He went to get his laptop to research theater superstitions, and she took her seat again, still warm from Grant. She shook her head. She shook out her hands. She reread the words she and Grant had written, and she got to work.

Rose typed on Grant's laptop furiously as Marty spoke. She took down every word, and her mind raced. She tried to think only of Marty and his story but instead thought of everything all at once, including things she hadn't let herself think about in weeks.

After Rose and Grant kissed, back at the end of junior year, she thought she understood what was going to happen. Grant would break up with Mer. She wouldn't text Taj again—not that she'd been planning to, actually. She and Grant would continue to make out on a regular basis, probably have sex. (She hadn't with Taj, not for any particular reason, and she kind of wished she'd gone for it, because she bet Grant had with Mer and she would've preferred starting out with him on an equal footing.) She'd make an amazing paper that would win dozens of MREJs, go to Northwestern, and so on, and so forth, forever.

None of that happened. She wasn't sure why. But the gap

between what she expected and what had actually come to pass allowed a bunch of other unwanted feelings to creep in: doubt and jealousy and resentment. Eventually, enough of those uncomfortable feelings piled up that they were all she could feel, and she forgot what it was she liked about writing a story: putting the facts in order, finding the space and structure for the words to tell their story.

This story, though—Marty's story—was too good. Everything she'd ever liked about being a reporter came flooding back. Pow.

Rose held her hands over the keyboard, listening.

"Shhhhh," she whispered, interrupting Marty. He cocked his head—he'd heard something, too. Coming from the hallway.

A few voices? Footsteps? Neither of them breathed, waiting for the sound to come back.

There—she could definitely hear footsteps running through the hallway outside, and doors opening and closing. "Shhhhh," she whispered again, though she didn't know why. Marty wasn't moving or making a single noise.

The footsteps were coming from the classroom next door. Rose looked at Marty Caulfield, shirtless, sheet in his hands, gun on the table between them; Marty, her oldest friend's greatest love. She made a split-second decision.

She stood and grabbed his hairy arm. "Do exactly what I say. Yes?"

Marty nodded. The footsteps came to the door. Someone tried the handle. Locked—for now.

This was probably a mistake. But she was doing it anyway.

When Rosie's number popped up on Grant's phone, he leaned bonelessly against the nearest wall.

"Grant? Are you sitting down?"

At the sound of her voice he slumped to the floor.

"Yup," he managed to say.

"You're not going to believe what happened. This is not just a story. This is the Holy Grail of stories. Plus we literally have someone's life in our hands."

"Don't drag it out, Rosie," he said. He felt his face with his free hand. It was smiling.

"So I went to the *Gazette*—"

"Oh shit, Rosie, I'm sorry—"

"Don't worry about it. It was my decision and if I hadn't I wouldn't have found Marty and that would've been a shame for us and probably an even bigger shame for Marty."

"You found him? Are you—did he—"

"No, no. It's much weirder than that."

This was better than her being alive and safe; this was the best thing that had happened to him in months. All he had to do was keep her talking. "I should've known. It's Marty we're talking about."

"I know, right?"

Rose was safe and there was a story here—a story! He'd told Rose something would happen, and something had happened, and now something even *more* was happening? Even he didn't believe that the gods could be so generous. It was like being in a dream, but not the one where he opened the paper and all the articles were written in gibberish, but the one where he knew exactly the words to make the world line up exactly the way it should, justice served to those in power, a voice for the disenfranchised, Rose looking at him adoringly—

Even now Rose was still talking, and saying the most wonderful things.

"So here it is, in brief. Dateline: Hackenstrat's office, right after Marty crashed prom and declared his love for Jenna. Oh god, Jenna—she's out there somewhere—"

"I thought she was with you."

"She was, but she left because she was convinced something bad was happening to Marty, and I'm not even in the school anymore—"

"I thought you went to the *Gazette* room."

"I did, but the SWAT team came through and escorted me

out. They're evacuating the building—probably get to you soon. So I'm in Fisher Louis's rented limo right now."

"Excuse me?"

"Don't worry, the privacy screen is up, and the driver is out smoking a cigarette anyway. He lent me his charger—he's cool. It's me, a disco ball, and fifty cans of LaCroix peach pear—oh, and I stole your laptop—hope you don't mind."

Grant's brain felt as if it was tripping up stairs. She was okay. Marty was okay. She was in a limo. LaCroix. Cigarettes. Charger. "I don't mind."

"What was I— Oh, Jenna! Jesus. I probably can't talk to her on the phone. If they're really still looking for him, they might be monitoring her phone, though maybe that's paranoid—"

"I thought the SWAT team swept through the *Gazette* room."

"Yes, well. Marty wasn't there anymore when they did. If you'd stop interrupting, I could tell you."

"You've been interrupting yourself, actually."

"I'm sorry—should we take a break and fight about it?"

"I concede. Go on."

"Thank you. So. Rewind to right after Marty crashes prom and gives his big speech. Marty's in Hackenstrat's office and Hackenstrat's reading him the riot act. After all his pranks, blah blah blah, how dare he ruin things for other students, et cetera. Then Hack calls for a security guard to escort him off the premises. Wants to scare him a little, I think."

"Plus Hackenstrat's always had a thing for extra security."

"Right. Wants to feel like his hired muscle are there for a

reason. Remember that I said that, by the way. It's going to be important later." Rose breathed deliberately, as if trying to slow herself down. Grant imagined the breath tickling his cheek and neck where he was holding the phone. "Anyway. Hack comes out of the office because he hears me and Jenna in the hall. While he's out with us, Marty notices something wrapped up in a Hawks High athletic bag, right in the middle of Hack's desk."

Rose paused, and Grant's mind skipped and stumbled as he realized what she was saying. He sat up so fast, he startled a group of math-team kids next to him. "No!"

"Yes."

"In the athletic bag . . ."

"Yes. There's a gun in the bag. Sitting there. As if waiting for Marty to come in and find it. Not even locked up somewhere. I mean, for all we know the safety wasn't even on—not that me or Marty would know if a gun had its safety off or on, of course, but if it hadn't—"

"Rosie," Grant said, because he could tell she was in a chatter spiral. This happened sometimes when her brain and her mouth were both working too hard to stop, and they could go on forever like that in a perpetual motormouth feedback loop.

Rose stopped and started over. "Right. Right. So Marty's staring at this gun. He's not thinking straight—if he ever really thinks straight. When Hack and the rent-a-cop come into the room, they see Marty's got a gun in his hand, and they freak out and try to tackle him, but he gets free and makes a run for it. And Hackenstrat initiates the lockdown and here we are."

Grant stood and started pacing the center of the gym. Everyone was clustered in groups around the edges, but the dance floor was open and his rented shoes made a very satisfying click with every step.

Here we are.

"I'm in the gym. You're in the limo. How soon can we publish?"

Rose had her feet up on the leather seats of the limo and Grant's keyboard in her lap. While she was talking to him, she made notes in an encrypted document that saved directly to a thumb drive, so that when they were on the school's Wi-Fi, the document couldn't be accessed by the school's cyber security, assuming the school had any, which was an open question. They'd managed to shut down Hackenstrat's password-collecting plan, but who knew what other invasive technology he'd sneaked through without making a big deal out of it.

She and Grant had started covering their digital tracks after reading a bunch of Cory Doctorow, watching *All the President's Men*, and hearing Grant's stepmom describe the Edward Snowden case. It had always seemed kind of sophisticated and mostly silly, and made her feel a little bit like a spy in a dumb movie. But for the first time she started to wonder if it was enough. What if the school had not only the usual spying controls but more advanced, less obvious ones? What if they were monitoring her screen from a remote location right now?

Her instinct was that they were too stupid to do any of that, but she tended to underestimate her adversaries. "You can't really know what's in someone's head, so better to treat them like they're potentially the smartest person in the world," Grant had told her once, when she'd botched an interview with a nervous sophomore candidate for class treasurer. Rose had pointed out that she knew for a fact the sophomore was not the smartest person in the world. "Yeah, and she knows you think that," he'd replied.

Better safe than sorry. That's what she'd told Marty—better safe than sorry.

She'd gone over the whole story a hundred times in her mind as the SWAT team escorted her out, as she chatted with the limo driver, as she reassured her mom she was fine and it was all a false alarm. She had to be safe. She couldn't underestimate the police or Hackenstrat, and what he might do to prevent the story from coming out.

"How soon can we publish?" Grant asked.

"Well, we don't actually have access to the site right now."

"Nick knows the password. I can make him give it to us."

"I thought he was in the library?"

"He owns a phone. I'll call."

"Good. I also think we need to do one other thing."

"Whatever it is, let's get it done quick before Marty gets caught and talks to someone else. Where's Marty now?"

"I can't tell you," she said.

"Why not?"

Here was part one of the conclusions she had come to that would decide her and Marty's fate: either Grant was with her and in it, or she was on her own.

"Because when they ask you, it's better that you not know."

Grant didn't answer right away. He would know what that meant. If Marty was wanted by the police and she believed he was innocent, she wasn't obligated to turn him in, but she also couldn't help him hide. At least not according to usual journalistic ethics.

She knew that . . . she did. Really. But it was Marty. She believed him. If he was right and the police shot him because they thought he was armed and dangerous, how could she explain that to Jenna?

And if he wanted to hide anyway, what was the harm in getting her story out first, before the rest of the world could get their hands on it—and him?

Rose looked up at the limo's open sunroof. Grant let the silence tick by. Rose counted twenty seconds. Thirty. She could see stars outside the sunroof. They were a little judgy, those stars.

"He's terrified," Rose said, trying to talk over the stars' judgment. "He knows that the story sounds nuts. He's convinced that as soon as they see him, they're going to shoot."

"If he surrenders . . ."

"Yeah, maybe, but he's worried about Hackenstrat now. Marty thinks Hack framed him."

Grant laughed, then stopped. "Wait. You think Hackenstrat might've done it?"

She shrugged, even though she knew Grant couldn't see her. "You said yourself he's been beating the drum for extra security forever. Maybe he set up Marty to prove his point."

"Rosie . . ."

"He wouldn't've thought that Marty would take off running with the gun. I mean, that's a little unhinged of Marty, if we're being honest."

"So you're saying it's possible that Hackenstrat left a gun in an athletic bag on his desk so that Marty would open it and Hack could find him with it and be called a hero and a visionary? I suppose he made sure Marty was going to crash prom in the first place, otherwise this whole conspiracy falls apart."

Rose tried to suppress a smile. This wasn't supposed to be fun; it was Marty's life. But sometimes talking with Grant felt like she could pass ideas directly from her brain to his, as easily as handing over a piece of paper. "I agree. I don't actually think Hackenstrat has the foresight or gumption to pull off something like this."

"So what . . . so wait . . . Why'd Hack have a gun in a bag on his desk, then?"

"Exactly."

"I see. You said you had to do one other thing—that's it, isn't it?"

"Yup. We can't have any holes in this, Grant. Not if we want it to stick—if we want people to believe Marty instead of the administration. Say the gun's Hackenstrat's, and he made the monumentally stupid decision to bring a gun to school, whether to frame Marty or for some other ill-thought-out reason. Is it registered to him? If not, where'd he get it? If it's not his at all, whose is it? How did it end up on his desk? Why was it there for Marty to stumble upon? That's the real story. The story that explains the story, rather than simply presenting an alternative version of the facts. They can't say Marty's making it up if we prove it."

"Hmmm . . ."

"And Grant, this is going to be big news. The police, the administration—they'll try poking holes in Marty's version of events every way they can, blame him for this, sweep all the rest of it under the rug. We can't be wrong about that when we publish—they'll use it as an excuse to discredit everything we said. Everything Marty said, too."

"I thought you said you believed him," Grant said softly.

"I do," Rose said, just as softly back. "But I'd rather be sure than wrong."

SOPHOMORE'S VISIT WITH FATHER UNSATISFYING

"Don't you want to be sure?" Grant asked Rose. "You don't have to, like, take Disney cruises with him or whatever. But if you go in, you'll know one way or the other."

Rose and Grant stood in front of an office in a strip mall in a town near the Indiana border. It was Valentine's Day, sophomore year, and there were light flakes falling from the gray sky.

"Do you think he's noticed us?" Rose asked.

"Oh, no. We're only the two teenagers staring into his window from the otherwise empty parking lot."

Rose glared at Grant, then pulled on his elbow and yanked open the office door.

There were two desks in a small room, both piled high with paper. An angular white woman sat at one desk, her hair carefully curled under her chin. At the other sat Adam Escarra-Lopez.

He was older than she'd thought he'd be, even though he was

younger than her mother. He had gray mixed in with his brown hair, and lines around his eyes and mouth. His skin might have been a shade darker than Rose's, though it was hard to tell because he was wearing a cream sweater over a blue button-down.

"What can we do for you?" the woman asked, but Rose and Grant ignored her and stared at Adam.

"Hi," Rose said. She felt Grant hovering behind her, not quite touching her shoulder. "I'm Rose."

"Hello, Rose. I'm . . ." Adam looked at her, squinted, and looked longer. His mouth fell open. "Holy shit, Rose. Uh, sorry. Excuse me. Your mother didn't say— I didn't know you were coming."

"Hi," Rose said again.

"Oh," the woman said. She stood up from her seat and walked through a door in the back of the office. Adam looked after her, sighed, then looked back at Rose, putting on a grin. It looked so familiar that Rose was too startled to smile back.

"Wow. Rose." Adam leaned back in his chair. "You wanna get out of here? We should talk. It's been forever, man."

"What about . . ." Rose nodded at the back of the office.

"What, Jaclyn? Don't worry about it. She's got it under control here."

Rose hadn't been worried so much about the workload as the look of despair on the woman's face, but Adam was already putting on his coat and hustling them out the door and down a few storefronts to a Chinese restaurant.

"This place is the best, I'm here all the time, it won't be too crowded so we can sit as long as we want," Adam said, along with a lot of other stuff about the weather and the traffic and the convenience to the highway and the details of small business leases. Before Rose knew what was happening, she and Grant were sitting in a booth across from Adam as he joked with the waiter and ordered them all tea and egg rolls.

"I'm a fiend for tea now," Adam said, leaning back with his arms up on the back of the booth, a tiny teacup in his hand. "I don't party anymore, so it's all green tea and meditation. Does your mom meditate?"

"No," Rose said, but Adam didn't seem to hear—or care.

"You know, Rose, it's crazy to look at you. You were so little last time I saw you. I kind of always thought you'd be a baby, you know, needy, crying. But you're like a real person now." He shook his head in disbelief. "What are you— I mean it's fine you're here, good to see you, but—what's the occasion?"

"Nothing," Rose said. *Mistake mistake you've made a huge mistake.* "I wanted to say hi."

Adam put down his tea and scratched at his wrists, pulling the shirt high enough to reveal the ends of a few tattoos. *Mom's are better,* Rose thought, though she couldn't see enough of them to know for sure. *Mom doesn't hide her tattoos, anyway.* "It is a trip to see you," Adam said. "Just wild."

He laughed uncomfortably. Rose felt absolutely no desire to join in.

"We found you on the internet," Grant said, though it was

really Grant who had found Adam, after asking Rose all about her family history.

Grant had been shocked when he learned that she and Adam weren't in touch. He wouldn't let it go.

"You don't even know what city he's in?" he asked. Rose shook her head and Grant leaned forward over the lunchroom table. "When was the last time you saw him?"

"When I was . . . three, maybe?"

Grant's eyes widened in disbelief and he ate chips off her tray distractedly.

He kept mentioning it every couple of days: *How did your parents meet? How did they fall out of contact? Have you ever met your grandparents?* He would sit next to her in the *Gazette* room and lob questions her way while they worked. Rose told him—she wasn't exactly sure why. She and her mom barely ever talked about Adam. It wasn't a forbidden topic, but Rose's mom had always made it seem like there was no story there. "A lot of mistakes led to one good outcome, my special girl," she said, tweaking Rose's nose.

Rose answered Grant's questions because she trusted him. Besides, when he got interested in a topic, it was hard to extricate herself from his enthusiasm. Mostly that worked out well, when it came to articles and schemes to keep from failing chemistry and plans for the future. This hadn't seemed any different, at least at first.

"All I know is his name is Adam Escarra-Lopez and they

lived in a shitty commune in Wisconsin together. I talk to my nana in Florida on my birthday and Christmas."

Rose enjoyed her semiannual conversations with Nana Gloria, who was on her third face-lift and fifth husband and blamed herself matter-of-factly for her son's problems. Rose sent her clippings, sometimes, and got back effusive postcards with pictures of buff lifeguards on the front.

"Hmmmm," Grant said, and Rose thought that was the end of it. But two weeks later Grant proudly produced a printout of a lease agreement for an office in Calumet City under the name Adam Escarra-Lopez and told her they were going.

She hadn't asked herself if she actually wanted to go until they sat at the Chinese restaurant, across from her blood relation, who was still scratching his wrists nervously.

"I wasn't hiding," Adam was saying to Grant as Rose scrutinized him. "Rose's mom has my email. If she'd emailed, we could've all hung out. Man, that would've been crazy! Except for maybe Jaclyn . . ." He trailed off, then shook his head and brightened. "So that was the office. What did you think? We mostly do tax work, so it's our busy season. Jaclyn's probably wondering where I . . . But whatever. My kid's here! Jac'll understand."

Rose had to ask, though she knew the answer. "Who's Jaclyn?"

"She's my wife."

There was a pause. Adam downed a cup of tea and poured another. No one knew exactly where to look.

"Do you have kids?" Rose asked. "I mean, you and Jaclyn."

"No," Adam said. "No, Jac can't—that's not for us."

Another pause, much worse than before. Rose's entire journalistic training disappeared from her brain, and she stared miserably at the poster on the restaurant's wall, one of those generic watercolors of a dock full of sailboats, all the masts a jumble of lines, with seagulls drifting by. It was the ugliest fucking thing Rose had ever seen.

"Rose and I are on our school newspaper together," Grant said when the silence got to be too much. "We *are* the newspaper, really."

"Oh yeah, my mom said something about that. Gloria's got a binder of your shit. Cool, cool. Your mom must be really proud of you."

"She is," Rose said.

Adam nodded a couple of times and then jumped a little. "Oh, hey—do you need money?"

"What? No!" Rose flattened her back against the back of the booth, as far away from the table as she could get. "You think I came here to ask you for money?"

"Well, I don't know." Adam frowned, not exactly apologetic. "I know I haven't been around and that's probably been hard for you and your mom. And you come here out of the blue . . . Asking for money, it's what I would've done if I were you. Have done it, actually. Though Gloria knows better now than to give me any."

Rose flushed. "You think I'm like you?"

Adam raised his eyebrows. "You're my kid. And your mom

wasn't exactly straight edge, back in the day. That's some serious genes."

Rose pressed her hands into the table so they would stop shaking. It didn't work. "I'm not here for money."

Adam shrugged. "If you say so."

Rose blinked, but before she could open her mouth, Grant had grabbed her shaking hand and squeezed. She squeezed back and swallowed the words she was about to say. Adam noticed Grant holding her hand and gave her an intent look, but she couldn't be bothered to care.

"I wanted to see you," Rose said, then took a deep breath, "out of curiosity. But I don't need anything from you."

She stood up, and Grant followed her. Adam slid to the end of the booth.

"Come on, don't be like that. I didn't mean anything by it. We can still hang out—Jaclyn can hold down the fort for a couple of hours." Rose didn't stop walking, and Adam followed them to the door. "Or whatever you want to do. You don't have to leave so fast. I'm not—I don't know how to do this, that's pretty obvious, but I could try?"

Rose's heart had stopped hammering quite so loud, and she took a deep breath. "It's okay, Adam. You don't have to be someone you're not. I'm really fine." She nodded out the door. "You should go back to Jaclyn. It's not fair to her for you to bail during the busy season."

Rose and Grant were still holding hands when they got to Rose's mom's car, but as soon as she noticed, she dropped his.

They were halfway home before either of them said anything.

"That guy . . ." Grant started, then gathered himself up. "He was . . . something."

"I feel bad for Jaclyn."

"I feel bad for the waiters at that restaurant."

Rose kept her eyes on the road. "I don't know what I expected."

"It was weird and the money thing was awkward, but he seemed happy to see you, right?" Grant said.

Rose made a noncommittal noise.

"Will you hang out again?" Grant asked.

She could tell Grant wanted her to say yes, that this mission had been a success. But she didn't want to have to *try* with Adam. To learn, together, how to be a father and daughter. The thought made her recoil. The idea of having to keep talking, even when she didn't want to, even when he pissed her off—having to meet Jaclyn—the idea of being saddled with another person who wanted to know her and expected she would tell him all her secrets—

"Nah," she said.

"Are you . . . okay?"

"Yup," she said.

She half expected Grant to keep asking her questions like he always did, pushing and prodding into the tiniest nuances, trying to convince her to change her mind. She half hoped he would at least ask one more time if she was okay, because then she'd tell him the truth: that she didn't know. That she felt guilty and angry and sad. That a part of her even wished she'd taken Adam's money, because, goddamit, she and her mom deserved it.

But he kept quiet, letting her sit with her own thoughts. And maybe that was better, after all. She didn't need Adam Escarra-Lopez—and she didn't need Grant Leitch to fix her life. She wasn't like her father, no matter what genes she had. She was Rose Regnero, and she could take care of herself.

FIVE

Grant thought that the SWAT teams had come to evacuate them from the gym, but it was only a group of chaperones tackling Fisher Louis.

"I can take him!" Fisher shouted, shaking off the teachers' grips. "Little asswipe like Marty Caulfield? Let me at him!"

Grant watched, curious, for perhaps longer than the scene warranted. But it wasn't every day that you saw the prom king lose it on a group of teachers and parents.

"Hey, Grant," Mer said. Her hair had started to fall out of its updo, and she'd chewed off all of her lipstick. "Can I talk to you?"

"I'm a little busy," Grant said. His phone's battery was in the red, and he still had to call Nick. Mer hesitated for a second, then nodded and drifted away.

Grant knew why they'd dated for so long: he was too scared

to break up with her, and she was too nice. But he still wondered why she'd agreed to go out with him in the first place. He didn't know what he was doing and had never dated anyone, but she'd had a couple boyfriends before him. Surely she should've known better.

"Nick!" he yelled into the phone, and then toned it down when he saw a group of volleyball girls glaring at him. "Nick. Buddy. How are you and Ollie doing?"

"Fine," Nick said.

"Great, great. Crazy time, isn't it?"

"Yeah. They came by to evacuate us but they didn't say what was—"

"Yup. Very dramatic. Very secretive. Listen, I have a favor to ask."

"Okay," Nick said slowly.

"Don't sound like that, Nick. You know I only ask for things when they're really important."

Nick sighed, which crackled through the phone's speaker. "Yeah, but you think everything you do is super important."

Grant thought about it and laughed. "You know, you're probably right."

"I am?"

"But this is different. Rosie's writing a story—"

"She is?"

"Yes, keep up, Nick. There's lockdown at prom, I don't know if you noticed. So Rosie's writing a story, and we need you to—"

"No," Nick said.

"It's a stupid little password. You're going to graduate in three days. Who cares?"

"Is that your argument? Ignore my principles because I'm leaving anyway?"

"Principles." Grant almost laughed again, but stopped himself. Nick wouldn't appreciate the pun, and would probably think Grant was laughing at him. "Come on. I don't have much battery left. Give it up."

"Ask Hackenstrat if you're so determined to get something up on the site."

"We can't."

"Why not?"

"It's complicated." Grant heard his voice getting louder and took a deep breath. "Hand it over, Nick. You owe me."

"For what?"

"I've been your best friend for thirteen years—"

"And, what, I should be so grateful for your company? I should be thanking you for every time you deigned to acknowledge me?"

"Maybe, yeah," Grant said. The story was *right there*, they had it in their grasp, but they wouldn't be able to do anything with it unless Nick gave them the password. "You're so afraid of everything, Nick. If you break this little rule, nothing's going to happen except that you might actually do something interesting for once instead of being a coward."

Nick didn't answer right away. Grant counted the seconds nervously. When his phone died, he'd be cut off. It wasn't the meanest thing Grant had ever said to Nick, and Nick had always forgiven him in the past. So he needed to skip to the part where Nick forgave him and did what he was told.

"I'm not the coward here," Nick said finally. "The cowardly thing would be to give you whatever you want. The cowardly thing would be to wait until the last possible minute to manufacture a crisis in order to spend a little more time with the girl whose heart you already broke a million times."

Grant blinked. He heard a roaring in his ears. "Oh, this is rich." His voice raised. He saw chaperones heading for him and turned to the wall, because there was no getting quieter. Not now. "Thanks for the lecture. Why don't you ask Ollie if you're going to be together next year, if you're so convinced you're such a noble, brave, principled stalwart—"

His phone beeped. He looked at the screen—not dead, not yet, but Nick had hung up on him. Grant swore and tapped his head—not quite cracked, but close—against the concrete wall.

He'd let Nick cool off and try again later. Nick would have to give him the password; he'd understand eventually what this meant. It wasn't some sort of a ploy to spend time with Rosie. She had called *him*, after all. This was *news*, not some sort of romantic adventure.

And what did Nick mean, that he'd broken Rosie's heart?

Rose's heart had never been broken. And certainly not by Grant. He knew her better than anyone and he'd never seen her cry. She'd never sat around with tubs of ice cream watching Nicholas Sparks movies. If she'd been heartbroken, she'd have shown up at the paper in the same pajama pants five days in a row with unwashed hair, and he'd definitely have noticed if something like that had happened.

No. Rosie had always been capable and funny, the same as always. They'd fight and flirt and work really hard, same as always. They'd go to the diner, same as always.

If he'd hurt her, he'd *know*. Wouldn't he?

SENIOR DUMPED

Grant got dumped on the second day of senior year.

Mer hovered outside of the *Gazette* room as staffers gathered around the conference table. Grant waved at her, but she didn't head off for the dance team like she usually did, so he eventually had to go out and see what was the matter.

They had been dating for almost a year, but he hadn't seen much of her over the summer. He'd had his job and she'd gone on one of those service trips where you pay an obscene amount of money to build a school in a developing country. He'd said something slightly disparaging about the trip before she'd left, and she'd gotten a hurt expression. "Are you saying those kids don't deserve a new school? Because we're paying money to come help?" He'd tried to explain that no, that wasn't what he was saying, he was only suspicious of a trip like this because some kids sign up for them in order to put something nice on their college applications, and it often ended up harming the local communities more than helping them—voluntourism, it was called; he'd read an article about it on Medium—and she'd gotten even more offended. "That's not why I'm doing it," she'd said, and then the movie started and they didn't have to talk anymore, which had been a huge relief.

She stood in front of him, her golden skin extra tanned because of her summer in the sun building the school, while he had gotten paler than ever and had had to increase his glasses prescription by a full point in each eye. (At least he'd grown another three inches. He could see over Mer's head now if he wanted to.)

"We should break up," Mer said. The only indication that she was apprehensive about this conversation was the way she was worrying a ring around her pinky.

"Um," Grant said. His shoulders relaxed; he hadn't been aware that they were tensed up. "Okay."

Mer stopped turning the ring and tilted her head at him. "Okay?"

"Yeah. If that's how you feel."

She opened and closed her mouth. "Did you want to break up with me?"

He wouldn't have said that he was unhappy with Mer, but he'd forgotten why he thought it was a good idea to have a girlfriend in the first place. Nick and Oliver seemed to get happier and happier the more time they spent together, but that hadn't been the case with Grant and Mer. He found himself on an extremely even keel with Mer, somewhat happy and mostly comfortable from week to week, with occasional bouts of awkwardness like the argument over the service trip or the hiccup of doubt and confusion he'd felt after making out with Rose. And yet there was no reason to break up with her, so he hadn't really considered it.

"Not really, I guess."

Mer's bottom lip quivered. "Were you—are you—do you love me, or what?"

"Why does that matter? You said you wanted to break up. So, fine." Something occurred to Grant, and he considered Mer. "Who is it?"

Mer's cheeks reddened. "Who's what?"

"Who are you breaking up with me for?"

"Grant!" Mer exclaimed, but she didn't deny it. Grant waited. Finally, Mer dropped her shoulders, sighing. "Fisher Louis."

Fisher Louis. They'd devoted a full page of the sports section last spring on his run at the state championship; Rosie had written the in-depth profile. "Trading up, I see."

"Nothing's happened, Grant. I swear."

Grant thought of last June's grad issue and the night spent in the back seat of Rose's mother's car. He smiled uneasily. "It doesn't matter if it did."

"It didn't, though! It's only . . . I wanted something different this year. Fisher goes to parties, he's got his swim-team friends, he's serious about swimming but it's not his whole world."

"Like the paper is for me?" Grant suggested. He glanced

back into the *Gazette* room and saw the staff waiting for him, all sitting around the conference table, laughing at something Rosie was saying. "Thanks for letting me know, Mer. I'm sure you'll have a great time at Fisher Louis's keggers. All the best to you."

Mer flinched. "You can be such a jerk sometimes," she said, and turned away.

"I'm a jerk? You're the one who's breaking up with me!" he called after her, then saw the entire *Gazette* staff staring at him through the open door. He had a moment of embarrassment— he'd been dumped, after all, weighed against Fisher Louis and found wanting—but he quickly covered it up with a roll of his eyes.

When Nick asked him later if he was okay, he'd said "of course" automatically, and then when Nick went back to his work, Grant thought about it seriously. Was he upset? Had Mer broken his heart?

He felt . . . blank.

No, there was a little bit of emotion in there. Something jittery and sensitive, cringing away from his scrutiny.

He felt . . . guilty.

Well, that didn't make any sense at all. Except for that one time with Rose, he'd been devoted to Mer. Although . . . maybe devoted was too strong a word. He'd been dependable. Hmmm, even that felt like he was overstating it. At the very least, he'd been *present*.

Clearly he was better off without a girlfriend at all, as he'd always suspected. That way he wouldn't have to ask himself if he was upset or guilty or anything else—he could just be. No one would expect him to be anywhere or do anything, and he wouldn't disappoint anyone with his focus on the paper.

He wouldn't have to feel guilty for no reason at all.

Rose had the phone to her ear and it was ringing, slowly and endlessly.

While she waited for the voice mail to pick up, she watched the limo's small flat-screen TV, which covered one of the windows. She'd turned it on to local news, which was broadcasting live twenty feet from her. Rose had the out-of-body feeling of being on TV and watching herself on TV at the same time. On the TV and out the window next to it, she saw a dozen police cars and half a dozen fire trucks on the street in front of the main school doors. Local TV vans clustered around the corner. Four or five reporters had set up in a row on the baseball diamond and were narrating in pools of aggressively bright light.

Dozens of parents gathered at the edge of a police barricade in the parking lot. Not Rose's mom—she'd offered to come but

Rose had told her to stay home, that Rose was fine, that she'd be home as soon as she could.

It wasn't clear how much, if any, of that was true. Was she fine? Her heart hadn't fully recovered from seeing Marty with the gun in the *Gazette* room, and she couldn't focus on anything for longer than ten seconds at a time. She'd write a sentence, look up at the TV, check her phone, write a sentence, and go through the whole thing again.

And would she be home as soon as she could? No way. Not as long as something was happening.

The phone stopped ringing and the voice mail beeped.

"Jenna, where are you? We need to talk," Rose said into the phone, knowing full well Jenna wouldn't ever listen to the message. She felt better leaving it, though—like she was doing all she could to try to get in touch with Jenna without compromising her source over the possibly bugged phone. She sent another vague text, too, to be thorough.

So that was done. She should really call JB. He'd be wondering how she was.

"Sorry, I'm writing an article for a paper I quit, but don't worry, it's only because I was compelled to by circumstance." "Sorry, JB, I've been talking to my former best friend/never-quite-boyfriend for the past twenty minutes, but I can't tell you anything about what we said." "Ooops, forgot about the time because I've regressed into a version of me that forgot you existed."

She shook her head and tapped at the screen of her phone

nervously. Open the texts, close them. Unlock the phone, put it to sleep. Check the TV—more of the same. Write a sentence of her story. Delete it.

She pulled up the photos on her phone, then zoomed in on the first photo. The gun was dull black, hard and heavy, with a scuff on one side of the handle. (Marty didn't know if the scuff had been there when he picked it up or if it had acquired a mark while in his possession.) "Glock" was engraved near the end of the barrel, along with some numbers and "Austria." She scrolled through her photos of the phone, looking for a serial number. There was a series of letters and numbers stamped into the side of the barrel. Hard to read with the flash, and her hand must've shaken slightly because zooming in didn't make it any clearer.

Rose put the phone facedown on the seat next to her and took a deep breath. Even looking at a picture of the gun made her queasy. The noise it made when Marty set it on the table. The dark and dangerous glint of it in the nearly empty *Gazette* room.

On the TV and fifty feet away from her, Vice-Principal Hackenstrat was talking to a reporter. Sweat shone on his forehead. "I'm confident that we will find the young person before he hurts anyone, but if we'd instituted the reforms that I suggested last year—including monitoring student social media presence—an incident like this could've been prevented."

The frowning reporter took the microphone back. "What can you tell us about the student police are searching for?"

"Martin Caulfield has had a history of unstable behavior. I'm shocked that it came to bringing a weapon onto school property, and yet at the same time, his history suggests that he is capable of violence."

He meant the parrot, Rose supposed, but that had been an accident—even those most angry with Marty had understood that he killed the parrot out of carelessness and not out of malice.

She turned to Grant's computer and started Googling "tracing a gun" and "gun laws Illinois." She didn't expect to stumble upon a site where she could type in the gun's serial number and out would pop the owner, but she kind of thought that's what the police would do once they got their hands on the gun. But that wasn't what she found at all.

"No way," she said out loud to the screen.

By law, there could be no central electronic record of gun sales on the state or federal level, so when the ATF did run traces, they had to go through paper records to find who had bought it. In Illinois, gun stores didn't have to report sales to law enforcement. They did have to respond to law-enforcement requests within twenty-four hours, but Rose wasn't law enforcement, nor did she have the first idea where her local gun store might be, and she seriously doubted a gun store would give that information to anyone other than an official with a warrant.

So basically, if the gun was purchased legally, and if it was purchased in the last ten years, and if it came from a store in the general vicinity, the cops might be able to find out who it had originally been sold to. Maybe. In a couple of days.

What the hell?

If it was purchased illegally, or legally in another state, or if it was old or stolen, then it would be even harder to trace where it came from. Not impossible, but nowhere near as easy as plugging a number into a database.

It was enough for a person to lose her faith in the rule of law. For the first time since Rose had heard the lockdown alarm, her panic and excitement were replaced by a righteous fury. She could've written a scathing editorial on it, if there had been time and if she had still been on the *Gazette* and not temporarily called to duty under extenuating circumstances.

Rose kept clicking around. Second Amendment activists were against a gun registry because they figured it would be an easy way for the government to come and round up their weapons. Yeah, well, no shit. Maybe they should. Too many people had clearly proved that they weren't capable of handling the responsibility of gun ownership.

Rose slammed the computer closed. Her head was starting to pound. She ran her hands through her hair, dislodging half a dozen bobby pins, and as her updo collapsed, the pain receded. She stared for a second at the bobby pins littering the floor of the limo. She'd been so engrossed in her computer, she'd forgotten that she was in a limo, in a fancy dress, with full face and hair. How was it that she was still at prom while all of this was happening? She shook her head, sending another handful of pins flying.

On the TV, Hackenstrat was called away by official-looking people in trench coats. Marty wasn't wrong—this whole disaster was suspiciously great for Hackenstrat, who'd been so afraid of his students for so long. Now he'd been proved right.

But Hackenstrat—with his security proposals and crime stats—had to know this stuff about gun ownership and registration, and that in the end the authorities would catch up with him. The penalty for bringing a firearm to school was huge; he'd know that, too. Rose wouldn't be able to trace the gun, but the police could—eventually. That made it unlikely that Hackenstrat had brought in the gun to frame Marty. It was too risky—too likely that the truth would come out, or that the gun would be discovered before he could set up the frame job.

Hackenstrat couldn't have known that there was a gun in the bag on his desk. He would've sounded the alarm as soon as he saw it, for one thing, and he certainly never would've left Marty alone with the gun while he went into the hallway to talk to Rose and Jenna and wait for the rent-a-cop. He wanted tougher security, but he didn't have a death wish.

She should tell the police where Marty was so they could get the gun and start looking for its real owner.

Unless . . .

Maybe there was a way to find out whose gun it was without involving the police and the gun stores. If the gun came from someone in school, someone *else* had to know about it. No secret was that well kept. A gun wasn't tossed into the vice-principal's office in an athletic bag in a vacuum.

She texted Grant quickly, then checked the rest of her texts. Nothing from Jenna yet. And she still hadn't responded to JB.

PROMISING DATE DECLINED BY SENIOR

When JB had first asked Rose out, she'd said no. He was a swimmer, for starters, and ever since she'd written a profile of Fisher Louis, swimmers had given her the heebie-jeebies, even a year later. Plus, when he asked, it was February of senior year, and she was still deep in the paper—in particular an article about teachers' salaries that the administration wanted very badly to stop and that she and Grant wanted desperately to keep. (Hackenstrat took it to the school board, and the *Gazette* lost that one.)

The Midwest Regional Excellence in Journalism Award had arrived the week before. She'd submitted a series of articles she'd written about the group of Syrian refugees who had moved to town the year before. Sami and Amena had been through terrible trauma and were now dealing with the casual consumption and subtle racism of Hawks High, and they let Rose hang around with them for weeks, getting to know them, their families, their daily routines. She'd submitted the series knowing that the topic would be appealing to the judges, but also believing that it was some of the best writing she'd ever done. She'd written it well because she cared about the subject. Because she wanted to get it right. It was gratifying—and, if she was being honest, not entirely surprising—to have won.

When the trophy arrived in the newsroom, Grant had commandeered it and put it in a place of honor on his desk so that it was the first thing anyone saw when they walked in the room. He peppered regular conversation with references to the award—"As an MREJ winner, Rose would be the best person to write that," "That type of thing isn't going to win you any MREJs," "Everyone scoot down—our MREJ winner needs a booth seat"—and Rose rolled her eyes but it felt good, the moment of recognition, of standing out, of being valued.

Of course the recognition only extended through the *Gazette*. No one else cared—not even her mom, who had nodded and smiled condescendingly when Rose had told her about it. "Big honor," her mom had said, and Rose couldn't be entirely sure that her mom wasn't mocking her.

Sometimes the disconnect between how she was perceived in the *Gazette* room and how the rest of the world saw her was jarring. She was constantly being reminded that no one gave a shit about her.

Maybe that was harsh, but they certainly didn't notice her—not really, not in a way that counted. They thought of her as that *Gazette* girl or not at all. It would be an exaggeration to say that she was lonely, because Grant and Jenna and Nick and the rest of the *Gazette* staff saw her for who she was—Grant made sure of that, with all his MREJ talk—and that was enough. Or at least it should be. Shouldn't it?

JB sat next to her in French and kept volunteering to be her conversation partner even though her French was abysmal. She couldn't have said why JB wanted to be partners with her—if asked, she probably would've guessed that he thought he had to, based on the alignment of their seats.

All Rose knew was that he couldn't be talking to her because of her work on the *Gazette*, because he was a civilian, and he didn't know or care about anything she did on the paper. And that was the only reason Rose could imagine anyone taking the slightest interest in her whatsoever.

"*Qu'est-ce que vous . . .* uh . . . *Qu'est-ce que tu as fait ce week-end?*" Rose asked, doodling in the margins of her notebook.

"*J'ai nagé, surtout,*" JB said.

"*Nagé?*"

"Swimming. *On a eu une compétition.*"

Competition. She got that much. "*Comment avez-vous . . .* uh . . . *commencé . . . à la . . . piscine?* How'd you get into swimming?"

JB leaned back. "I know you're not trying to say black kids can't swim."

"Oh my god," Rose said, stricken, then saw JB smile. She took a breath. "I mean, *mon dieu! Je suis désolée. Ce n'est pas mon . . .* intent."

"*De rien. Quand même,* you've heard of Cullen Jones, right? Anthony Ervin?"

Rose shook her head.

JB laughed at her, and their teacher glared in their direction. "Look them up," he said, then pointed at her notebook. "*Qu'est-ce que c'est, ça?*"

"Umm . . . *mon cahier. Pour l'ecrire . . . la* Gazette. 'Gazette' is French, isn't it?"

"*Oui,*" he'd said. "*Toujours, tu écris dans le cahier.*"

"Yeah. I mean, *oui. C'est mon passion.*" She didn't know how to say "I won an award" in French, and as soon as she started mentally translating it, she realized it would be an absurd thing to say anyway.

"*C'est adorable,*" JB said.

"*Oui?*" Rose had looked at her notebook suspiciously. "It's supposed to be serious and important. *Sérieux. L'important.*"

"*C'est ça, aussi.*" JB poked at the edge of her notebook. "I'd say this in French but I don't think you'd understand me. Do you want to go out sometime?"

Rose laughed, then stopped suddenly. "Oh! I'm sorry. I thought you were joking."

"*Non. Je suis sincère.*"

"You don't want to go out with me."

"Why not?"

"No, I mean—I don't believe you." She stopped talking, seeing the confused look on his face. "Oh god. You do? Really? That's so nice of you."

"I don't feel like this is going very well," JB said, but he didn't seem embarrassed. "Should I start over in French?"

"No, I'm sorry. I'm only—do people actually ask each other out? Is that a thing?"

JB shrugged. "I could text you, but I don't have your number."

Madame called the class to order to go over some conjugations, which gave Rose a chance to compose her thoughts.

She hadn't dated anyone since she'd stopped calling Taj, if you could call what she had with Taj dating. It had been occasionally fun, but in the end it had made life more confusing than it was worth.

And now she and Grant were both single. He hadn't said anything to her yet. . . . They hadn't kissed since that one time, ages ago now. But they spent all their time together. They were each other's *person*. They didn't have to say anything about it for it to be true.

If she went out with JB, it wouldn't be casual like it was with Taj—that was obvious. She could tell based on their interactions so far—even in French—that he wasn't an ass like Fisher. And JB wouldn't be wishy-washy like Grant. He'd be a good boyfriend, the type of guy who wanted to meet your parents and would plan dates that involved food and an activity. He'd hang out with her friends. He'd like all of her Instagrams and share her articles on Facebook.

For a brief second, that sounded wonderful. Then Rose came back to reality.

"Thank you for asking," she whispered, when she completely

lost track of whatever Madame was saying. "But I don't think I have time to date anyone right now."

JB nodded and held out his hand. "Give me your phone." She handed it over while Madame's back was turned, and he typed under the desk. "In case you change your mind."

So a couple of weeks later when she did change her mind, after Northwestern, all she had to do was go to the entry marked "JB (Google Anthony Ervin)" and type out a message.

Rose pulled up JB (Google Anthony Ervin) on her phone. She tried to block out thoughts of Marty and VP Hackenstrat and the gun, and focus on her boyfriend. Jason Baxter.

When this was over, she would be returning to normal, and normal meant JB. She was writing a story, but that didn't mean she was trapped again with Grant on the *Gazette*—they weren't even on the *Gazette* anymore. Rose had to think about the future. She had to at least try to be happy and not get caught in the same empty spiral she'd been in before.

I'm sorry, she texted JB. Everything's fine. The SWAT team got me out and I'm in the limo. How's the gym? How are you?

He responded right away. I'm glad you're okay. It's not so great in here. Antsy.

I can't imagine you antsy. You always take things in stride. She took a deep breath and typed with her eyes mostly closed.

That's one of the reasons I like you.

Pause. It was true and all, but it was so sincere, Rose considered barfing into the limo's ice bucket.

Hope this ends soon, he wrote. Then we can get back to our date.

Won't be any prom left.

We could hang out. Or there's Fisher's after-party.

But we don't have to go to that if you don't want to.

A party at Fisher Louis's. Rose had heard of such parties but had never actually attended one before. Putting aside her disgust with Fisher Louis, it would be so normal. So classic. She could see exactly how that would fit into her article: "Hours after the lockdown, the students of Hawks High gathered to commiserate over their close call—a lockdown at prom that could easily have become tragic."

She had to go.

Fisher's party sounds like fun.

There was a pause as JB typed.

It will be if you're there.

This was what it was like to text someone who said what he meant. Rose appreciated the thought, but at the same time she feared something in her personality made her more likely to believe a compliment if it was buried in an avalanche of constructive criticism.

Grant turned from bashing his head into the wall and imme-diately jumped backward into it. Fisher Louis stood in front of him, all six-six of him, arms folded across his chest, grimace twisting up his features.

"Jesus. Fisher. What's up?"

"You're writing a story about the lockdown," Fisher said, not a question.

"Yeah," Grant said.

"You're investigating Marty Caulfield."

"Yeah." The urge to spill Rosie's scoop bubbled up, but he knew he had to keep quiet until they managed to write the story and get it up on the *Gazette*. Fisher Louis was unlikely to sell them out to another reporter (or Hackenstrat, for that matter), but you never knew. Better to keep quiet about it—let Fisher believe whatever he wanted to believe about Marty until Grant could point to his evidence proving otherwise.

Fisher nodded continually, his scowl deepening. "I want to help."

"Oh," Grant said. "Um. I don't know if there's anything . . ."

"I want to *help*," Fisher said, taking another step closer to Grant, whose back was already flush against the wall.

Grant felt the phone buzz in his hand and he glanced down, expecting to see a message from Nick with the password. Instead, it was a text from Rose. Grant smiled.

"Awesome," Grant said to Fisher. "Let's do this."

Rosie's text had been short but clear. Ask Owen Pettibone. Grant understood exactly what she meant, and it was a great idea. He should've thought of it himself, but that was why he had her around.

Grant and Fisher went from group to group in the gym, looking for Owen. "You sure he came?" Fisher asked. "It doesn't sound like something he'd do."

"He was on Ms. Davis's list," Grant said. "And even dirtbags deserve a nice prom, don't they?"

Fisher grunted. "We should be out there talking to Marty Caulfield."

"They're saying he's armed and dangerous," Grant said, hedging. "That's kind of the whole point."

"Yeah, maybe," Fisher said. He glanced Grant sideways. "You know where he is, don't you?"

Grant raised his hands in surrender. "I'm looking into a story. That's all."

Fisher stared at Grant for a long couple of seconds, then went back to their search for Owen Pettibone.

They found Owen lying underneath a table at the very back of the gym, farthest from the doors and the chaperones gathered around them. He had a vaporizer in one hand and held on to the bottom rung of a chair with the other. When he saw Grant, he exhaled a mouthful of vapor very slowly.

"Want a hit?" he asked. "This shit is stressful."

"Owen. Dude." Fisher looked disgusted. "They drug-test at Princeton. I gotta go."

"Bye-bye," Owen said.

"Thanks a ton for your help, Fisher," Grant said. Fisher stuck his middle finger up as he practically ran back to the safety of the other swimmers. "How's it going, Owen?"

"Peachy."

"Listen—you don't know about anyone bringing a gun into school?"

Owen blinked at Grant. "Is this . . . a trick question?"

Grant knelt next to Owen's head. "Not Marty Caulfield. You heard it was Marty who set off this lockdown, right?"

"I heard."

"So did you ever hear of Marty having a gun? You ever sell him one?"

Owen rocked his head back and forth slowly and took another hit off the vaporizer. "I don't sell guns, Mr. Officer Grant."

"Come on, Owen. Maybe you don't sell, but you know people who do."

Owen widened his eyes. "If my mother heard that I was up to naughty business like that . . ."

"I'm not here to rat you out. I wouldn't print a word of what you tell me—deep background only. All I want is information."

Owen pulled himself to sitting, but couldn't keep his balance and leaned both elbows on the seat of the chair. "I never heard of Martin Q. Caulfield having a gun. But he could've gotten it all secret-like, for all I know. Happy?"

"Who does have a gun that you know about? Hackenstrat?"

Owen laughed so hard that tears came to his eyes.

"Fine, not Hack. Someone else?"

Owen stopped laughing and narrowed his eyes. "Why you asking? You looking to form a posse, ride or die?"

"No. I'm trying to figure out if anyone might've—"

"Ohhhhhh. You think the gun Marty's waving isn't Marty's."

Grant nodded, conceding the point. "I don't think the gun is Marty's."

"Well, that's interesting. What's it look like?"

"What does—the gun, you mean?" Grant had his phone out and was texting before he finished the question. Seconds later, Rose sent a picture. Grant showed it to Owen. "Here. Look familiar?"

Owen stared at the photo, then glared up at Grant with red-rimmed eyes. "Where the hell did you get that photo?"

"You don't want to know."

"And that's the gun that Marty has? For real?" Owen shook

his head and slid down to the floor. "Oh man oh man oh man."

"Why? What is it? Whose gun is it?"

Owen deliberately put the vaporizer in his mouth and inhaled, keeping eye contact with Grant. The light at the end of the vaporizer glowed blue.

"If you know whose it is, you should tell me," Grant said.

"Why? Otherwise you'll tell the po-po?" Owen spoke while barely exhaling, and gestured at Grant's phone. "If you do, I'll have to tell them about that picture. I don't think you'd want that."

Grant rocked back on his heels.

"Bye-bye, newspaperman," Owen said. "Run back to your friend Fisher. Tell him you came up empty."

Rose answered the phone before the first ring ended.

"Rosie, you're a genius," Grant said.

"Of course I am. Why, specifically?"

"Owen Pettibone."

"He knows whose gun it is?"

"Possibly. He won't tell. But he had a weird reaction to seeing the picture of the gun. We need leverage."

Rose bit her thumbnail. "What kind of leverage could you get on someone like Owen? All his sketchiness is right there on the surface."

"We'll think of something. Rumor is we're about to be evacuated, so I'll see you soon."

Rose's heart leaped, but she managed to keep her voice even. "Great. Do you have the password from Nick?"

"Well . . ."

"I've been writing this story for nothing if there's no password."

"I know, Rosie, and I'm sure he'll come around, but right now he's—"

The call cut off. Rose tried to call him back, but it went straight to voice mail.

Fine. They'd finish the evacuation and she'd see him soon. Together they could convince Nick to give up the password. If Rose had to guess, she'd bet that Grant had asked Nick too harshly, without explaining the reasons he wanted it, and Nick had reacted defensively. The two of them might be best friends, but they sometimes needed a translator to properly communicate.

There had to be something she could dig up on Owen Pettibone. If he knew whose gun it was, they wouldn't need the cops and the stupid gun shops and gun laws to find out why the gun was in Hackenstrat's office. They could have the story ahead of everyone. A real story.

Rose went to Owen's Twitter page and scrolled through idly. A lot of it seemed to be written in code, or it was too stupid to be understood. "Red leather yellow leather red leather rawr." "Underwear underwhy overeasy ha ha ha." And then, along with a picture of a dog at a tea party, "PWNED!"

Owen—owned—pwned. That at least made sense. Sort of. It reminded Rose of something. . . .

She closed the laptop and opened her Instagram, scrolling through picture after picture of a dark gym lit up with tiny keychain flashlights. She wasn't exactly sure what she was looking for, but she kept scrolling, chasing the feeling that she had seen "pwned" someplace before.

After another dozen dark pictures she threw the phone onto the seat next to her and reopened the laptop. It would come to her or it wouldn't; in the meantime, she had a story to finish.

Grant stared at his dead phone. He was cut off. He would have to wait to get out, like everyone else in the gym.

This whole thing was taking too long. They'd been stuck in the gym for an hour, but it felt much longer. If Grant still bit his nails, they would be bleeding by now, but he'd stopped biting them the summer after junior year post-Rosie-kiss because she'd held his hand and it became suddenly clear to him what a gross habit it was.

He put the dead phone in his pocket and clenched his hands into fists.

"Hello! Hi, everyone. Hello," Ms. Davis said. She'd borrowed the DJ's pineapple mic. At the sound of her amplified voice, everyone stood and surged toward the dance floor. "Whoa, whoa. Okay. So. I know this has been frightening, and I appreciate all your cooperation. I wanted to let you know that I've received word that the SWAT team has nearly finished its sweep, and they'll be escorting you off the premises shortly."

Grant started elbowing his way to the front of the crowd.

"They're asking that you please not congregate in the parking lot or anywhere near the school. Okay? So some of your parents are here, and you can go home with them. Or get a ride from a friend. The important thing is: go home." Ms. Davis handed the mic back to the DJ, who started playing a song. Ms. Davis shook her head at him, and he sighed and turned it off.

"Fuck that!" Fisher Louis shouted. Ms. Davis glared at him, but he only grinned at her. "You're all invited to my house for the best after-party in the known world!"

A bunch of students cheered Fisher's invitation. The other, more serious-minded ones shushed him.

"Did they catch Marty, Ms. Davis?" Grant asked. He didn't shout as loud as Fisher had, but the people around him heard the question and looked up at the stage for the answer.

Ms. Davis glanced around helplessly. "They're asking you to stay away from the school. It's still a potential crime scene."

That sounded like they hadn't found him. Those closest to the stage exploded in chatter, spreading the news to the rest of the gym. Fisher came up and pounded Grant's back.

"Still investigating?" he asked.

"I seek the truth."

Fisher nodded and pointed at Grant with double finger guns. A little tasteless, but it was Fisher. "You're coming to my party. I'm going to help you find this little turd."

"Thank you."

"No problem, man. What the cops can't do we have to do ourselves, am I right?"

Fisher didn't wait for Grant to agree but plowed his way to the front of the line for the door.

Grant followed, slightly less aggressively. He would straighten everything out once he got outside. He'd find Rosie, and they'd find Nick and get the password, and then they could decide what to do about Marty and the gun and the best story of their lives. Out there in the world, there were phone chargers and Wi-Fi. He ducked ahead of some slow-walking girls in five-inch heels and found himself behind JB.

A fanciful part of him wanted to arrive in the parking lot at the same time as JB, and for Rose to see Grant first, run to *him*, do that Rosie-chatter thing to him until he had to interrupt her. But the realist in him knew that if he and JB showed up at the same time, she'd be more likely to run to JB. Either way, if he stood exactly in the right line of sight, by the time they reached her, he would know one way or the other: was she back, or was she lost for good?

Or he could avoid that moment entirely.

He grabbed a prom program from the floor and ripped out a page. He had a pen in his lapel pocket—because you never knew—and he wrote quickly with the paper resting on his hand. The ballpoint occasionally poked through the page, but he kept writing and writing, and when he was done he folded it twice and then tapped JB on the shoulder.

The note would be his insurance. If his plan worked, great. If it didn't . . . well, it wouldn't hurt to cover all his bases.

"JB, we meet again," Grant said. "I guess we do have reasons to talk after all."

JB frowned, as if he didn't remember the conversation Grant was referring to. "Good thing Marty didn't hurt anyone."

"We're a lucky bunch. But I also heard he might be innocent."

"You hear things, huh?"

"I find things out. There's a difference." Grant crossed his arms nonchalantly. "Rosie told me. She went to the *Gazette* room and saw him."

"She what?" JB seemed genuinely surprised.

"Oh, she didn't say?"

"Hey, man," JB said, turning away from the front of the line and stopping traffic flowing toward the door. "I'm not jealous or anything, but you need to give it a rest with Rose."

"If you're not jealous, then that's a weird piece of advice. Is it supposed to be for my own good?"

"Yeah, maybe it is."

"Thanks, but I can take care of myself."

"Like you took care of Rose?"

JB had four inches on Grant, and facing off with him made Grant feel like a freshman again, shorter than everyone in the school. Luckily, that year (okay, two years) had given him practice doing battle when physically overmatched. "You've got nothing to worry about, Jason Baxter. Rosie's writing a story, that's all."

"She's writing a story?"

Grant savored JB's look of surprise for a split second. "Yes. She didn't tell you?"

"She didn't—"

"Has she been in touch at all?"

"Sure, she texted—"

"Oh, I wouldn't read too much into it. She's been so busy and it's been a hectic time. That's probably why she told me to tell you to meet her."

"She what?"

"Right, yeah, sorry, so much has been happening, I nearly forgot." Grant smiled through a twinge in his conscience. "We were talking about the story a little while ago, and she said if I ran into you, I should tell you to meet her at the *Gazette* room."

JB shook his head. People pushed past JB and Grant to get to the door. "She wants me to go into the school? Now?"

Grant lowered his voice and ducked closer to JB. "Between you and me, Marty is not a threat to anyone, so don't worry about it. She really wanted to see you."

"I should give her a call—" He looked and his phone and frowned. "It died."

Grant sent a silent prayer of thanks for his good luck. "Yeah—mine, too, otherwise I'd let you borrow it. And hers probably died as well, and that's why she didn't let you know herself. Along with the fact she's been so busy with this story, and sometimes she forgets things, and anyway she told me to tell you and probably figured that it had been taken care of."

JB considered this onslaught of information.

"She wants me to go into the school," he said. "Even with all the cops . . ."

"Oh, come on. They've cleared it. You can sneak out, can't you? You sneaked out earlier when you and Rose went to the *Gazette* for her MREJ." JB's forehead creased even further. "The award," Grant clarified.

"I guess," JB said.

"Obviously you don't *have* to go. You'll see her tomorrow, probably."

"She texted that she wanted to go to Fisher's after-party."

"And she probably does! But she's in there"—Grant pointed behind him, to the interior doors to the school—"not out there." He pointed at the line and the cops ushering people through the door.

JB looked between the doors doubtfully. Grant almost couldn't stand it. He wasn't sure if he would burst out laughing or crying. JB was a better person than he was, and Grant had proved it. Grant shoved the note into JB's hand and started backing away. "When you see her, give her this, okay? Thanks a ton, man. Well, okay, good luck to you, bye now," Grant said, rejoining the line.

He didn't look back, but no doubt JB had taken the bait, because why would Grant lie?

REPORTER'S SOURCE COMPROMISED

Fall of sophomore year, Grant heard a rumor that there was hazing happening on the football team, so he started going to practices. Nothing ever happened out in the open, of course, but he got a sense of who everyone was, and he identified a freshman who he thought would talk to him. Young-looking. Shorter than the other guys. A little worried. Basically, a kid who reminded Grant of himself.

Every morning for a week, he waited at the kid's locker before school, before the rest of the team got in, and tried to convince him to talk. *Everything you tell me would be between the two of us. We won't publish your name and no one will find out it was you. You'll be doing a favor for the rest of the kids on the team who aren't brave enough to talk to me. I promise, it'll all work out.*

On Friday, the kid walked into the *Gazette* room before the game. Grant was the only one there—Rose was covering the game, Nick had gone home sick, and the rest of the staff actually went out and had fun on a nonclosing Friday. Grant tried to stay professional even as his mind raced with excitement, writing and rewriting before he even heard what the kid had to say. *Thank you for coming. Why don't you sit down and tell me everything?*

The kid confirmed: Yes, there was hazing. Mostly annoying, sometimes dangerous. He described having to wear other kids' jockstraps on their faces and only being allowed to crawl on the locker-room floor. He told Grant about freshmen being given so much to drink they blacked out, and being forced to clip helmets to their skin until they bled. He said the coach knew but turned a blind eye.

The kid's story became Grant's first front-page article.

What Grant hadn't realized was that there were just enough specific times and places and incidents in the story that careful readers—like, say, the kid's teammates—could eliminate each suspected leaker until only the kid remained. He was the only one who had seen all the things the article reported on—the only one who could know the precise combination of facts to paint that particular picture.

So all of Grant's promises of confidentiality and protection came to nothing.

Grant didn't like to think of the kid's name. He hadn't used it in the article, not that it mattered, but he felt that naming the kid, even in his mind, made the whole thing worse.

The kid ran into the *Gazette* room after school the day the article published. He was holding a copy of the paper and he was crying from anger and fear.

"You're a liar," he said, throwing the paper onto Grant's computer keyboard. "And you're going to get me killed."

"What's the matter?" Grant asked, alarmed.

"They can tell it's me!"

"But I didn't use your name," Grant said.

"So what? They're not idiots. Not like you." All other activity in the newsroom stopped as the kid's volume increased. He pointed at Grant and shouted, "Don't trust him! He'll use you, and he doesn't care!"

No one knew what to say when the kid ran out again. Rose twisted her mouth sympathetically and went back to the story she was writing. Nick hummed and put in his earbuds. The editor in chief came over to Grant's desk and asked him if he was okay.

"Should we . . . tell someone?" Grant asked him.

The editor in chief shrugged. "Who are we going to tell? The administration read the story. They can do something if they feel like it."

"Maybe we shouldn't have published it."

The editor in chief backed away from Grant's desk, holding up his hands. "Hey, you wanted the front page. I didn't make you do anything."

"I'll be more careful next time," Grant said, and the editor in chief snorted.

"You'll do something worse next time."

The next day, the kid came to school pulped. He had two

black eyes, a gash in his cheek that needed stitches, and a broken rib. He couldn't play football anymore—not that he wanted to.

It had been a good article, but had it been worth getting the shit kicked out of someone?

Bad things happened to people all the time, whether or not their stories were in the paper. The kid *wanted* to tell Grant about the hazing, or he wouldn't have talked. And the hazing stopped after the story went public, so it had accomplished something concrete and positive. Grant and the kid had done that, together.

"Would you have done it, if you were me?" Grant asked Rose and Nick that day at lunch.

"Absolutely," Rose said.

Nick looked startled, as if Grant had ripped off a human mask and revealed an alien underneath. "Wait. Don't tell me you feel bad about this?"

"Um," Grant said.

"Oh my god, Grant has a conscience!"

Rose rolled her eyes at Nick and punched Grant's shoulder. "Come on, Grant. It was a good story."

"Right," Grant said doubtfully.

"You worked really hard for this. You couldn't have known it would be so easy to identify him, before he told you everything he knew."

"Hmmmmm."

"And anyway, everyone will forget this in a week. They'll be on to the next thing."

The kid won't, Grant thought. *The kid will remember this forever.*

That night he found himself in Rose's kitchen with Rose's mother while Rose herself took the garbage out to the curb.

"Do you think I'm a bad person?" he asked her.

His own mom would've said "Of course not" and given him a lecture about all his stellar qualities, but Rose's mom considered the question. "I don't think people are good or bad in and of themselves. Are you doing good or causing harm?"

"What if doing good causes harm?"

She tilted her head, thinking, as Rose stomped up the back stairs. "If you're honest with yourself, you'll know if you're doing something for the right reasons, Grant."

But he wasn't sure he would know the right reasons if he saw them. When he was investigating the hazing, he hadn't been thinking about whether it would be good or bad. He could tell himself after the fact that it was good, but that wasn't why he'd done it. He'd decided to pursue the story and the kid because of his own selfish preference about the outcome—he wanted a front-page story.

It was almost as if trying to decide whether something was good or bad was an impossible task, and instead he should skip to what was best for the paper. That way it wasn't up to him and his sense of judgment and his guilty conscience—he could offload all his decisions to his higher power. He wasn't religious, but he could see how this type of shortcut for decision-making could be useful. (Though he suspected religious people wouldn't care for his description of it as a shortcut.) The question was simple: What did God—aka the *Gazette*—want him to do?

Thinking about it that way, he'd *had* to tell the kid that he'd be safe, because he needed the kid's information, because it made a great story. The *Gazette* wanted him to lie.

Every time he told a source or an interviewee what they needed to hear, it got a little easier, until it started to feel to Grant almost like he was telling the truth. If he still felt guilty about the kid or any number of other things he had or hadn't said or done, well, that must be because he didn't believe in the *Gazette* hard enough, and he'd try even harder.

He thought about it sometimes, though.

The kid's bruised face.

The gash where his cheek had caught the side of an open locker.

Grant's article, above the fold, on every desk of every homeroom.

Grant telling the kid, "Don't worry. I'd never compromise my source."

Movement at the gym doors caught Rose's attention through the limo's window. She saved the story she was writing, clicked out of the internet research she'd done (she'd figured out Owen's "pwned," thank god—that was one stroke of luck), and put Grant's laptop on the seat next to her. Then she opened the limo's roof window and stood on a seat to get a better view.

A single one of the gym's outside exits had been opened. SWAT-team cops formed a line leading away from the building, watching the well-dressed promgoers leave one by one. Some kids ran to their parents and hugged them, sobbing, while others strolled up nonchalantly and shrugged off their concern.

A group of parents yelled at Ms. Davis and demanded to talk to Mr. Hackenstrat, who had disappeared after he finished his last round of TV interviews. The rest of the teachers and students and parents got into their cars and, once in them, tried to exit the lot all at once. Cops attempted to direct traffic as everyone let off steam by screaming at one another through the windows.

Rose searched the faces for Grant. He'd said they'd meet out here as soon as they could. She checked her phone, but there were no new messages.

"Look who it is," Fisher Louis said, strolling up to the limo. "Where've you been?"

Rose stifled a shudder. Fisher Louis still gave her the creeps, and by far the worst aspect of dating JB meant that she was forced to enter Fisher's orbit on a regular basis. She remembered the profile she'd written on him, and she got the sense he remembered it, too, and was laughing at her silently.

"I got caught out in the school during the lockdown," she said, affecting breeziness.

"And now you're drinking all my booze." Fisher waved at the limo driver, who had been chain-smoking on the curb, and pointed to the limo. As the chauffeur stubbed out his cigarette and got back into the driver's seat, Fisher rolled his eyes at Rose and sighed impatiently. "You didn't see Marty when you were in there, did you?"

"No," Rose lied.

"No one seems to have spotted that kid. He can't even go postal right."

Fisher ducked into the limo and opened up the cooler of beer that Rose hadn't noticed. Rose kept her head out the sunroof so she could keep searching and also avoid being alone with Fisher in the back of the limo.

Everywhere she looked there was another boy in a tuxedo who wasn't Grant. And cops—cops everywhere, discouraging those left behind from congregating. The police made her jumpy. No one knew she'd seen Marty in the *Gazette* room—Fisher had seemed to believe her, like the cops had—but she worried.

And there was Grant, finally—his tux slightly bedraggled, his glasses and hair askew, elbowing and ducking his way to her. "Rosie!" he called.

She ducked down into the limo. Fisher refused to move, so she had to crawl over his legs to the door, which she did as quickly as possible, leaving Grant's laptop on the bench seat and slamming the door behind her. "Grant!" she said as they stood across from each other by the side of the limo.

She hadn't been running, but she found it hard to take a full breath. Standing across from Grant like this made Rose think of the time they'd started kissing outside her mother's car, probably only a few parking spaces away from this one, and she wondered if Grant was thinking the same thing. His face, visible only in the flash of police lights and headlights, beamed at her, and his eyes met hers with total focus, as if they were standing in an empty room, alone. There were enough people talking and shouting and cars honking that no one could hear them even if anyone was paying attention, which they weren't. But they leaned their heads together anyway.

"Have you seen Nick?" Grant asked, and at the same time, she said, "I know how to get to Owen."

They laughed and Rose raised her hand to talk. "Haven't seen Nick, but I think I know how to get Owen to talk."

"Perfect. And the story's done?"

"Ready for you to read—laptop's in the limo. Did they . . ." She hesitated, and Grant shook his head.

"I don't think they found Marty. They're acting squirrelly about it."

"Have you seen Jenna?"

"She didn't show up in the gym."

Rose frowned, the spell of Grant's arrival temporarily broken. "Maybe she'll be at Fisher's. Owen'll come, so that's where I'm going."

"Nick and Oliver will probably be there, too. Impossible to find them in this madness."

"I guess I'll see you there."

Grant tilted his head at the limo. "This is Fisher's? I bet he'd give me a ride. He's been trying to help out with the story."

"He has?" Rose frowned deeper. That didn't make sense. Fisher wasn't a helpful sort of person. Her head started to pound as she imagined Grant riding in the limo with her and Fisher and JB—

She spun around and stood on her tiptoes, searching. "Where's JB?"

Grant didn't answer. When she stopped looking for JB and

focused on Grant again, his nose scrunched up as if smelling something unpleasant.

"What did you do?" she asked.

"Nothing!"

"Where is he, Grant?"

"He's fine! I think. He's probably fine."

Rose pushed Grant in the chest with both hands. Not super hard, but he cringed away. "Tell me what you did."

"So suspicious. It's not a good look on you."

"I could give a shit what you think looks good on me," she snapped.

"Frankly, I'm offended that you think I'd interfere with your boyfriend. I want nothing but perfect happiness for you, Rosie, you should know that, and if Jason Baxter is your soul mate, then I wouldn't dream of keeping you apart."

The more he talked, the more her stomach sank. "I know I shouldn't expect better, because it's you being you, but still. I expected better."

Grant rubbed the back of his neck with his palm and stared above her head. "We're supposed to write this story," he said, no more bombast, and for a second she could see how small he'd made himself, sneaking around and lying and avoiding confrontation. She felt sorry for him. "He's waiting for you at the *Gazette*."

And then her pity evaporated.

Fisher stuck his head out of the sunroof. "It's time to move!" he called. "Leitch. Come on, dude. There's room."

Grant got in the limo, but Rose hovered outside the door.

Fisher snapped his fingers at her. "Rose. In or out."

"I have to go get JB," Rose said.

"Your funeral," Fisher said, and made a face. "Bad choice of words. You can meet us there, but the host is departing now."

"JB's your friend," Rose said.

"And he's your date. You're the one who lost him."

Fisher banged on the divider between the back seat and the driver, and the limo started to move. Grant looked out the window at Rose. "Rosie—"

"Don't talk to me."

The limo crept through the crowded parking lot. Rose pushed against the flow of traffic to head back to Hawks High.

SIX

PROM DIVIDES SENIOR *GAZETTE* STAFF

Marty asked Jenna to prom on their fourth date, at the beginning of March of senior year. "And you said yes?" Rose asked Jenna as they rehashed the date over doughnuts the next morning.

Jenna blinked slowly, smiling like she had a secret. "Of course."

Everyone knew Marty—he was the type of person who made himself known, whether on purpose or from the natural expression of his exuberant personality. Rose had never considered that he might want to date someone, and she never in a million years thought that her best friend would fall in love with him. But that was what happened, suddenly, out of nowhere. One day Jenna was a caustic free spirit who had pissed off and befriended the alternative art crews in a dozen area high schools, and the next day she was in love with a gangly, inept prankster with a huge white-dude 'fro.

"He took me up to the pedestrian bridge over the highway

to ask me," Jenna said. "And he'd rigged up electric lights in the chain-link fence and dressed up in this plaid suit and everything."

"The pedestrian bridge?"

"Yeah, you know at the very edge of the park there's that big hill that's actually hiding the highway? There's a bridge to cross over."

"In case you need to stroll across six lanes to the next town over. Sure."

"You are entirely missing the point. It was *beautiful*."

"On the pedestrian bridge above the highway."

Jenna breathed out through her nose. "The pedestrian bridge, yes! Your mockery is obviously a shield for your intense jealousy."

Rose picked at her red velvet doughnut. It had been a long time since she'd hung out with Taj. She hadn't kissed anyone since the day she and Grant had kissed, and that was months and months ago. She'd been busy with college applications and the MREJ deadline and a couple of big issues of the *Gazette*, so time had passed without her noticing.

"Now you have to get a date," Jenna proclaimed. "You should go with that hot guy who gave you his number in French."

"JB? I thought you said he was boring."

"He's a sure thing, though."

Rose made a face. "Thanks a lot. But maybe I should go with someone I'm actually interested in."

Jenna shook her head. "Nuh-uh. There's no way Grant's going to ask you. You know that, right?"

"Maybe I'll ask him."

The old Jenna might've rolled her eyes at that. The old Jenna—pre-Marty—might've challenged Rose, asked why she thought she'd suddenly start taking charge with Grant when she'd done very close to nothing about him for years. The old Jenna might've said that Rose could do better.

The new Jenna squeezed Rose's hand and stole the remains of her red velvet doughnut. "You totally should," she said. "Enough of this sexual tension. Jump his bones already."

Jenna and Marty had started having sex, and Jenna had become an evangelist for doing it. She'd always been open about hooking up with her previous flings, guys or girls, but she hadn't been quite so fervent about it before. Rose got a sort of funny queasy-jealous-embarrassed feeling when she thought about what might have precipitated the change in her attitude.

Rose didn't have any objections to having sex if it felt like it was the right time, but it never really felt right in the cars or park benches where she and Taj had hooked up. But then again sometimes she thought about licking Grant's ear and felt all the blood in her body rush to the surface of her skin, and she suspected that if she managed to find herself alone in the back seat of a car with Grant again, she wouldn't worry so much about whether it was the perfect location.

Jenna was right. She should jump his bones.

She didn't know why she couldn't quite manage to do it. Whether it was Grant subtly pushing her away or her own self-preservation instincts kicking in . . . she couldn't cross the invisible barrier.

A couple of days later, Rose and Grant were the last ones in the *Gazette* room, as usual. They'd been talking about regular things for a while—Nick worrying himself sick about staying together with Oliver next year when he was at college, which of the disappointing underclassmen was going to be named the next editor in chief, the latest challenge from Hackenstrat—when the topic of prom came up on its own. Rose was writing a series of articles about the cost of tickets, so it had been bound to come up eventually, but she still felt unprepared.

"Are you going?" she asked. "To prom, I mean."

Grant waved his hand dismissively. "It's closing night for the grad issue."

"But you won't be editor in chief anymore. It'll be someone else's problem."

"Still, I'll probably be here."

Rose didn't say anything for another minute.

She called upon the spirits of Susan B. Anthony and Gloria Steinem and Amy Schumer. She shouted down the self-preservation part of herself that was running and waving frantically, signaling that there would be danger ahead.

"Maybe we could go together," she said finally, pushing the words out with every bit of courage she could muster.

"Ha. Yeah. Maybe we should run for king and queen, too. Really blow everyone's minds."

Rose shook her head. "That's not what I meant. . . ."

"Oh, or were you thinking of something a bit more

Carrie-esque? I could start working on my telekinesis, though I haven't made much progress over the past seventeen years."

"Jenna's going with Marty Caulfield," Rose explained before Grant could go on another riff. "She wants us all to go together. Nick and Oliver could come, too."

"Oh." Grant's expression flattened. She couldn't read it, but the lack of smile made her nervous. "Jenna wants us all to go together. A big group."

Rose didn't know how to disagree with that statement, but she tried. "I thought it would be fun."

Fun. Jesus, Rose. You're supposed to be a writer.

Grant's mouth twisted. "Seriously?"

The floor dropped out from underneath her. She fell, wind rushing past her ears. "So . . . that's a no?"

"I didn't think it was your scene. The expensive tickets, the puffed-up pageantry, everyone pretending they're suddenly on the red carpet, the forced nostalgia . . ." He shook his head. "It's ridiculous."

"You don't want to go to prom with me."

Grant's scowl deepened. He seemed mad, which didn't make any sense. Why would he be mad that she wanted to go to prom with him? "No, I'm saying I don't think *you* want to go."

"Why would I bring it up if I didn't want to go?"

"I don't know. Maybe you think it's something you have to do for Jenna, going along with her lovesick, clichéd plans. But you don't, Rosie."

"Don't call me that," she said. Her voice shook. As apprehensive as she had been a second ago, now she was furious, a white-hot column of anger burning a hole through the ceiling. If he was angry with her, she would give him a fight. "Why won't you answer the question instead of giving me all this bullshit about what I should and shouldn't want to do."

Grant pushed his glasses up his forehead and rubbed his left eye. "I don't know what you want me to say."

"Tell me. Once and for all. Do you want to go to prom with me?"

Grant dropped his glasses back into place and shrugged as if ducking out of an awkward embrace. His voice had an edge to it, even as he tried to play it off casually. "Sure, Rosie. If it's that important to you."

"No," Rose said. "No, no, no. Not like that. Forget about it. Forget I said anything at all."

"I mean, if it's such a big deal—"

"It isn't."

Grant shifted at his desk, pushing proofs from one corner to the other. She pretended to read something on her computer, blinking hard.

She wasn't nervous or full of white-hot anger anymore. She felt curiously empty, like a soda bottle shaken and then sprayed, as if every emotion she'd bottled up had burst out all at once. But there was nothing left once it was done.

Grant cleared his throat. "I'd rather be at the *Gazette* than prom," he said.

"Yeah, I got that."

"No, but, listen—I'd rather be here with you."

Rose gave up pretending to read; the screen was too blurry with pent-up tears. "You'd rather spend the night at the *Gazette* than go to prom with me."

Grant looked at her. She could feel him looking, even if her blurry eyes meant she couldn't see his expression. "Wouldn't you rather be here than anywhere else in the world?"

Rose could've killed Grant. So typical. It was always what Grant wanted to do—always on Grant's schedule, always his itinerary. He'd spent too long as editor in chief and expected the entire world to line up on his command.

And at the same time, she owed him a thank-you. If he hadn't tricked JB, she might've been fooled into continuing on with the story and the paper. She'd've fallen off the wagon and woken up tomorrow with a *Gazette* hangover, wondering how she'd managed to sacrifice her entire prom for what Grant wanted. Again.

JB's phone went straight to voice mail, so it must've died like everyone else's. Rose tapped her screen, grateful for the limo driver's charger, and sent JB a message.

If she waited, maybe the police would bring JB out when they completed their search. Only they'd already cleared the *Gazette* room—when she'd been brought out—and so it seemed unlikely that they'd think to look in there again. JB was stuck in there. Or maybe when he realized she wasn't meeting him, he'd try to wander out and accidentally get shot. Maybe he'd find Marty and Marty would shoot him.

Damn Grant, leaving her with this shitshow, speeding away in a limo. In *her* limo. With *her* story.

Not that the story mattered anymore. She'd gotten distracted—Grant had made her get distracted. She should've known. She should've been on her guard, waiting for him to pull something like this. He wouldn't ask her to prom—he wouldn't go to prom with her if it was her suggestion—but he'd manipulate her into ruining her own party for the good of his precious paper.

(Admittedly, he didn't plant the gun in Hackenstrat's office and start the whole catastrophe. . . . Oh my god, he didn't plant the gun, did he? No. No. Even Grant wouldn't go that far. He wouldn't. He had limits. They were tough to find sometimes, and they shifted around unpredictably, but he had them.)

Now she had to rescue her boyfriend. She felt less like a hero and more like a janitor cleaning up Grant's messes.

Two cops stopped Rose before she could get to the gym doors. Their flak jackets bristled with weapons, making them appear larger than they were. When she told them she needed to get back inside, they laughed at her.

"My boyfriend's in there," she said.

"You're the killer's girl?" Cop A asked. "The detectives and agents have been looking for you."

"No, I'm—" She stopped. "You've been looking for Jenna?"

"If Jenna's the girl's name, yeah. If you're not her, then what do you mean your boyfriend's in there?"

Rose filed away that information for later. "I'm telling you he didn't evacuate. My dumbass former friend told him I was waiting for him inside. In a classroom."

The cops looked at each other. Cop B spoke into the walkie-talkie on his shoulder. "Yeah, do we have any kids still in the building?"

The answer came back after a couple of seconds of static. "Negative. We made a clean sweep."

"He's out here, honey," Cop A said. "Maybe look a little harder in the parking lot?"

Rose looked over their shoulders at the school's doors, open, but still fifty feet away. If she made a run for it, would they shoot her? Probably best not to risk it.

They thought the school was empty except for a hiding Marty. What would happen if they spotted JB in their search? Sure, Marty was white and scrawny and completely unlike JB in almost every way, but the fact that JB was a black teen stuck in a locked-down school didn't seem like a huge plus, no matter what Marty looked like. JB needed her.

She squeezed her purse, searching for a pen, but the only things that would fit in her tiny wristlet were her phone, ID, and a lipstick. Normally she always had a pen, and it had given her a twinge of anxiety not to pack one, but at the time she wasn't supposed to need one. Regular people didn't need an emergency pen in case they had to do impromptu interviews at their senior prom. Her fingers twitched.

"What are your names?" she asked.

Cop B raised his eyebrows at her. "We're a little busy here, so why don't you go—"

She smiled at them sweetly. "You can't tell me your names?"

"Officer Laughton," Cop A said.

"Officer Washington," Cop B said.

Rose's interview brain took over, and she started asking them questions. The key to interviewing was to ask questions fast enough that her subjects didn't have time to think about whether or not they should or wanted to answer the questions, which meant starting the next question before they finished the last syllable of the last word of their answer.

"What precinct are you from? How long have you been there? Where were you before that? Where'd you go to high school? Have you ever been to a lockdown before? Have you ever fired your service weapon? What do you think's going to happen to Marty when they catch him? Why do you think he did this?"

She could ask these questions without thinking too hard about them—interviewing required being able to float from question to question without pausing and sounding doubtful. If the interviewer sounded like she didn't know what she was talking about, her subjects could remember themselves and decide not to answer.

While she asked and nodded and inserted friendly asides, her mind turned over the situation. There had to be a way to get into the school—or at least for the cops to take her seriously when she said that there was still someone in there.

Of course, she happened to know that there *was* someone else still in the building. Someone the police wanted very much to find.

She'd get herself in a tremendous amount of trouble. She couldn't even properly guess how much trouble it would be—and it would seriously mess up the article she'd written.

But it was Grant's fault. He'd put her in this situation. He'd be furious—but what did she care if he was mad? Maybe it was his turn to be mad, and her turn to shrug and tell him to suck it up. *So sorry, Grant,* she imagined telling him. *Maybe if you'd been a little less* yourself, *this wouldn't have happened.*

She stopped asking questions and waited for the cops to come to the end of their answers. Then she took a deep breath.

"I know where Marty Caulfield's hiding."

EXPLORATION AND INNOVATION AT THE *GAZETTE*

Rose got the idea sophomore spring, as she lay on the *Gazette* floor staring up at the foam drop ceiling, trying to come up with a headline for a story about Hawks High's losing baseball team. It was a Friday and everyone else had gone home, including that year's editor in chief. Nick had left to find snacks, so Rose and Grant were alone.

"Good effort," she said to herself. "Solid effort. Solid attempt. Noble attempt. Hard-fought battle. Battle. Batting. Batting average. 'Batting Average'?" She rolled over, raised herself onto an elbow, and glanced at Grant, who was typing on a computer at the desk next to her.

"Good, but too mean," Grant said.

Rose sank back onto the floor. The ceiling was an ordinary school ceiling: pieces of mottled fiberglass board, about two feet square, with regular breaks for fluorescent lights.

"Why is the ceiling in here lower than the ceiling in the hall?" she asked.

"Because this is a drop ceiling," Grant said. "Better acoustics for classrooms."

Rose looked at the edge of the room, where the fiberglass squares appeared to continue on over the top of the wall. "Huh," she said. "Do you think the walls between the rooms go up to the real ceiling, or is it empty space?"

Grant stopped typing. "I'm not sure."

Rose stood and pulled a chair to the edge of a desk, then climbed the chair and the desk. She pushed at one of the squares, and it lifted easily away from the metal frame. She rested it to the side and stood up on her tiptoes, shining her phone's flashlight toward the wall. "I think it goes all the way over," she said. She blinked, looking in the direction of the light and not at Grant. "You know, if we were careful, we could climb into any room in the school this way."

"That is . . . interesting," Grant said.

"We could spy on the teachers' lounge. Get a bunch of juicy leads," Rose joked, but neither she nor Grant laughed.

When Nick came back with chips from the vending machine, Rose and Grant were on their computers and the ceiling square was back in place.

By the time the limo parked in Fisher's huge circular driveway, the party was in full swing. He must've left the door unlocked— or someone had climbed in a window in their eagerness to get the party started. It was as if the stress of the past couple of hours had exploded into a frenzy, and everyone considered it their personal responsibility to get shitfaced in order to show the world how resilient they were.

Grant didn't feel like celebrating. Maybe when they found out who owned the gun. Maybe when the story was up.

That was what was bothering him. Not what happened with Rosie. It was the story, always.

The house itself was a massive stone mansion, lit up with floodlights that showed the multiple turrets and columns and windows of all shapes and sizes gleaming brightly. Grant didn't exactly live in a shack, but he could've comfortably tucked most of his house into Fisher's house's three-car, two-story garage.

Grant had never been to Fisher's house before. He hadn't been to very many parties, period. And by "very many" he meant "none at all, unless you count drinking schnapps in Nick's basement while watching *Stop Making Sense*."

He tried to let Fisher and Mer go ahead of him, fussing with his laptop and his phone in the limo driver's charger and finishing his LaCroix peach pear, but Fisher hung back, keeping up a stream of questions about where he thought Marty could've gone.

"He's hiding," Grant said when he couldn't drag his feet any longer.

"No shit," Fisher said. "I think we're going to need to get a little more specific than that, right?"

Grant watched Fisher. Rose had seemed surprised that Fisher would take such an interest in the story, and since she'd mentioned it, it didn't seem entirely normal. It had taken Grant longer than it should've to notice the oddness, because as Nick had pointed out, he generally believed that things that were interesting to him were interesting to everyone, no matter how often that was proved untrue.

Fisher propped open the double-height wooden front door with an angular metal object from the sculpture garden on the lawn, then waved Grant into the house. People sat in their tuxes and gowns on the curving, carpeting steps in the foyer and filled the multiple sitting rooms all the way back to the kitchen, where competing stereo systems pumped a confusion of pop songs.

There was a line of people in front of a phone charger lying on a side table. In the kitchen, a table full of alcohol had appeared like magic, and girls mixed drinks in expensive-looking crystal goblets. From there, a wall of French doors opened onto the back porch. Fisher's backyard led out to the golf course, giving the illusion of acres of open fields.

Mer disappeared once they reached the kitchen, and Fisher poured Grant a drink that was half pineapple juice, half vodka. Grant sipped the drink and sent mental good vibes and ocean breezes to the prom DJ, wherever he'd gone.

"So what's next? How do we nail this guy?" Fisher asked. He gulped his drink as if it were Gatorade.

"Rose said she had a way to get Owen to tell us what he knows," Grant said.

Fisher shook his head. "A of all, no way that dude knows jack shit, and secondly, I doubt he'd tell you anything even if he did. And C, Rose ain't here."

Grant shifted uneasily. "It's true, Owen did not seem particularly forthcoming the last time we spoke."

Fisher used his glass goblet to poke Grant in the chest. "You need to talk to Marty. He's the only one who knows anything."

Grant stepped away from Fisher, hopefully without giving the impression that he was running away. "The other thing is, I have to find Nick," he said. "You really don't need to help me. Enjoy your party."

"I'll enjoy it when they catch the little asswipe." Fisher caught Grant by the lapel and pulled him closer, as if Grant weighed nothing at all. Grant's feet were not quite flat on the floor. "You'll let me know if you find him, won't you?"

Grant made himself smile out of instinct. He didn't know what Fisher would do if he knew Grant was scared, and that scared him even more. "For sure," he said.

Fisher let him go and Grant took a swig of his drink. Fisher clapped him on he shoulder. "Who's that guy—Encyclopedia Brown? No, no, you're more like the dude on *Blue's Clues*."

"Steve?" Dumb, Grant. Just because you know something doesn't mean it has to fly out of your mouth.

"Yeah, Steve. That's totally you. It's hilarious."

Fisher shook his head, unsmiling, and then spotted someone touching a painting. He left Grant to go yell at the offender. Grant put down his drink to straighten his jacket and then decided not to pick it up again. He had the computer—and if he was going to be the only one reading the article before it was posted, he needed his full mental capacities.

The only one.

His stupid, impulsive plan to waylay JB had backfired, and now he was alone. Even worse, Rose was out there somewhere—with her boyfriend—totally pissed at Grant.

He wandered down hallways at random, looking for a quiet place to sit and write, but the party had taken over every room he came across. Strip poker in the study. Dance party in the den. Kissing in the kitchen. Will there be boning in the bedroom? Crosswords in the closet? *Come on, Rosie, help me think of a third.*

Logrolling in the laundry room? *You could do better than that, if you were here.*

He opened the door of what turned out to be a bathroom and saw two guys making out by the sink. He let out a happy shout. "Nick! Ollie!"

They broke apart. Oliver looked away, and Nick glared at Grant. "What the hell?"

"I am *so* glad I found you. We need to talk about the password."

"Jesus, Grant!"

"What? You're not still mad at me, are you?"

"Consider the fact I might be mad about something different, now!"

Grant closed the bathroom door behind him and sat on the closed toilet lid. Oliver had composed himself and lounged on the edge of the enormous Jacuzzi, cane resting against his thigh. Nick still stood in front of the sink, face beet red from anger and embarrassment.

"Oh, we're all friends," Grant said, waving his hand.

"Do you sit in on the intimate moments of all your friends?" Oliver asked mildly.

"When it's important."

Nick tried to take a deep breath, but it got caught, and his face turned even redder. "Tell me."

"Tell you what?"

"Tell me what this stupid story is, you asshole! I know you're not going to leave until you do, so go."

Grant held up his laptop. "Read it yourself."

They rested the laptop on the edge of the marble sink. Grant read over Nick and Oliver's shoulders. Rosie was so good. Grant knew that, of course, but the way she'd distilled the entire story into a couple of clear, direct paragraphs made his heart palpitate.

"We wanted to find out whose gun it is," Grant said. "But Rosie's not here—"

"Shhh," Nick said, and he kept reading.

"Rosie wanted to have proof that it wasn't Marty's gun. She thought people wouldn't believe us otherwise."

"You could always post an update," Oliver said. "When you find out whose it is."

Grant shot Oliver a grateful smile, and he nodded benevolently.

Nick took a step back from the computer. Oliver reached out and held his arm. "Nick," Oliver said.

"Yeah," Nick said.

They sat in silence for another few moments, until Grant couldn't stand it anymore. "So . . . you agree, right? You think this needs to go up?"

Nick shook his head, and Grant reminded himself not to scream. "You could send this to a real paper, you know," Nick said. "The *Trib*, the *Sun-Times*, the *Sentinel-Journal*."

"Are you saying the *Gazette*'s not a real paper?" Grant asked.

"No, I mean—you didn't need me. Not really."

Grant inhaled sharply. "Of course I need you."

"Right," Nick said, unconvinced.

"If it isn't on the *Gazette*—it isn't really ours. Yours and mine and Rosie's." Grant held his breath as Nick and Oliver communicated with their eyes. Finally, he couldn't wait any longer. "So are you going to give the password or not?"

Nick rolled his eyes. "Yes."

Normally closings took hours—arguments and adjustments and stressing over every last comma. This time, they had the story up in five minutes. A couple of formatting tweaks and a brief debate over the best headline, and it was live.

STUDENT CLAIMS HE FOUND GUN
IN VICE-PRINCIPAL'S OFFICE
BY ROSE REGNERO

The cops brought JB out of the school in handcuffs. He looked shocked and scared, and Rose wanted to take a picture and send it to Grant so he could see what his stupid plots and plans actually did to a person. And then she felt even worse, because her first instinct was to shove this in Grant's face, instead of wanting to make that scared look on JB's face go away.

"JB!" she called.

He saw her and tried to wave, but he had to raise both hands. "What's going on, Rose?"

"Yes, Ms. Regnero, I'd like an answer to that, too," a detective in a boxy pantsuit said. She trailed behind JB, and unlike the rest of the cops, she seemed unarmed and unarmored. When they reached Rose, she stuck out her hand to shake, examining Rose intently. "I'm Detective Hart. There wasn't anyone in your secret hiding place. Only this young man in the classroom, who said he was waiting for you."

Rose drew in her breath and held it. Where had Marty gone?

Detective Hart waited for an answer. The longer Rose paused, the more guilty she would seem. She let out her breath slowly. "No one believed me that JB was still in there."

"You lied to us?"

"I was right about JB, wasn't I?"

Hart put her hands on her hips. "So you *don't* know where Marty Caulfield is?"

Rose shook her head and pressed her lips together tightly. That was true—now. He could be anywhere (the moron).

"And your friend Jenna Chen?" the detective asked. "She and Marty are a couple, aren't they? And you're Jenna's best friend."

"Nice work, putting that together," Rose said, nodding. "I've been looking for Jenna since the lockdown. Have you seen her?"

"I'm the one asking the questions."

"You need to pick up the pace. You're leaving a lot of dead air for me to think in."

Hart frowned and took another step toward Rose, when there was a sudden hubbub from the reporters on the baseball diamond. They shouted over to the cops, asking questions that Rose couldn't make out. Detective Hart's phone rang, and she picked it up.

"Uh-huh. Uh-huh." She stared at Rose. Rose reached for JB's hand, but he didn't take hers. She pretended she had meant to swing her arm instead. "And who wrote it? Rose Regnero. Really."

"Oh boy," Rose said, starting to get an idea of what might have happened.

"Rose, what's going on?" JB asked.

"Things are about to get interesting," Rose muttered.

"They weren't interesting enough?"

Detective Hart hung up. She smiled at Rose, but it wasn't a kind smile. "Ms. Regnero. You're a reporter."

"Yes," Rose said. She could make out a few of the questions coming from the reporters by the baseball field. The words "framed" and "Hackenstrat" and "whose gun" were repeated again and again.

"You spoke to Marty Caulfield tonight, after the lockdown," Hart said.

Rose nodded.

"You *did* know where he was hiding, didn't you?"

Rose shrugged.

"Where is he now, Rose?"

"Beats me."

Hart shook her head, disappointed. "You're going to have to come down to the station to answer a few more questions."

"I'm seventeen. So I think you should probably call my mom, and also I would like to speak to a lawyer, if it's not too terribly much trouble."

The detective's smile sharpened and soured. "Of course you would."

All Grant had to do was tweet the link to Rose's article to a few local reporters, and he saw it run from outlet to outlet, gaining steam with each repetition. His phone exploded with messages, asking follow-up questions and requesting comments. But the only call he made was to his dad, because he had a feeling that his dad's services were about to be necessary, so he might as well wake him and get him up to speed.

When he hung up, Nick was staring at him. Oliver had gone to find drinks and snacks. While talking on the phone, Grant had slid into the dry Jacuzzi and rested his feet up on the spout, with the laptop perched on his lap. Nick sat on the side of the tub, crossed his legs, and folded his hands over his knee. Party noises drifted in through the closed door.

"What's the matter with you?" Nick asked.

"Nothing. I don't know. What makes you ask?"

"You should be bouncing off the walls, but you look like you're about to take a nap."

Grant shrugged, which made him slide deeper into the tub.

"Is this not the picture you had in mind when you thought about your senior prom?" Nick asked.

"Always hated prom. Never thought I'd actually go."

Nick's lip quirked. "Me, too. But here we are."

Grant tilted his head at the bathroom door.

"Things are good with Ollie?"

Nick sighed through his nose. "Bestowing nicknames upon people against their will is one of your more grating habits."

"And?"

Nick shrugged. "We talked about it."

"About next year?" Grant pushed. Nick nodded. "And . . . what did you say?"

Nick jammed his hands deep into his pockets. "Our lives are going to be totally different this time next year. We don't know what exactly is going to change, though—if we'll even be the same people, have the same feelings, or anything. So I don't know how it's going to work."

"So you're going to give up?"

"No!" Nick looked up at the bathroom's gilt ceiling, searching for the right words. "It's like—story meetings at the *Gazette*, right? Everyone comes with their ideas for stories for the month's issue, but no one knows what's going to pan out—who's actually boring and what team is going to win and why something becomes more important. We can try to make a plan, try to picture what will be on the front page and what will fill the rest, but in the end we have to deal with the stories that come in. And it always works out, somehow."

Grant knew what Nick was talking about. "So you're saying you're going to . . . *believe* it will be okay."

"Yeah. I mean, I love him. It seems stupid to throw that away because there may be hot guys in New York or Oliver may get sick of me or we both might fall into a volcano and perish."

"Huh," Grant said.

"Nice deflection, by the way. I believe I asked you what your problem was."

"I don't have a problem."

"Are you worried about Rose?"

Grant shook his head and nodded at the same time, which knocked his skull into a Jacuzzi vent. He wasn't worried about Rose. He knew her well enough to know that she would be fine. He was worried about himself in relation to Rose. He was worried that despite the best story in the world, she might still be gone.

"She quit," he said.

Nick nodded.

"I miss her," he said.

Nick smiled sadly. "Finally, you admit it."

"I miss her," Grant repeated. That was exactly it, in three words: He missed her. He missed talking to her. He missed looking at her. He missed having the other half of his brain. He missed her so, so much. "When she brought up us going to prom . . . I thought she was doing it because Jenna wanted her to. But I guess what she really wanted was someone who would get her a corsage and all that crap."

"Come on. I don't think she quit the *Gazette* because you didn't buy her flowers."

"I pissed her off somehow."

"You are a person who pisses people off. But she knows that about you."

Grant considered filling the bathtub, dunking his head underwater, and holding his breath. It would be quiet there and give him something to do. Instead he got out his phone. No new messages.

"Before, when we were fighting about the password, what did you mean when you said that I'd broken her heart?" he asked Nick.

Nick didn't answer but instead grabbed the phone out of Grant's hands.

"Can I give you advice for once?" Nick asked, holding Grant's phone out of reach.

Grant pointed between the two of them. "That's not the way this thing works."

"Try something new."

Grant nodded reluctantly. "All right, give me your advice. We'll call it your graduation present."

"That's it. That's the advice." Nick gestured widely with Grant's phone. "Try something new."

"Can you be a little more specific?"

Nick held out the phone to him, and Grant grabbed it back

but didn't start texting immediately. Nick giving advice warranted a moment of contemplation, at the very least.

"All I'm saying is," Nick said, "have you truly been happy with the way things have been going? Is this the way you want to end high school? Are you really as self-satisfied and smug and superior as you act?"

"Nice alliteration."

"Proving my point," Nick said. "Anyway, you're you, I get it, I accept that. But maybe it's worth thinking about changing if you being you isn't producing the results you're looking for."

Oliver rapped on the door and Nick opened it for him. He had a bottle of whiskey in one hand and three goblets tucked under the crook of the same arm, plus a bag of chips between his teeth. As Nick relieved him of the whiskey and goblets and started pouring, Grant scootched up to a seated position in the tub.

"Do people change, Oliver?" he asked.

"No," Oliver said through clenched teeth, and in response to Nick's reproving look, he shrugged and took the bag of chips out of his mouth. "Not who they are. Not on the inside."

"You're not helping," Nick complained.

"You can't change who you are. But everyone can change what they do."

Grant toasted Nick and Ollie. He could drink to that.

SOPHOMORE CONTEMPLATES MORTALITY

In the spring of Grant's sophomore year, his mother was diagnosed with breast cancer (thereafter referred to only as Fucking Cancer), had surgery, and began chemo and radiation.

Before the surgery, Grant moved into his dad and stepmom's full-time, and his grandma moved into his bedroom in his mom's house. His mom was sick as hell or she never would've allowed such an arrangement, but her anger about the divorce had been totally overwhelmed by her anger at Fucking Cancer, and Fucking Cancer made her unable to teach yoga or drive him to school or do much of anything but lie on the couch.

His parents' divorce had been acrimonious, that official word that attached itself almost solely to painful divorces. Julie was already pregnant with the twins when his parents split up. His mom had sued for sole custody of Grant, and only after a year of bitter court appearances did she agree to primary custody with regular visitations. At one of the court dates, the judge asked nine-year-old Grant who he wanted to live with, and Grant had said "both of them," which had made everyone equally ticked off, including the judge. The family therapist they'd hired told Grant that no one was mad at him, but Grant could tell an aggrieved sigh when he heard one and didn't need condescending reassurances.

At first, Grant found his dad's house big and loud and weird. His dad didn't know what to say a lot of the time so didn't say much at all. The twins seemed to hate him, based on how many times they farted in his face. Julie kept asking how his mom was doing, as if saying her name all the time would make it less awkward the next time she did it, which it never seemed to do.

But his mom's house was much worse.

The Fucking Cancer was advanced enough that the doctors weren't kidding around; they threw everything they had at it right away. His mother went from healthy (seeming) to raggedly thin and sallow and grumpy in the space of a few weeks. She wasn't stoically facing her illness with good humor—she was pissed, and Grant was, too. Together they railed against Fucking Cancer and fate and the feel-goodery and do-nothingry of the pink ribbons. When she had the energy, they complained about his liar dad and the smells and sounds of living with two six-year-olds. Grant had gotten a lot of his fight from his mom, people said, and they bonded over their shared anger.

It was exhausting, keeping up vitriol for so long.

And there was something horrifying about the way his life had been divided. There were firm boundaries between his worlds, and to go between them he had to become a totally different person. With his mother, at the hospital, he was one Grant. With his dad and his stepmother and brothers, he was another. At the *Gazette* he was one Grant. Talking to his grandma about taking out the trash, he was another. It was as if he'd chopped off pieces of himself and they were each walking and talking and acting like a full real human, but really they were each only a pair of eyes or an arm or the back of his knee.

The only person he could be both Grants and all Grants and sometimes no Grant at all with was Rosie.

She drove him (with her newly acquired license) to the hospital and kept his mother from dwelling on the worst of her complaints. She distracted the twins by letting them color in their Berenstain Bears books. She chatted politely with Julie and his dad. She listened to Grant brainstorming ideas at the *Gazette* and clarified what he meant when he couldn't find the right words. She kept up a conversation with his grandma about reality TV when he was too tired to speak. She sat with him in her mom's car in the driveway of his dad's as he cried.

The day of his mother's final chemo treatment, he asked if they could go to the diner before he went home. They sat in their usual booth. Rose drank an iced tea while Grant, too nervous to eat or drink, tied the paper from her straw into knots.

"What if it didn't work?" he asked.

"Then the doctors will try something else."

"But she's going to die," Grant said, swallowing hard. "I mean, eventually. No matter what."

Rose nodded.

"I don't . . . ," Grant started, and then held his breath until the tears disappeared back into his eye sockets. "I don't want to move back home. I want to stay at Dad's. Is that awful?"

Rose thought about it. He could see her thinking, see the thoughts flash in her eyes, but he did not see judgment. "I don't think it's awful. If it's what you want."

"I want . . ." Grant couldn't explain it out loud, not even to Rose. It was sort of that he was afraid to be alone in the house with his mom. Sort of that he couldn't imagine being Angry Grant full-time, constantly railing at the specter of Fucking Cancer. Sort of that he didn't want his mom to get worse and for him to have to watch. Sort of something else entirely that he couldn't name.

All the things that had annoyed him about his dad's house at first turned out to be the best parts about it. The twins were hilarious—and nothing ever bothered them, at least not for more than five minutes. He liked Julie's careful questions, the way they made him feel that she both respected him and cared about him, but without making a big deal about it. And his dad—well, yeah, he didn't know what to say. But at least he gave Grant some space. At least he wasn't trying to make Grant feel exactly what he felt all the time.

Then there was the big thing, the thing that had made his parents split up in the first place. His dad had cheated. His dad had wanted a different family, not Grant and his mom at all. He wasn't supposed to ever forgive his dad for that, but the past few months all he could muster to think about it was *so what?*

The family therapist might have been right all along, and their divorce might not have had anything to do with him and how much his parents loved him.

Rose held his hand across the table, covering the shreds of straw paper. "You're not awful," she said firmly. "You love your mom. You've been through some shit. That's all."

"She's going to be so upset. I have Dad and Julie and the kids, but she doesn't have anyone else." Grant didn't want Rose to let go of his hand but he felt too jittery not to gesture, and started picking at the paper scraps. "What if you left your mom and went to live with Adam and Jaclyn? Wouldn't she be devastated?"

"Are you kidding me? She'd hunt me down and murder me."

"Very reassuring."

"Your mom isn't my mom. You should ask. See what she says."

So Grant talked to his mom, and as Rose predicted, she wasn't as upset as he feared she'd be. Maybe enough time had passed that she wasn't as pissed at his dad and the world as she used to be. Maybe, like all the inspiring movies and books said, being sick had Changed Her and given her a mellower outlook on life (unlikely, but possible). Maybe she needed some time on her own, too.

And it wasn't like he went to the moon. He was a mile away, and saw her almost every day. He missed her but he also felt better than he had in months. Less like three or four different scrap-heap people, more like himself.

Grant sat in the bathtub, finishing Nick's and Oliver's drinks. They'd gone out to mingle and he'd promised to follow, but something kept him hiding a little bit longer.

His mom had gotten through the chemo and had been free of Fucking Cancer at every checkup since. Grant had been living at his dad's for almost two years. He thought about what Rose had said in the diner all the time. Not the words themselves, but the fact that she'd sat there with him and listened to him and believed him when he said what he wanted.

In his darkest moment, when he thought he was doing the worst thing a person could do, she'd been there to tell him he wasn't a monster. She'd seen him as he was, not as he wanted her to see him or feared she'd see him.

But could he think of any times he'd done the same for her?

Been there for her when she needed him? Unconditionally, completely, honestly, and truly?

He thumbed open his phone and scrolled through the contacts. He'd kept Adam Escarra-Lopez's number saved for the past two and a half years, both his office's number and the personal cell that Grant hadn't told Rose he'd dug up. There had been no reason to use the numbers, but he liked having them available to him.

His finger hovered over the call button.

He liked to think he'd been there for Rose that day, when they went and found her father. She didn't want to talk about it and they never really had. But he kept the numbers anyway.

He didn't really know what he'd say if Adam answered the phone at one in the morning. He kind of wanted to yell at Adam, but even in his imagination the yelling was only a jumble of syllables and nothing specific. WHAT THE FUCK IS WRONG WITH YOU, THAT YOU ABANDONED ROSIE. IT'S YOUR FAULT SHE DOESN'T WANT TO TALK TO YOU OR LET ANYONE IN, mostly.

But Rosie wouldn't want him to call Adam. So he didn't.

He'd gone to prom even though he'd rather have been anywhere else. He'd tried to stop JB from meeting up with Rosie. He'd published the best article either of them had ever worked on. The fact that he was even considering calling Adam meant that he was scraping the bottom of the barrel.

He had no moves left.

Officers Washington and Laughton escorted Rose and JB to the back seat of a police cruiser. JB wouldn't look at her directly. The police car drove away from the school with lights flashing but no siren.

Deep silence filled the car. They'd been driven to prom in a limo and were leaving in a cop car. Rose thought that was sort of funny but guessed JB wouldn't find it particularly amusing.

"I'm glad you're okay," Rose said. When he didn't respond, she felt her nervous chatter taking over. "I know this might seem a little grim right now, but it's going to be totally fine. I'm innocent and you're extremely innocent, so this shouldn't take long and we can get to the party and the night will continue exactly as it's supposed to."

"There's not different types of innocent," JB said. "You did something bad or you didn't."

"Agree to disagree," Rose said, smiling and shrugging slightly.

"I hate that expression. If we disagree so much, what's the point of talking to each other?"

Rose tried to scoot closer to him, but her seatbelt kept her firmly on her side of the seat. "Hey. I'm sorry about all this. But it's Grant's fault in the first place, and secondly, I got you out, didn't I?"

"Yeah." JB sighed. "I really didn't need to be cuffed and put in a police car tonight."

"I'm sorry."

He shook his head. "You don't know how bad this could've gotten."

"I do. That's why I had to tell them—"

"No, Rose. Come on. Believe me when I say you don't understand what it's like to be black with a SWAT-team rifle pointed in your face."

She took a deep breath. He was right. She'd thought about what might happen to JB, but only abstractly. She didn't think about how it would feel to be JB—to be the person stuck in an extremely dangerous situation, alone. And maybe she was imagining it, but she felt a subtle dig that she *should* understand as a person of color—but she never felt right speaking or thinking of herself like that, as if being biracial didn't count, somehow. And hell, she knew she was blind to all sorts of things that JB or Jenna or Taj probably knew without thinking about it.

She had the uncomfortable feeling that she was only seeing

a small sliver of this story, and that the bigger one would always be just outside what she could understand because of parts of herself she couldn't change.

JB's trip into the school was Grant's fault, yeah, but JB wouldn't have been in this situation at all if it weren't for her. So it was her fault, too. "I'm sorry. You're right. But I did try. I told them—"

"Yeah, what did you tell them? A bunch of lies?"

"Not entirely." She tried to make it sound like a joke, but JB shook his head.

"Please, Rose." He dug in his pocket and pulled out a folded-over piece of paper torn from a prom program. Rose could see Grant's scrawl through the white page. "Grant left this with me."

"I don't want it."

"I told him I would give it to you."

The note had been written quickly, in dim light, and Grant's handwriting wasn't easy to decipher in ideal conditions. The back of a police cruiser wasn't ideal by any stretch of the imagination. But Rose had a lot of practice interpreting Grant.

Dear Rosie,

If you're reading this, you're probably very angry with me.

I don't know how to write this. Definitely part of it's an apology, but also part of it isn't.

I thought the paper was who you are, but that's backward. Even if you're not on the paper you're still you, and I'd rather spend time with you than do anything in the world.

But I'll stop now. You've made your decision, and I'll leave you alone. Be happy, Rose.

Yours,

Grant

That was as close to an apology as she was likely to get from Grant. He was letting her go.

Good. That's what she wanted.

JB watched her face, and when she attempted and failed to smile at him, he looked away—sank into the back of the seat and gazed out the window.

She crumpled the paper and squeezed it against her chest. Her heart had been trying to jump out of her rib cage since she'd opened the note.

She would not cry, because she never cried, and she would especially not cry when there was nothing to be sad about. It was over—that's all. She'd gotten what she wanted. She was free. As free as a person could be while trapped in the back of a police car on the way to the station.

This must be what freedom felt like, that's all. Like she had to hold up the collapsing whole world all by herself.

SEVEN

Grant wove through the rooms of the party, feeling the effects of Fisher's mixed drink and the whiskey goblets he'd drunk with Nick and Oliver. People cheered him when he came into rooms, holding up their phones with Rosie's article on them. They bombarded him with questions. His phone didn't stop ringing, so he stopped feeling the vibration, though he checked it every once in a while to see if Rose or his dad had called.

They hadn't.

He lost track of Nick and Oliver, which was only fair; he didn't want to be a third wheel. At a prom after-party that was kind of what he had to be, though. Everywhere he looked, people had paired off.

It felt like the end of something. *Cliché, Grant.* It was the end of high school. Everyone knew that.

But Grant's ending felt even bigger than that. When the sun

rose, he would be someone he didn't recognize, as if he'd shed his original skin and revealed a new, worse Grant underneath. Someone who wasn't smart or charming or any of the words he'd used to describe himself in his most confident moments.

He'd been chickenshit. Textbook, run-of-the-mill, inhumanely farmed chickenshit.

He'd had so many chances in the past year to tell Rosie how he felt about her, but he'd put it off again and again. And he wasn't a person who put things off. *Be bold. Ask for what you want*, his mom had always told him, and he had. He'd become the editor in chief. The best editor in chief the *Gazette* had ever had. When things were important, he'd step up—for the paper, for truth, for fairness. Except when it came to Rosie. Then he'd backed off. Ducked out of the way. Made excuses. Deflected. Anything not to have to tell her the truth.

He circled the party like a lost ant looking for his hill. This room, that room, look and leave, keep moving.

Through the door to the patio, he saw Mer sitting alone on a glass table, her prom queen crown flashing in the light from the pool. She turned her head as he came out and raised a hand to gesture to him to come over.

Everywhere he went, Mer kept showing up. Not the girl he wanted to see, but a particularly vivid example of the clueless chickenshit he'd been. He'd only asked her out because he was too scared to admit he wanted to ask Rosie instead.

He dragged his feet on the way to her, then heaved himself up on the table next to her.

"That was a good story Rose wrote," Mer said.

"I like your crown."

She made a face. "You don't have to do that."

"I thought we were exchanging pleasantries, but if you'd rather skip them, that's fine with me."

"Fine," she said. "I wanted to tell you—"

"I was a bad boyfriend, wasn't I?"

"What?" She appeared genuinely confused. Maybe he hadn't made enough of an impression to rate, but, hell, they'd been together for nearly a year. "You were fine, Grant. That's not what I—"

"Because I shouldn't have asked you out. I should've asked Rosie instead."

"Jesus Christ," Mer said. Now she was pissed, and Mer never got pissed. "Are you drunk?"

"I've had some drinks."

Mer stood up, leaving Grant wobbling on the table alone. "No one made you do anything. You know that." She took off her crown and shoved it at his chest. "This was giving me a head-ache."

Then she stomped into the house, elbowing aside people as she went. Well. Apparently Mer was having a mental breakdown. On a normal night, that would be news, but tonight it hardly made a ripple.

FRESHMAN CONTEMPLATES DATING

Rose was the first girl to really talk to Grant. When they met, Grant had been in school for nine of his fourteen years—ten, if you counted preschool—and girls had always been there, but after fifth grade or so, they had their own thing. Grant and Nick could talk about TV or games or school, but every time he tried to talk to a girl in the same way, she'd laugh and say something he didn't understand and go back to her friends.

Within the next year or two, some of his acquaintances started going out with girls, which seemed simultaneously wonderful and exciting and awkward and terrifying. Grant wanted very much to talk to girls, but he'd overthought it to the point where he couldn't come up with a simple original normal greeting. He started making elaborate jokes instead, and doing funny voices, and quoting TV shows and movies and local commercials.

Some girls found that funny, which felt good, but it didn't lend itself to a meaningful back-and-forth.

"Should we be concerned that girls don't seem to like us?" Grant asked Nick.

"No," Nick said, and Grant let the subject drop.

A couple of months later, Nick paused *The Fisher King* in the middle of the movie. "I think I'm mostly gay," he said.

"Oh," Grant said. He felt like that shouldn't be the end of the conversation, but he wasn't sure where to take it next. "I think I'm mostly straight."

"Yeah, I figured that."

"So you're going to go out with guys?"

Nick snorted. "Like anyone would want to go out with me."

"But if they did, you would?"

"Yeah. Wouldn't you go out with a girl if she wanted to?"

"No," Grant said, deciding in the moment. "It would be a distraction."

"From what?" Nick asked.

"From taking over the world."

Nick nodded and pressed play.

By that point Grant had so far alienated himself from regular conversation and standard interaction with girls that the idea of one wanting to go out with him seemed farcical, so it didn't cost him too much to decide he didn't want to date anyone. All the girls in his class were taller than him, too, except for Ashleigh Albertson, who was a gymnast, and she was mean—plus she was already going out with Zed McCloskey (the first in the class to hit six feet).

When high school started, Grant joined the *Gazette* and set his course for world domination. He wrote stories and interviewed people and talked freely to the other *Gazette* staffers of any gender. The *Gazette* made sense out of the chaos. If he viewed the world through the lens of the *Gazette*, he knew exactly who he was and what he was supposed to do.

Then there was Rosie, sitting next to him at a computer, getting his jokes, making jokes back, and existing, undeniably, as a girl in the world.

Weirder still, she seemed to like him, and Grant liked her. He liked the way she talked and the shape of her smile and how she'd try to get better stories than he did. He liked her laugh and the way she wrote and the way she rolled her eyes. He wanted to spend all his time with her—and he got to, because she was as invested in the paper as he was.

"Are you going to ask her out?" Nick wanted to know after Rose and Jenna had joined their lunch table, officially, in October.

"No," Grant said.

"Why not?"

"Because I'm too busy."

"You're scared," Nick said. "Which is stupid, because I think she'd say yes."

"I'm not scared. I'm practical."

It wasn't only practicality that kept him from asking her out, either. (And it wasn't being scared. Nick must've projected that—Grant wasn't scared of anything.) The issue came into focus one Saturday, during one of his dad's court-mandated bimonthly weekends. Grant asked Rose and Nick over to watch *The Paper* and Nick canceled at the last minute. So he and Rose watched the movie, along with Grant's dad, when he wasn't chasing around a naked kindergartner or two.

After Rose left, his dad hovered in the entrance to the living room. "She's nice," he said.

"Yeah," Grant said.

"Are you two . . . ?"

Grant stared at his dad. The question hung in the air between them.

Grant's dad cleared his throat. "Bud, if you want to talk about it . . ."

"Nope," Grant said.

"It took a while for me to figure out how to ask a girl out, you know."

"But you don't really have that problem anymore, do you?" Grant said. He didn't have to inject very much venom into the question in order for Grant's dad to wince and leave him alone.

Grant wished he hadn't said it (because he wasn't even really that mad anymore, and his dad was trying), but at the same time the interaction had made everything clear. He didn't have to go chasing after the first girl who actually talked to him. His world made sense now—the paper, Nick and Rose, high school. It might be nice to have a girlfriend, but it would definitely mess up all of that.

It was weird, actually, that his dad couldn't see that, after everything he'd gone through. But it didn't matter. Grant wasn't his dad. Grant could be friends with a girl without it blowing up his whole life.

Rose could not remember the last time she cried.

Sometimes a tear would escape during a sad movie—or, more likely, a manipulative commercial—but as far as she could remember, she hadn't sobbed since she broke her arm at Girl Scout camp in fifth grade.

Jenna cried all the time—when she was angry or happy or bored—but Rose's emotions tended to twist into her chest more tightly, winding the motor in her heart that propelled her to work harder and faster and better. Crying would mean giving up those controls. And then people looking at her could know exactly how much and what feeling she was experiencing.

Rose didn't cry when she saw her mom sitting on a bench just inside the police station doors. Her mom had on her grungiest leather jacket and her scariest scowl, which Rose knew was for the cops, not for her. When her mom spotted Rose, her face crumpled into something softer and incongruously maternal, and still Rose did not cry.

But as soon as she saw Grant's dad, wearing a faded Yale sweatshirt and the old-man version of Grant's glasses, tears spilled out of her eyes in rivers. She didn't understand where they came from, but she couldn't make them stop.

Her mom hugged her, smelling distinctly of cigarettes, and Grant's dad patted her arm. "Grant called and asked me to take care of you," he said. "We'll figure it all out. Don't you worry."

She didn't know how to say that she wasn't worried, that she felt completely safe and taken care of and worthless and faulty and confused, and she was crying too hard to say anything anyway.

"Are you her parents?" Detective Hart asked.

"I'm her mom," Rose's mom said.

"And I'm her lawyer," Grant's dad said, then pointed at JB. "His, too."

At this, Rose cried harder.

She cried so hard, she couldn't hear what Grant's dad was saying to Hart. Even when he started to yell, and Hart and the other cops yelled back, she couldn't follow the argument.

Their conversation returned to normal volume, and after a while Detective Hart started nodding reluctantly. Grant's dad turned to Rose. "Detective Hart has very kindly agreed to let you and JB go home for the night and come in tomorrow for some questions. You don't have any idea where Marty went, right, Rose?"

Through her tears, Rose shook her head.

Hart gave her a lecture before she left—something about looking out for her fellow students, and her responsibility to the community, and how if they found out she had anything to do with Marty and his gun they would not be happy.

Rose cried and cried and cried.

REPORTER ASSAULTED

Fisher Louis grabbed Rose at the end of their interview. She didn't think of it as assault right away, because she'd spent an hour talking to this person, and it didn't make sense that someone whose words she'd carefully recorded and copied by hand into her notebook could reach out and grab her tits—both of them, both hands, as he came in for what Rose thought was going to be an end-of-the-interview hug. When she'd jumped back, slapping his hands away, he'd laughed as if he'd made a joke, and that, too, kept the word "assault" from her mind. Because maybe it was a joke she hadn't gotten yet.

She didn't mention it to Grant afterward because it seemed stupid and embarrassing and still not assault, and she knew Grant would be both outraged on her behalf and a little nervous that they were talking out loud about her boobs.

She thought she'd shrug it off, but it stuck in her mind,

Fisher's large, strong hands abruptly on her, the suddenness and the brazenness shocking her into a frozen half second in which he *squeezed*—and the question she got stuck on was what made this different from Taj at the paint party. Didn't Rose and Taj grab each other, too, without even talking before at all? There had to be some difference between the events that she couldn't quite grasp, why she'd responded to Taj's overture and rejected Fisher's move. No, not a "move." A "move" was quaint, hopeful, with at least the goal of reciprocation. What Fisher did wasn't a move.

Then she thought: *I am describing an assault.*

And then: *Fisher Louis assaulted me.*

Rose always wanted to find the best, most accurate word to describe an event, and her brain told her that "assault" was the correct one to name what had happened to her. But her entire body resisted the description. She could *not* have been assaulted by Fisher Louis. There had to be some other way to think about it.

As Rose and Taj drove around a couple days later, she tried to bring it up with him.

"The paint party," she said.

"Yeah," he said.

"When you kissed me—"

"You kissed me."

"Well, we both sort of . . ." She trailed off, and Taj didn't pick up the conversational slack. He didn't mind silences; in fact, he seemed to prefer them. He drummed his hands on the steering wheel, and Rose shuddered, thinking of hands. Taj had graceful artist hands, not big beefy sports hands like Fisher's, but they were both boy hands, with hair on the knuckles and rough fingertips, bigger than hers. "I've been thinking. About us at the paint party. Why wasn't that assault?"

Taj's hands stopped drumming. He kept his eyes on the road. "You think I assaulted you?"

"No!"

"Because like I said, you kissed me."

"Yeah, we kissed each other."

"No," Taj said emphatically. "If anything, you assaulted me."

"What?"

"Yeah."

Rose frowned. "Okay. Forget I said anything."

She looked out the window. They usually drove around for a while before going to the forest preserve or an old empty elementary school playground or the parking lot of an office complex and making out for a while. Taj passed by three promising parking lots and didn't slow down.

"Did someone hurt you?" Taj asked at a red light. He looked at her, finally, and she found she couldn't look back.

"What? No."

"Guys are dicks. Tons of girls get—you know. Raped."

"I did not get raped."

"Okay." He paused. The light turned green, but he did not go. "*I* didn't rape or assault anyone."

"I know."

"I mean. You could talk to me, if you wanted."

Rose clamped her lips shut. She could tell Taj what had happened. He would be sympathetic and supportive, in his quiet way. He would never be her boyfriend but he could be a friend. All she had to do was open her mouth.

Fisher Louis assaulted me.

It would change the way he looked at her. She liked the way he looked now, most of the time, prior to this conversation: as if she were an amusing diversion, and he was watching her antics from three rooms away. She didn't want him any closer than that. She didn't want that expression to get any more intent.

What would be the point of telling him? Of telling anyone? It wouldn't make her feel any better. If she told, she could maybe see Fisher punished, but would that be worth the whole world looking at her with pity and suspicion? She supposed Fisher's punishment for grabbing her would be a slap on the wrist anyway. Would it be worth becoming the story?

She'd have liked to think if Fisher had hurt her in a way that left a mark—if he'd raped her—she would've gone to the police. But maybe she wasn't as brave as she'd always assumed.

She could tell the truth in her stories—about other people's lives. But the thought of her own life being exposed, even to Taj, or Grant, or Jenna, or her mom—made her shut down completely.

A sour taste filled her mouth. Fisher's hands grabbing her.

She should've pushed him off harder or faster. She should've called him a dick. She should've screamed. At the very least, she should've put it in her article about him.

She was angry—at Fisher, and beyond Fisher, the whole world. Herself. She could write all the stories, win all the awards, and inside she was still weak and confused and not grown up at all.

Her three years on the paper—what had they been for?

"I'm fine," she said to Taj. "Drive me home."

"You sure?"

"Yeah. I'm tired."

"But nothing's wrong."

"Right."

He drove her home. As she was getting out of the car, she stuck her head back in through the door. "There's nothing the matter with me. Okay?"

Taj nodded, unconvinced. He didn't say anything, and she knew he would not be calling her again, and she would not text him, and in a couple of months they would be completely erased from each other's lives. She had no photos of Taj, no box of mementos. The only friend who'd ever even met him was Jenna.

She could return to her life and pretend none of this ever happened.

Rose had been so sure she didn't need anyone looking out for her. She could handle her own shit—hadn't she successfully suppressed the memory of Fisher Louis assaulting her, to the point where she could sort-of-calmly go to prom in the same group as him? Hadn't she dealt with the Northwestern question entirely on her own, without needing to rip open her heart to anyone? Didn't she know exactly what she wanted and needed, without input from anyone else?

When she'd read the note Grant had left with JB for her, she'd really thought Grant was going to leave her alone.

And then she saw his dad at the station—and she knew he hadn't abandoned her. She hadn't noticed with all the bluster and the planning and flirting, but Grant had been looking out for her the whole night. More than that—he'd looked out for her their whole friendship. He'd been there helping her get the MREJ. He'd been there when they'd found her dad. He'd been there urging her to stay late when they were freshmen, impressing the upperclassmen together and making her feel welcome at the diner.

Every time he'd texted annoyingly or checked up on her or sent her conflicting assignments, he'd been looking out for her. Checking in on her. Making sure she was still there—like echolocation. She knew where he was; he knew where she was. Ping. Ping. Ping.

She cried with relief.

She'd thought she was alone, but Grant had been there the whole time, and he wasn't going to leave because she dated someone else or kept a few secrets or quit the paper.

On the police-station steps, Rose stopped and turned to JB. His parents had come, too, and stood behind him with shocked expressions. They'd never warmed to Rose. When she went over to JB's house, they were perfectly polite but treated her warily, as if she'd say or do something outrageous at any moment. She'd thought it was her mom's influence, or maybe the cultural divide. But maybe she was someone parents *should* be wary of. Considering the situation, they'd been right to hold her at arm's length.

Rose wiped her eyes and attempted to collect herself. She pulled off the corsage JB had given her. In the last few hours, it had lost most of its petals, and the few that remained hung raggedly off the metal backing. "I am really, truly sorry, JB."

"Yeah. I think we're done," JB said. He didn't say it warningly or angrily or bitterly. He stated it as a matter of fact and let the words hang there.

She could've batted the words away, changed her mind, put on a pretty smile.

She could've stuffed down the relief until it blended in with all the other anxiety and fear and yearning she'd been stuffing down for months.

She could've kept denying what she truly felt in order to keep those pesky feelings where they were.

She could've kept trying to go with the flow a little bit longer.

But she wasn't a go-with-the-flow person. She liked the fight, the complications, the challenge.

She would always look for the story. Always write the truth, even if she didn't always tell it. And speaking of the truth, it was time she started telling it in real life, not only for the paper.

Grant knew when she needed help, even if she couldn't say it out loud. He knew all her flaws and cared about her anyway. It wasn't fair to JB for her to argue for them to stay together, because despite everything, she still cared about Grant. Loved him, actually.

"You deserve better than me," she said.

JB wiped away one of her tears and smiled for the first time since he'd been brought out of the school by the cops. "Yeah, that's probably true."

She tried to smile, but it didn't feel like the normal smile shape.

"Well. Thank you for the corsage," she said. Then she turned away before she could throw more words at him and make everything worse.

She couldn't stay. She had the rest of a story to write.

Grant put aside Mer's crown and got out his phone. As he looked at it, it started to ring, and he nearly dropped it in his hurry to answer the call.

"Dad?"

"Hey, bud."

"What happened? Is Rosie okay?"

"She's fine. We're all coming back to the station in daylight to give official statements. I don't think they're going to press charges for her hiding Marty—I think they actually believe the story you published."

"They should. It's true."

"Of course it is," Grant's dad said smoothly. Grant couldn't tell if there was irony in his tone or not. "How are you? Coming home soon, I hope?"

"Probably."

"Did you call your mom?"

"Yeah." He had, before he left the bathroom, and let her rail at him for a good five minutes without taking a breath.

"Not the best prom, was it?"

"I don't know," Grant said. "It was kind of epic."

Grant's dad didn't respond, and Grant closed his eyes. He should go home. If he had one more drink, he'd be really drunk, and he'd already mostly forgotten what he was doing here.

The story went up but it wasn't over. Right. Because someone had brought a gun to school, but it wasn't Marty.

He could keep doing what he did best—chase the story—but it felt like a slog without Rosie.

"You may be interested to know," Grant's dad said, picking his words carefully, "that I don't think Rose and Jason Baxter are on the best of terms anymore."

"Really?"

"I would guess that they've broken up. Based on careful observation."

"Huh," Grant said. "Did you . . . observe her going home?"

"She left with her mom. As her lawyer, I promised the police she would go straight to bed, in order to come back refreshed tomorrow. Or later today, as the case may be." He paused. "But did I see her go home? No, I did not."

Grant sat straighter. The cloud of gloom lifted ever so slightly. Mer's cheap plastic crown seemed to sparkle like diamonds in the light from the pool. "Thanks, Dad."

Grant's dad sighed. "That thank-you sounds like you're not coming home after all."

Grant had learned all the best lawyer tricks from his dad, which meant that he didn't answer. And his dad knew exactly what that meant.

"Stay safe, bud."

Grant grinned.

SENIOR FALLS THROUGH CEILING

Rose fell through the ceiling once. It was the fourth (and last) time they'd opened up a fiberglass panel and climbed up to spy on the teacher's lounge, during second period in October of senior year. Grant was the only one sitting in the *Gazette* room—they only climbed up through the ceiling when no one else was around—and he'd dispatched her to see if Hackenstrat would say anything about rumors of a new pool being built in the senior parking lot.

Grant replaced the ceiling tile she'd gone through in case anyone came by the *Gazette* room while she was gone. Then he went back to the piece he was editing. He tried not to worry about Rose up in the ceiling, creeping over dead rats and live wires and below her the entire humming life of Hawks High.

Then there was a creaking, and crack, and one of the tiles split in half and Rose tumbled down onto his desk. It happened in slow motion, seemingly, because Rose could tell what was happening and tried to grab at the next tile over, but that tile split from the sudden weight, too, and then Rose dropped the rest of the way onto the desk.

She lay there for a minute, covered in dust, coughing. "Do you think anyone heard?" she asked when she could take a breath.

"They'd be here by now if they had," he said.

"Oh, good." She rolled over and dropped her head back onto the desk.

"Are you okay?"

She opened her mouth to answer, but instead of speaking, she laughed.

He laughed, too. He closed his laptop and laughed so hard, he had to bend over at the waist. Tears of laughter streaked the dust and dirt on her cheeks.

When it seemed like they'd stopped laughing, they started laughing again.

Rose shoved pieces of fiberglass off of her and wiped her eyes. She still had a huge grin on her face. She shifted to her side and held up her head with her hand, her elbow resting on a pile of old page proofs.

"So," she said. "You want the scoop or what?"

In the car on the way home, Rose's mom turned off the radio at a stoplight and stared at Rose.

"What?"

"That was the first and last time I'm going pick you up from the police station," she said.

"I'm sorry, Mom, I promise it won't—"

"Oh, don't promise, Rose. Every time I got picked up by the cops, I would promise my mom, and then it would happen again. I don't need you to promise—I need you to stop being an idiot."

Rose wiped the last of the tears from her eyes and shifted uncomfortably in her seat. "I'm not an idiot. And how many times did you get arrested, anyway?"

"You *are* an idiot. You can't help it."

"Thanks a lot, Mom."

"I still love you, of course, but you're a total idiot. Just because you're not into drugs and tattoos doesn't mean you're not."

Rose thought of JB riding home with his parents, who probably didn't call their son an idiot. They were probably very supportive and sympathetic, which was why JB had turned out so upstanding and she had ended up the way she had.

But then again there were Jenna's parents, who had expected her to be a rule follower and had found themselves continually disappointed. Jenna had been born to rebel, and maybe Rose had been born to take the difficult path.

The light turned green. "Did Jenna stop by the house, by any chance?" Rose asked her mom.

"Her parents wanted to know the same thing. And no, she hasn't."

"Weird. If she'd gone to Marty's, the police would've picked her up by now." Rose frowned, thinking. "Or if they'd accidentally shot her, presumably they'd know where she was."

"Presumably," Rose's mom said drily. "Where else could she have gone?"

Rose shrugged. "She could be anywhere within walking distance. Not school, not the police station, not her house, not Marty's, not ours . . ."

"Maybe she managed to find Marty and they're making out madly someplace very romantic."

"Gross, Mom. But that is what she wanted to do in the first

place. Find Marty." Rose tapped her forehead against the side window, thinking.

She sat up and grabbed the dashboard so fast, her mother swerved out of her lane. "Turn around. I know where she is."

The pedestrian footbridge over the highway was exactly as romantic as its name. A set of narrow, rusted stairs led over the embankment to a metal bridge barely an arms' span wide. Chain-link fencing arced overhead and groaned in the wind. The cars and trucks passed below at full speed and volume.

Rose climbed the stairs slowly, her hand hovering over the dirty handrail. As soon as she could see the bridge itself, she abandoned caution and ran up the last couple of steps.

"Jenna!" she shouted over the roar of the cars.

Jenna sat in the center of the bridge, cross-legged, the skirt of her dress stained and shredded around her. When she heard her name, she raised her head, then lowered it again, defeated.

"What the hell, Jenna? Everyone's been looking for you."

Jenna shrugged one bare shoulder.

"You can't stay up here all night. You don't have to go to the cops, but come with me—my mom's waiting in the car. Your parents are freaking out."

"Don't care," she muttered.

"Oh, come on," Rose said. "Snap out of it."

Rose tried to grab Jenna's arm, but Jenna leaned sideways, practically lying on the bridge to escape Rose's reach. "My parents were right, weren't they."

"What?" Rose asked.

"I should've been good. I should've studied and listened to them."

"Um. No. Then you wouldn't be Jenna."

"Exactly." She screwed up her face. "Why did you let this happen to me?"

"Let what happen?"

"You let me . . . fall in love. With this guy. Who we didn't even know."

Rose crossed her arms over her chest. "You think there was any way I could've stopped you?"

Jenna let her shoulder and head drop slowly to the bridge, then rolled onto her back. Rose sat next to her in order to hear over the sound of traffic below. "As my friend you should've tried."

"Jenna. Come on. If I'd fought against Marty, you would've liked him even more."

"Nuh-uh. I would've listened to you. You're my best friend." Jenna closed her eyes. "You could let people in every once in a while."

Rose leaned back into the chain-link fencing and then, when

it groaned, hastily scooted away. "I don't think I'm shy about expressing my opinions."

"Yeah, your smartass thoughts. But no one knows what you *feel*. It's like if you admitted a feeling, you might explode."

Rose leaned back into the fence again, ignoring the creaking. She thought she had five secrets from Jenna, but those were only the ones she knew about. Maybe there were even more she hadn't even considered.

That was the way she'd been built, with a fortress around her heart to shield her when things inevitably went wrong.

But things fell apart whether or not she said out loud how she felt about them. Pretending not to have feelings didn't make it easier to see Grant ask someone else out; it didn't make Fisher's assault any less disgusting and embarrassing; it didn't make her dad less disappointing. In no way did it protect her from slights and pain. Hiding her feelings only meant she had no one to talk to when she hurt the worst.

"I was a little jealous," Rose said.

Jenna opened her eyes, and her head lifted a couple of inches off the bridge. "You were?"

"Yeah. You guys seemed happy. It seemed . . . easy for you."

Jenna had fallen into true love with someone who loved her back. She didn't worry about it, make false starts, advance two steps and then take five back. She didn't wonder if Marty kept her around for the right reasons. She didn't second-guess herself and change direction suddenly and fear constantly that she was doing the wrong thing.

Nothing was that easy for Rose. She tried and tried and tried, and things still came out wrong. The *Gazette*, Northwestern, JB, Grant.

Jenna sat up and hugged her knees into her chest. "You think any of this has been easy for me?" she asked, mystified. "My family? Being me?"

Rose shook her head. "I know. But you asked me how I felt."

"Maybe that's a little how I felt every time you went off with Grant on one of your newspaper missions. Leaving me behind."

"Really?" Rose asked, and Jenna nodded. "I'm sorry, Jenna."

Jenna's chest rose and fell with ragged breaths. "Well, that's not enough, and it's too late anyway. You still let me get into this situation! And now he's . . . and now . . ." Jenna's tears gathered on the end of her nose and fell in a mini waterfall onto her dress. "He's crazy."

"A little wacky, maybe, but let's not call him crazy."

"He brought a fucking gun to school!" Jenna's face crumpled as she sobbed harder. "How could I be so stupid?"

"Oh my god," Rose said. "Did your phone die?"

Jenna nodded between wails.

"You don't know, then!" Rose grinned and clutched Jenna's arm. If Jenna had been standing up, Rose would've danced with her the entire length of the bridge. "You're going to love me forever, because I am about to give you the best news you've ever heard."

Grant made another circuit of the party, this time looking under tables and chairs for Owen Pettibone. When he saw Nick and Oliver holding court with some theater kids in a dark-paneled library, he told them to start looking, too. He must've sounded pretty persuasive because they actually did, with the promise to call Grant if they managed to find him.

In the far corner of a distant wing of the house, Grant opened the door to what looked like a solarium with a glass roof and walls and a white grand piano in the middle of a sea of potted plants. "Owen?" he called out.

It wasn't Owen who stood next to a Ping-Pong table covered with red Solo cups, but Fisher and Mer. They were on opposite sides of the table, Mer with her arms crossed, Fisher with his akimbo, as if they'd been arguing.

Grant tried to duck out of the room, but Fisher spotted him.

"Grant Leitch, you dog!" Fisher shouted. "You knew where Marty was the whole time!"

"Nope," Grant said.

"I've got to go," Mer said, and brushed past Grant on her way out the door. He tried to say goodbye, but she wouldn't look at him.

"Sorry I interrupted," Grant said.

Fisher shrugged. "You know Mer. She's 'emotional.'" He used elaborate air quotes around the word. "Come on in, come on in. I've got beer pong going, but I know I'd wipe the floor with you and that doesn't seem sportsmanlike, does it?"

"Actually, I—"

"Though, you know, it's not exactly sportsmanlike of you to not tell me what you knew about Marty. Especially when I'd been trying to help you."

"I'm not a sportsman, so—"

"It's exactly what a piece of shit would do, actually," Fisher said. There was a pause, and then Fisher smiled. "Messing with you. Obviously. Come tell me where Marty is now and we'll call it square."

Grant approached the Ping-Pong table but did not take the Solo cup from Fisher's outstretched hand. "What's wrong with Mer?"

Fisher shrugged, sloshing the beer in the cup. "I mean, it kills me. I don't know what she wants from me sometimes."

Grant nodded, not because he agreed but because Fisher

wanted someone to nod along with him.

"It's like, I'm supposed to be with her all the time, but then also not mind when she talks to other guys, or dances with them or whatever she does. But, like, which is it, Mer? Because if I'm supposed to be okay with her acting like such a slut, can I go home? Why do I have to be there to witness it, except if she's doing it to make me mad?" His voice got loud and raw. "Why does she have to be such a raging bitch all the time?"

Grant had stopped nodding a long time ago.

Fisher shook his red face, unbothered at Grant's lack of response. "You got girl problems, or are you gay with that gay friend of yours?"

"He has a boyfriend. Also, I'm not gay."

"So you have girl problems. I got ninety-nine, man. Ninety-nine."

Grant felt a correction bubbling up his throat. *Jay Z didn't have girl problems. He feels bad for you, son.* But for once Grant reined in his know-it-all tendency and managed to keep a stone face. Even smiling at this dude felt like agreeing to something that Grant wanted no part of.

"It's that girl reporter, isn't it?" Fisher said.

"Rosie?" Grant said. *Damn it, Grant.* Plug the know-it-all leak in one area, and it breaks through someplace else.

"Yeah, Rosie." Rose's nickname sounded dirty in Fisher's mouth. "She interviewed me once. You must like them spirited."

Rose had interviewed Fisher for the profile they'd done on him, sometime junior year when everyone still thought Fisher had a shot at the Olympics one day. The feature turned out well—some nice shots of Fisher in his Speedo celebrating wins that made him look like a bleached-blond Michael Phelps. Rosie hadn't said much about the interview except right after she got back to the *Gazette* room from the pool. He'd asked how it had gone, and she had twisted her face in disgust. "Euuuuuugggggghhhhhh," she'd said.

Grant had thought he knew what that meant, but now he realized he actually had no idea.

"Your reporter had Marty hidden away someplace this whole time. She looked me right in the face and lied about it, too. Cold-blooded little bitch."

"Shut up about Rose," Grant snapped.

Fisher grinned. He wanted to fight someone, Grant realized. Mer or Grant or anyone else who walked into the room. He needed to yell and loom large and take a swing. "And what exactly are you going to do about it?" Fisher asked.

Be bold.

Before Grant answered, he steeled himself to take a punch. He'd never been hit before, but it would be quick, at least from all the movies he'd seen. A swing and a crunch. He tried to take a breath but found he was already nearly hyperventilating.

Grant leaned forward and opened his mouth. "Well—"

A body threw itself against the glass wall of the solarium. Grant and Fisher both jumped.

The body was pale white and hairy and shirtless. He knocked on the window frantically with his fist. His eyes darted side to side, and as soon as he noticed Grant, he knocked more urgently.

"Grant, dude, hey, man, let me in let me in let me in."

Grant ran for the door, some instinct taking over even as he processed what he was seeing. From behind him, he could hear Fisher laughing.

"No shitting shit," Fisher said.

It was Marty Caulfield.

EIGHT

The only way that Rose's mom would let her go to Fisher's party was if she came along.

"But you're an alcoholic and addict," Rose pointed out.

"And you're seventeen and under police suspicion," Rose's mom replied.

"Touché," Jenna said. She had cheered up considerably after getting into the car, borrowing Rose's mom's leather jacket, and wiping her ruined makeup off with a stash of Wet-Naps she found in the pocket on the back of the passenger seat. She seemed almost like herself again, except for the torn-up skirt. Rose's dress had dirt streaks where she'd sat on the bridge, so at least they were a matched pair. "Really I'm the only one who should be allowed to go, seeing as the only reason the police want to talk to me is that I'm the girlfriend of a wanted man, and that seems pretty tame, comparatively."

Rose agreed to the conditions, which meant that she entered Fisher Louis's blowout after-party flanked by her mother and her best friend. They asked everyone they saw for Owen. Rose kept seeing Grant out of the corner of her eye, but when she'd turn her head, it was never him, only another kid in a tuxedo.

On the second floor, they ran into Nick, who was leaning his head out the doorway of a bedroom. "Rose! Have you seen Grant?"

"Not recently."

"He's not answering his phone." Nick nudged open the door, and Rose peeked in to see Owen Pettibone slouched on the foot of the bed, arguing with Oliver.

Out of relief and gratitude and perhaps a little bit of senior-year nostalgia, Rose hugged Nick, who patted her back awkwardly before stepping away and eyeing the hallway warily. "You brought your mom?"

"She's my girl Friday," Rose said.

"No, I'm the muscle," Rose's mom said, elbowing her way into the room.

Owen, blinking slowly, watched Rose and her mom and Jenna come in and close the door behind them. "This is going to be a weird game of spin the bottle," he said, and Rose sat down next to him on the bed.

"Rose," Nick said, shifting uncomfortably. "I would do a lot for Grant, and I *have* done a lot—especially tonight—but this is starting to feel like something we should involve the authorities in."

"Aren't I an authority?" Rose's mom asked.

"No offense, Ms. Regnero. I don't really want any part of whatever this is."

"We're not going to beat him up or anything," Rose said.

"Very reassuring." Nick pulled on Oliver's sleeve, and the two of them walked toward the door. "When an officer asks me what happened tonight, I think I'd rather be able to say I had no idea and mean it."

"Fair enough," Rose said. "And thank you, Nick. For this and for publishing the story."

Nick shrugged and reddened, and he and Oliver made their exit, closing the door behind them. That left Owen alone with Rose, her mom, and Jenna. Rose's mom stood by the door with her arms crossed over her chest, and Jenna went to the windows and yanked the curtains closed.

"All right, I'm into it," Owen said.

"Owen, you rapscallion," Rose said, throwing an arm around Owen's thin shoulder. "You're going to tell me whose gun Marty found in Vice-Principal Hackenstrat's office."

"And why would I do that?" Owen squinted at her and then squinted past her toward the now-closed door. "Is that . . . your mom? Nice ink, Mama Rose."

"You're going to tell me what you know, Owen, because I know why you came to prom."

Owen shifted, but his expression didn't change. "Because I love parties?"

"Because you're stalking Mairead Callahan."

"No I'm not," he said.

Rose held up her phone. "Fifty-six comments on a recent photo of hers, from eight different accounts? And that's one example. This goes back weeks."

"That's not me."

"It is, though, Owen, because six of those usernames are also used on a different gaming site with the same photo, which is originally found on your own Facebook page. All eight of the usernames contain 'own' or 'pwn,' which I assume is a clever-ish reference to your name. On the gaming site, you mention your school and the street where you live. Five of the accounts are on a list of banned users on a different site, for harassing and sock puppeting. One of them is used for an Instagram account of puppies wearing top hats."

"What do top hats have to do with Mairead?" Jenna asked.

Rose grinned at her friend. "Nothing, Jenna. Even scumbags contain multitudes."

While Rose's head was turned, Owen jumped off the bed and made a run for the door, but Rose's mom was faster. She tackled Owen and knelt on his back.

"Go ahead and try something, dickbrain," she said cheerfully, then turned to Rose. "Aren't you glad I came along?"

"Thanks, Mom. Owen," Rose said, kneeling to face Owen. "Spill. Or I'm telling Mairead."

Owen groaned into the carpet.

"I didn't catch that."

Owen turned his head to the side and spit out carpet fibers. "It's Fisher Louis's gun, okay?"

No one in the room moved.

"How do you know?" Rose asked.

"He showed it to a bunch of us at a party. I came to sell to them—drugs, not guns, FYI—but you know you've got to socialize for a while, build up customer relations."

"How do you know it was that exact gun?"

"I'm not an idiot," Owen said. "It's the same gun. Make, model. Scuff on the handle." Owen snorted into the carpet. "Fisher was telling people that the scuff came from it being shot in a drive-by. Like anyone believed that. I think it's his dad's."

"Why did he take it to school? How did it end up in Hack's office?"

"I don't know." Owen winced as Rose's mom dug her knee into his back. "I seriously don't know. I saw it in Fisher's bedroom, and then I saw that photo Grant showed me. I don't know anything about the rest of it."

Rose's fingers twitched again.

Grant had his laptop, because he'd uploaded her story to the *Gazette*—she could start writing as soon as she found him. She looked up from Owen, thinking. They'd have to call Detective Hart and tell her what they'd found out. After that, it was only a matter of time before it broke to the public.

She went for the door.

"Hold up, Rose," her mom said from on top of Owen. "You're not really letting this loser walk away?"

"Not at all. Mom, you can tell the detective all about it when we call her and let her know what we know about the gun."

"You said you wouldn't tell!" Owen whined.

"I said I wouldn't tell Mairead. I didn't say anything about the cops."

Jenna got out her phone, dialed information, and asked to be connected to the police, nonemergency line. Rose's mom half smiled, half scowled at her daughter. "And where are you going?"

"I want to get a comment from Fisher before the police start asking him questions. And I need to find Grant and his computer and get the update to this story on the *Gazette*."

"I'm coming with you," Jenna said, ending her call. Her chin jutted out and she had a malicious glint in her eye. "Fisher must've suspected the gun wasn't Marty's. He could've said something at any time, but he let people believe Marty was a bad guy."

"Great," Rose said. "Mom, I won't be long. I won't leave the party without you."

Rose's mom narrowed her eyes at Jenna, sizing her up and then taking the measure of Owen Pettibone. "You'd never be able to hold him down."

"My arms are basically made of straw," Jenna said, flexing weakly.

Owen squirmed and Rose's mom sighed. "Fine. Get your quote. Be safe."

"Nothing to worry about," Rose said. She tried not to think about Fisher grabbing her at the end of their interview. "There are a million people here. Besides, we know one thing for sure— he's unarmed."

The situation in the solarium disintegrated rapidly. As soon as Grant let Marty in, there was a flurry of pushing and shoving and tripping over his own feet, and Grant ended up jammed against the Ping-Pong table, knocking half-filled cups of beer everywhere, while Fisher held Marty against the piano keys. They clanged out of tune.

"Give me the gun," Fisher said, his face inches from Marty's.

"Fisher, calm down—"

"Get the fuck out of here, Grant—this is between men."

"The hell does that mean?" Grant asked, but he wasn't as unconcerned as he tried to sound; he had to fight against his instinct to leap over the Ping-Pong table and make a run for it.

"You stole that gun from me, you little shitstain," Fisher said to Marty. "And you're going to give it back before the cops find you and it and figure out where it came from."

Marty's eyes widened. So did Grant's, but no one was looking at Grant. "It was your gun?" Marty asked.

Fisher shook Marty, hitting more piano keys. "Don't play stupid. You took it from my locker. You're going to get us both thrown in jail unless you give it to me now."

"Fish, you brought a gun to prom?" Grant couldn't stop himself from asking.

Fisher, eyes red rimmed, glared at Grant. "So what? I wasn't going to do anything with it. No one would've known if it weren't for this loser."

Marty gulped for air and tried to twist out of Fisher's grip. If he'd been wearing a shirt, maybe he'd've been able to slip away, but since he was only in cargo shorts, Fisher had him by the throat. "I didn't take it from you. I found it in Hackenstrat's office."

"Liar!" Fisher shook Marty again. Marty's face had turned an apple red. "Not that it matters now. Give me the gun and you can get the hell out of here."

"But Jenna—"

"Fine, stick around for Jenna, get yourself arrested—what do I care?" Fisher punched Marty in the face with his left hand, casually, as if he punched people all the time, and maybe he did. The smack of the flesh and crack of the bones made Grant shudder. He was glad it hadn't happened to him, even as he cringed for Marty.

Marty's nose began to bleed, and he moaned. Fisher hit him again. "Make it stop, shitstain. Give me the gun."

"Fisher, dude—"

"Grant, you've been very helpful bringing me to this dead man, but you can shut the fuck up now."

"Well, now you're making me feel responsible for this beating, and that's going to be a problem." Grant took a deep breath. "Maybe you'd be interested to know that Marty didn't steal your gun?"

"What?"

"I keep telling you," Marty said through a stuffed nose.

"If he didn't steal it, how did it end up in the veep's office?"

"That is an excellent question," Grant said. "Who else knew you had a gun in your locker?"

As she went down the stairs, Rose nearly ran into Mer Montez on her way up. "It's you," Mer said, her face only betraying a slight annoyance.

"Mer, where's Fisher?"

"Why?"

"I need to talk to him."

"Good luck with that."

Mer turned away and attempted to keep climbing the stairs. Rose's thoughts tumbled over one another.

When Mer and Grant were dating, Rose had been friendly with Mer. It had been important to Rose not to be jealous, not to be possessive, not to show any sort of emotion whatsoever when it came to Grant's dating life. (Because why show emotion about anything. Especially Grant.) Since they all spent so much time together, it made sense for her to be friends with Mer, so she attempted to do so, and Mer had seemed to reciprocate. But something of Rose's true feelings must have come through, because as soon as Mer had dumped Grant, Mer had not talked to her again, except to exchange superficial pleasantries.

Partly this was because Mer had ended up with Fisher, who Rose despised. Rose didn't hate Mer—none of this was Mer's fault. But she'd always been so sweet and kind and bland. Rose hadn't thought there was anything particularly interesting about her.

Rose stopped walking in the middle of the staircase, but Mer kept going up, so when Rose snapped out of her reverie, she had to grab Mer's ankle to keep her from getting away.

"Hey!" Mer said, and kicked away Rose's hand.

"You know something," Rose said.

"What? No," Mer said, her eyes darting side to side guiltily.

"Rose, come on, the cops will be here any minute," Jenna said from the bottom of the stairs.

"The cops?" Mer echoed. "Oh god."

She sat hard on one of the steps and put her face in her hands. Rose sat two steps below her. At the bottom of the stairs, Jenna sighed and crossed her arms, but Rose ignored her and focused on Mer.

"What happened?" Rose asked.

Mer looked up, and tears were sparkling in her eyes. Even when crying, she seemed like a Disney princess. "I was trying to help," Mer said. "It was for his own good."

Rose held her breath. She shouldn't have thought Mer was

a Disney princess. Grant always told her not to underestimate people, and she'd done it again. *Stupid, Rose.* She'd nearly let Mer walk away.

"Fisher?" Rose said, and Mer nodded. "You knew he brought a gun to prom?"

Mer nodded again. "He brought it in the limo, you know. You were there with it, too."

Rose's skin prickled.

"I told him I wouldn't dance with him if he had it on him, so he went out and put it in his locker. He's such an idiot sometimes. Thinks he needs protection. Thinks *I* need protection, and somehow a gun is going to help with that."

"So what happened?"

"Nothing. Or nothing would've if Marty hadn't crashed the dance." Mer wiped the tears away from under her eyes. Her voice dropped, and Rose had to lean in to hear her whisper. "But it's not Marty's fault, either. Not really. None of this would've happened if it weren't for me."

"It's not your fault that Fisher's carrying around a weapon."

Mer shook her head and whispered even more softly. "I . . . I didn't want him to get in trouble."

"What did you do?"

"I took the gun from Fisher's locker and put it in Hacken-strat's office."

The slot machine in Rose's brain turned to three lemons in a row, and the lights and bells exploded.

"Why?" she asked.

"I didn't know what else to do! I thought Hackenstrat would know what to do with it. And at least Fisher wouldn't have it anymore, and neither of us would get in trouble."

"So when the lockdown happened . . ."

"I wasn't sure what must've happened at first, but when I started to hear about the office and poor Marty Caulfield . . . I knew." She sniffled delicately. "Fisher assumed Marty must've stolen his gun. He knew it was too big a coincidence, some other kid with a gun. Fisher didn't know it was me who put it in the office. He's going to be so mad."

"Why didn't you say something earlier? Like when everyone thought Marty was an active shooter?"

Mer shrank back, wounded. "I've been trying to tell Grant, but I can't seem to get him to listen to me."

Rose rolled her eyes. "Yeah. He can be like that."

"And Fisher's been with him most of the time anyway, trying to find Marty." Mer put her hands up to her face again. "He's never going to forgive me for this. It's my fault."

"It's not," Rose said.

"Can you, like, not tell the cops it's Fisher's gun?"

"They'll figure it out," Rose said. "But . . . don't tell anyone else, okay? I mean, for now. Don't tell any other reporters, that is."

"Rose," Mer said, and Rose looked up at her. She didn't look perfect or princessy at all. Her hair had fallen out of its pins and hung in hairsprayed chunks; her lips were raw instead of glossy.

"Am I . . . do you think I'm stupid?"

Rose didn't answer right away, because she didn't want to give Mer a glib answer.

Mer could've told someone about Fisher's gun earlier—like, before the lockdown earlier—but Fisher being Fisher, there was no guarantee anyone could've done something about it, and then he'd be furious with her, like she said. Rose couldn't imagine caring about Fisher that much—to risk her own safety by being with him, to try to help him even though she knew he would never appreciate it. But not understanding it didn't mean it wasn't real for Mer.

And in a weird way, she knew how Mer felt, keeping things to herself. Rose had never told anyone about Fisher assaulting her. She'd let him get away with it.

But it wasn't Rose's fault that Fisher was an asshole. And it wasn't Mer's, either.

"You're not stupid," she said, and she meant it. "Fisher will get what he deserves."

With every passing second, the solarium's walls closed in a little more. The piano and the Ping-Pong table and the potted plants seemed to jumble up on top of one another, crowding out all the air. Grant pretended the table was the conference table in the *Gazette* room, and this was a story meeting, and he was in charge. It sort of worked.

"Who else knew about the gun, Fisher?" he asked.

Fisher sneered at Grant. "Nobody knew I had the gun in my locker. Unless they were following me."

"So your theory is that Marty was following you and saw you put the gun in your locker."

Fisher rattled Marty. His butt played a minor chord on the piano. "Why not?"

Grant shrugged. "For one thing, how would he get into your

locker? Did he steal your combination, or did he have a pair of bolt cutters to snap the padlock?"

"I didn't have any bolt—"

"Hush, Marty. We know," Grant said.

Fisher shook his head. "I'm telling you no one knew about the gun. Except for—"

Fisher's face went slack and he froze. He dropped Marty, who sat on a cluster of keys before collapsing on the floor.

"Except for Mer," Rose said from the doorway.

Grant's heart leaped.

Rose walked into the solarium, keeping her eyes trained on Fisher but heading straight for Grant. "She took the gun from your locker and dropped it in Hackenstrat's office."

From the doorway, Jenna ran past Rose and straight for her boyfriend under the piano. Fisher looked down at them, then looked at Rose and Grant. "No fucking way."

"Mer didn't want you to get in trouble," Rose said calmly. As soon as she was within range, Grant grabbed her hand. They held on to each other tightly.

"I wouldn't—" Fisher blinked rapidly. "I needed to have it— no one would've—that *bitch*—"

"Yeah. It'll be kind of a bummer when Princeton hears about this."

"No," Fisher said. "No, I can't get kicked out."

"Dude," Rose said. "What did you expect to happen?"

Fisher stood in shock, until the hard clank of metal dropping to the floor broke the silence.

"Oops," Marty said.

Time froze, and then Rose and Grant ran toward the piano, and Fisher lunged for Marty, and Jenna threw herself over her boyfriend and screamed.

Grant ran toward the melee—only feet away—at the same time that Fisher got his hand on the gun and it went off, and the enormous pane of glass above their heads shattered, raining shards down on them all.

Rose threw her arms over her head at the same time that Grant tucked her under his chest and flattened them both to the floor. It was both terribly romantic and extremely uncomfortable, and it blocked her view of the action.

"Ow," Rose heard someone say.

She lifted her head and Grant tilted his to look at her. The look was so serious, Rose stopped breathing. She could've been shot. So could Grant or Jenna or Marty. It hadn't seemed real until that look.

"You okay?" he asked.

She nodded and forced herself to breathe. "Everyone alive?" she called.

"Yes," Marty said.

"Sort of," Jenna said.

"Uuuuuugggghhhh," Fisher said. He stood, blood pouring

out of a huge cut in his arm, staining his white tuxedo shirt red. He had the gun, and it was dripping blood. "If this cut nerves and I can't swim, I swear to god . . ."

"Someone could've *died*, you asshole!" Jenna shouted.

"Shut the fuck up," Fisher said, raising the blood-soaked gun in her direction.

"Jenna," Rose whispered, and Grant squeezed her closer to his chest.

"Drop it!"

The shout came from the doorway. Grant didn't turn around, because he knew if he took his eyes off Fisher, he'd die, the way he knew his own name and the layout of the last *Gazette* and that he loved Rose Regnero.

Fisher looked behind Grant and wiped one blood-splattered arm on his face, smearing red over his eyes. Some wild emotion flashed through them.

And then he lowered his arm and dropped the gun on the floor.

Grant exhaled.

The police took the gun. They took Fisher. They sent someone to find a way to sweep up the broken glass and mop up the spilled beer, and in the meantime paramedics checked Rose and Grant and Jenna and Marty for cuts and other injuries. Rose surveyed the damage to the solarium—glass everywhere, the shrieks and laughter of the dispersing party coming in from the shattered ceiling. Now that they were safe, it was all sort of beautiful and sparkling, like a snow globe.

"Where's the computer?" Rose asked Grant as a paramedic cleaned a cut in her hand.

Grant nodded at the floor a couple of feet from them. The laptop was propped against a potted plant, free from glass. "You in?"

Rose smiled, and the paramedic gave her a strange look. "It's my story, isn't it?"

Grant smiled back at her, the smile that was all hers.

Grant and Rose sat on the piano bench. Rose typed furiously, and Grant read over her shoulder, sitting perhaps a little closer than strictly necessary to read the screen. The police had told them not to leave, and several officers wandered around the solarium, occasionally conferring. Jenna and Marty inhaled each other's faces with enthusiasm and a total lack of self-consciousness. Rose's mom's leather jacket had a rip in the arm from where a piece of glass had caught on a buckle and Jenna had pulled it free, and Jenna's hair was tangled with dirt and leaves. She and Marty both had specks of blood on their hands and legs and faces. Marty's shorts—with their voluminous pockets, somehow capable of hiding a gun through a literal shakedown—slipped down his skinny butt. Everyone knew way too much about how happy Marty was to see his girlfriend.

Grant caught himself looking at Jenna and Marty, then

hummed and looked away. He met Rosie's gaze. She grinned and rolled her eyes. Her dress had stayed together better than Jenna's, but her hair was loose and tumbling over her bare shoulders. There were tiny shards of glass in it like sequins. She looked wild and happy and alive, and he wanted to kiss her so badly, even the noise of Jenna and Marty's kissing couldn't keep him from wanting it.

Be bold. Ask for what you want.

"Hey," he said.

She looked at him. Then she closed the laptop, placed it on the bench on the other side of her, and touched the lapel of his tuxedo jacket. "Yes?"

"I'm sorry," he said.

She tilted her head, curious. "Do you know what you're sorry for now?"

"I'm sorry I was a dick to JB," Grant said. "I'm sorry I didn't say yes when you asked me to go to prom. I'm sorry I didn't break up with Mer. I'm sorry I ever asked her out. I'm sorry I hid your MREJ trophy from you. I'm sorry I didn't tell you how much I wanted to kiss you, like, every single day I knew you."

Rose scrunched her nose. "Yeah, listing them all like that makes them sound a lot worse."

"Well, I am sorry."

"Grant. I'm sorry, too."

"For what?"

"I did get into Northwestern," she said. "But I told them I didn't want to go."

"Oh." Grant felt his stomach drop. He tried to summon something else to say. "Oh," he said again.

"Yeah. So. This isn't easy for me. But I'm going to say how I feel." She tried to smile, and what little he could see of it was radiant before she gave up and made a sour face. "Even saying that gives me hives. Thing is, I never really knew if you wanted *me* or you wanted your star reporter. I was terrified that if I told you I was having doubts about going to Northwestern, you wouldn't like me anymore—so I kind of took the decision out of your hands and bolted. But that doesn't matter. I mean, it does matter, but it also matters what I feel, and I love you." Immediately she blew out her cheeks and rolled her eyes and flared her fingers around her face. "Blaaaaaauuuuugggggghh!"

For once, Grant could not think fast enough to interrupt her panic babbling.

"It's actually more embarrassing than I ever thought possible to say that out loud! But it's true. So if you don't feel the same way and you want me to go back to being your best friend only, because that's all you've really got for me—fine. But the way I feel, well, I want more, too, all the time"—she blushed but didn't stop talking—"like, lots more. And I think you do, too. And there's a ticking clock because we're leaving for college in three months." She laughed a little bit, trying to cover the blush, trying to stop the nervous chatter. "So that's it. No more subtext. Think about it."

Grant's understanding of the past few months tilted sideways. Putting aside the fact that she loved him (if one could put aside such a monumental, life-changing fact, as if it didn't blot out the rest of rational thought like staring straight into the sun would blot out the rest of the world), she had said no to Northwestern and quit the paper.

If she'd quit the paper because she was disappointed about not getting into Northwestern, well, that was something Grant could almost understand. He'd've been pissed if he himself hadn't gotten in. He would've written letters, staged protests. But he couldn't conceive of getting in and then burning his whole life down anyway, the way that Rosie had done.

She'd lied to him, basically, by letting him believe she'd failed to get in. But the lie mattered less than the reason behind it: she didn't want the same thing he wanted, but had only been swept along by his enthusiasm.

Grant was constantly writing the headlines and arranging the front page of his life. What mattered, what didn't. What deserved attention, and what could be shuffled off to the funny pages. He had to stop trying to fix things for a minute and ask himself a question.

What did Rosie want?

He'd thought she wanted to go Northwestern. She didn't.

He'd thought she was okay with staying friends and never talking about kissing. She wasn't.

He'd thought she'd picked someone else. She hadn't.

So did he love the Rosie in his mind, or the girl in the real world?

(The girl who loved him. Rosie loved him. There was that fact, sneaking in again.)

That Rosie had goals and opinions and made decisions that were different from his—that wasn't a bug, that was a feature. She was her own spectacular person.

She'd said what she wanted. So what did he want?

Before Rose could find out what would happen next, Detective Hart called to them from the door.

The colors seemed brighter than usual, the earthy smell of the solarium's plants even stronger, the sound of the glass crunching under their feet even louder. Rose was reminded of the spike of adrenaline she'd had when the lockdown started—only this wasn't from fear but exhilaration. If she could live on the high of saying exactly what she wanted at exactly the right moment—without experiencing any of the repercussions or living through any of the consequences—she would give a speech like that every day of her life.

Grant shrugged at her ruefully and grabbed the laptop, and they followed the detective through Fisher's house, along with Jenna and Marty. The formerly packed house had been abandoned, as if the entire senior Hawks High class had been raptured.

Detective Hart lectured them about unsafe choices and asked them the same questions over and over, but Rose couldn't listen. She scrolled through the many, many messages on her phone. Grant called his dad and asked him to meet them at the police station again.

Rose's mother was waiting for them in Fisher's curved driveway. She hugged Rose so hard her bones creaked, and Rose thought she saw a couple of tears in her mother's eyes before she angrily wiped them away. "No more guns," she whispered.

"No more guns," Rose said, hugging her again.

The cops had found Rose's mom sitting on Owen and had taken him away for questioning along with Fisher. Hart let her mother drive the rest of them to the police station together. Rose crowded next to Grant in the middle-back seat, the laptop half on her knee and half on his. Jenna and Marty had to be yanked apart so that Marty could ride in the front seat, Jenna in the back.

"Can you drive really, really slowly?" Rose asked her mom, who had recovered her cool in record time.

"Certainly. I wouldn't want to disobey any traffic laws," her mom replied, and proceeded to make a couple of wrong turns "accidentally."

They had the basics of their story update ready to go, and Rose's mom was approaching the police station for the third time, when Grant's phone rang.

"Shit," he said cheerfully, and showed Rose the screen. RUTGAR HACKENSTRAT.

"You have Hack's cell-phone number?" Rose asked.

"Hackenstrat's first name is Rutgar?" Jenna asked.

Grant shrugged and answered the call as Rose's mom pulled into the police station parking lot. "Grant Leitch's phone . . . Well, hello, Mr. Hackenstrat. How was your prom?" Grant grinned at Rose. "Oh, you saw that, did you? Good reporting, I thought, and a compelling story. Do you care to comment about how a gun might have ended up in your office? No?" Grant's smile slowly faded, and his eyebrows drew together in concern. "You can't do that. Yeah, I know you *can*, but you shouldn't. Freedom of the— Uh-huh. Uh-huh." Grant, mouth set, stared at Rose as Hackenstrat talked in his ear. Rose grabbed his arm, and he mouthed, *Shutting down the website*. She fell back against the door. "And you're calling me, what? To gloat?"

Rose let go of Grant's arm and grabbed her own phone, scrolling through the contacts to get to Frances Haddad from the *Sentinel Journal*. Frances had been messaging with her all night, and had even sent a compliment when the story went up on the *Gazette*. Rose held the phone up for Grant to see, and as he read, his whole face relaxed.

"So what you're saying, Mr. Hackenstrat, is that we can't put out any more stories under the *Gazette* masthead. Got it. We've graduated anyway, so it's about time we've moved on." There was a pause, and Grant nudged Rose with his elbow. "It's not really your concern," Grant said, dripping condensation, "but as a courtesy, I can tell you we've heard from the Chicago *Sentinel Journal*, and they'll publish our new, updated story. . . . Yes, there's been a development. You haven't heard? Well, unless you have a comment on how the gun found its way to you, I guess you'll have to read about it in the paper tomorrow."

Grant hung up, and everyone in the car broke into a round of applause.

"You think she'll really publish the story under your byline?" Grant said quietly.

"We'll have to make it so good that she has to," Rose said.

Rose's mom's Subaru became the *Gazette* room in miniature, all the chatter and urgency and the feeling of pulling toward a common goal, except that Grant couldn't move an elbow without jostling the computer while Rose was trying to type, and Rose's mom and Jenna and Marty weren't even on the paper. Still, it felt exactly the same.

He didn't have much time to think about the fact that this would be Rose's first article written for a real paper—and for an editor who wasn't him. He managed to forget entirely that they were in the police-station parking lot, scamming off the public library's free Wi-Fi, delaying the moment when they had to go into the station and answer a bunch of potentially tricky questions.

While they worked, Rose's mom went into the station to talk to Grant's dad and stall the detectives. Rose read the story one more time. Grant read it two more times. Marty offered to read it and they ignored him. Rose read it once more after that.

When they'd stared at every character at least a dozen times, Rose hovered the cursor over the send button. She made eye contact with Grant and bit her lip. Grant briefly forgot all about the article, then snapped back to himself.

"Ready?" she asked.

"Do it."

She pressed send, then closed her hand into a fist and spread it open again. "They might not accept it."

"They will."

"They might rewrite it entirely."

"They won't."

Rose smiled and ran her hands over the laptop's keys, like a pianist at the end of a concert. "I know. It's pretty spectacular."

Grant watched her.

His Rosie.

Grant had loved their everyday high school life, the day-to-day existing they did together. Afternoons at the *Gazette*, nights at the diner. Story meetings and text messages and editing each other and teasing and not-quite-touching. It had seemed perfect. But it didn't anymore.

How could it be perfect when it wasn't being honest? How could he be satisfied knowing there was an even better life out there, if only he could be bold?

"Marty and Jenna, get out of here," Grant said, but he didn't take his eyes off of Rose.

Marty and Jenna obediently opened their doors and tripped out of the car.

Grant took the laptop from Rose, closed it, and placed it on Jenna's now-empty seat. He looked at Rose's dirt-streaked dress, at her waterfall of hair, at her dimples, at the soft skin of her shoulders, at her mouth. He saw her eyes lit up and happy and looking directly at him.

"What?" she said.

"I didn't know what to say," Grant said. And then he leaned forward and kissed her.

Rose kissed Grant. His hand held her waist. Her hands reached up and took off his glasses and tangled in his hair, without her instructing them to do any such thing. Her body closed the distance between them.

She had thought saying out loud that she loved him was exhilarating and terrifying and satisfying, but words had nothing on kissing. She remembered the feeling of kissing him from the last time, but back then it had been laced with a twinge of guilt—Grant shouldn't have been kissing her, and she hadn't been truthful about her feelings with Grant. This time, without guilt and silence mucking things up, she could forget everything else. She could be hands. Lips. Skin. Breath.

Exactly right.

NINE

When the police finally let Grant and Rose go, the sun was starting to rise. Grant looked to the east, stretched, and felt his entire back crack. He caught a whiff of the underarms of his rented tuxedo and quickly lowered his arms before Rose could get within sniffing distance.

Detective Hart stood on the steps of the station with Grant, his dad, his mom, Rose, and Rose's mom. Jenna's parents had picked her up already, and even Marty had been let go before they had, since he probably understood the least of anyone how the night's events had transpired.

"Well," the detective said, rubbing her eyes. "I guess I should thank you for your help straightening this out, but I have to admit it doesn't feel very straight."

"What's going to happen to Fisher?" Grant asked.

"You asking as a member of the press?" Hart almost smiled, but pulled back at the last second. "Fisher Louis brought a gun onto school property, which is a serious crime."

"On the other hand, he also has his parents and their unlimited resources," Grant said, thinking of that absurd palace of a house, and the parents who hadn't shown up the entire time.

"We'll see. Though I wouldn't put any bets on Princeton welcoming him with open arms in the fall."

"What about Owen Pettibone?" Rose asked.

"We gave him a good talking-to. I think he'll leave that girl alone."

"That's it?" Rose glared. "You know, it wasn't that hard to figure out who was behind the stalking. It's almost as if you didn't try to find out what happened—like cyberstalking isn't a priority."

Detective Hart rolled her eyes. "We do the best we can with our resources. Save it for your next editorial."

"I will," Rose said, so fiercely that the detective actually took a step back. Grant grinned.

That was his Rosie.

His dad ushered them down the steps and away from the station, muttering to Grant that he should "take the exit you've been offered."

Before he got into the car with his dad to head home, his mom took him aside. "You scare me sometimes," she said, hugging him tightly.

"Same," Grant said.

"But I love you, you jerk."

Grant, still hugging his mom, hid his eyes in the crook of his arm. "Same."

No one's parents could be convinced that they should go to the diner for breakfast—even the most permissive parents had limits, especially after a night of lockdowns and no sleep—so Rose drove home with her mother.

"Other than nearly dying, this has been an interesting night," Rose's mom said. "I don't see how you quit the paper, if it's always that exciting."

"It's definitely not that exciting most of the time."

"Still. You really seemed in your element."

They passed Hawks High. All the TV news crews had abandoned the baseball field, and there were only a few cars left in the lot. With its empty windows and locked doors, it looked as if the building had closed its eyes to take a long nap. After graduation, Rose would have no reason to ever return to the building. She'd never go to the *Gazette* room again. Never pass Grant and

Jenna and Nick in the hall. Never run to her locker to grab her notebooks before running out again to cover a game or a meeting.

"I'm proud of you, Rose," her mom said. "You're kicking ass. You know that, right?"

Rose nodded but didn't say anything.

They were at an endless stoplight at a deserted intersection when Rose took a deep breath. "Last year Fisher Louis grabbed my tits at the end of an interview."

Rose's mom turned around in her seat and the car drifted forward into the intersection. She punched the brakes.

"I didn't say anything. I didn't *do* anything. I wrote the stupid profile." Rose laughed, but not because anything was funny. "Not exactly full of ass-kicking."

"What a piece of shit," Rose's mom said with heat. "That's on him, Rose. That's not you."

"But I didn't tell anyone."

"Not even Grant?"

Rose shook her head. She hadn't wanted to tell him before. Would she tell him now? It couldn't possibly be as embarrassing as admitting she was in love with him. But somehow it seemed worse.

Rose's mom reached out a hand and held Rose's tightly. "It's okay, Rose. You're telling me now."

Rose held her mom's hand and nodded. She'd keep telling people things until it didn't feel so scary. Or maybe it would always be scary, but having her mom and Grant and Jenna on her side would make it worth the risk.

As soon as his dad fell asleep, Grant took a quick shower, said goodbye to Julie and the twins (who were up for breakfast), ran to the gas station, bought every *Sentinel Journal* they had, and then ran the half mile to Rose's house, holding a stack of papers to his chest.

He couldn't breathe when she opened the door, so he pushed the papers into her arms and collapsed onto her front steps, clutching the stitch in his side. There went all the good the shower had done him.

She sat next to him, the stack of papers on her lap. She'd changed from her prom dress into sweats and a holey T-shirt, and her hair was stuck up in a messy bun. She stared at the story—front page, below the fold—for a full minute without moving. When Grant could breathe again, he reached an arm around her shoulder, and she rested her head on his chest and moved the paper so he could read it, too.

PROM LOCKDOWN CAUSED BY
DISCOVERY OF STAR ATHLETE'S GUN
BY ROSE REGNERO

"I mean . . . ," she said.

"I know," he said.

He nuzzled the side of her neck and she laughed. It was strange and wonderful and comfortable and right to be this close to her, finally, sweaty or not. And he was finally not a chicken-shit, and the worst had not come to pass, because the best had come to pass instead.

In fact, he felt so good about not being scared, maybe he could be the bravest person in the world. A person who abandoned his entire life plan for love. Wouldn't *that* show the old scared, frozen Grant who was boss.

"Hey," he said, waiting for her to look up at him. "If you don't want to go to Northwestern, I can transfer to Michigan."

"What?"

"Yeah," he said, pretending he hadn't suggested something outrageous. "I don't care where I go. I want to be where you are."

Rose stared at him for several very long seconds. U of M was a very good school. This would be fine. He'd get to be with her all the time. He'd major in . . . something. They didn't have a journalism major, he vaguely recalled. But they had a good paper. What was it called? He'd known it yesterday. Why couldn't he remember? It was good, though, whatever it was. Right?

Oh god, what had he done.

"No way," she said finally.

He was relieved, but also a little bit hurt. "You don't want to go to the same school?"

"No." She sat up a little; her hair fell out of the bun. "I appreciate the offer, Grant. But I need to do this on my own."

"If you say so," Grant said.

"And I wouldn't make you give up Northwestern."

"Well. If you insist, Rosie."

She put her head back on his chest and looked up at him, and he kissed her, and they looked at the paper again in silence. On the sidewalk in front of Rose's house, an old man walked a small dog. A breeze rustled the trees. No cars passed by.

"So when's your first day of school?" she asked.

"Not till after Labor Day. You?"

"Same."

"That's forever from now," Rose said.

"Eons. Ages."

"Do you think you'll ever publish a better story?"

Grant considered it. He thought about all the things that could happen to human beings: The infinite variety of ways they screwed up, the multitude of ways they were caught. The moments that made them heroes, the moments they became villains. The fact that Grant was only one tiny speck in a huge universe, with only his own two eyes to observe everything that had ever happened.

"I don't know," he said, honestly. "But I'd like to keep trying."

"Me, too," said Rosie, gazing at the paper again.

"And you wanted to quit."

"Oh, enough with that already."

"You have to admit this is pretty great," Grant said.

She looked up at him and smiled. His chest was a balloon close to popping. "This is pretty great."

Rose arrived at her dorm, a four-person suite with its own bathroom, before any of her roommates. She put her bags on a bottom bunk and sat next to them.

Her mom was finding a parking space. Rose had made Grant stay home for her drive to Ann Arbor, even though Northwestern didn't start for another couple of days. It was all a part of her brilliant plan to do her own thing.

A thing that felt very lonely, now that she was all alone in her new dorm.

She unzipped her backpack and pulled out her old, beat-up laptop. It had terrible battery life and the trackpad didn't work, so it lived on her desk with a mouse. She looked around for a desk near an outlet and froze.

There, on the center of the desk closest to the window, was the Midwest Regional Excellence in Journalism trophy.

She approached the desk slowly. The circular award was definitely hers; she didn't need to get close to the engraving to be sure, but she checked anyway. *For Excellence in Feature Reporting and Writing, Rose Regnero.*

She placed her laptop very carefully next to the award and picked it up. A piece of paper fluttered away from the metal base. She knew who it would be from. She didn't know how he'd gotten in—or when he'd driven up here—or that he'd even been back to the *Gazette* offices after prom to retrieve the award.

She picked up the note.

The Michigan Daily's *offices are only two blocks away. They have an orientation meeting today at 3 p.m. You don't have to commit; you can go and see what they say.*

And then, on the other side:

Love you, Rosie.

Rose had spent so long letting the paper and Grant tell her who she was. Rose Regnero, the star reporter. She'd bent the rules and followed leads and done whatever it took to find the story. But it wasn't the stories she wrote that made her who she was; it was the other way around. She was the person who was too stubborn and curious and suspicious to let the stories go. Even if she hadn't written a word, that drive would still be in her somewhere.

She still didn't know what she wanted to be or what path in life would make her truly happy, but she'd go to the orientation meeting. She could write for the paper and not be defined by the paper. Or at least she could try.

She held the note to her chest and laughed.

ACKNOWLEDGMENTS

First off, I offer my undying fealty and love to my favorite movie, the 1940 Howard Hawks film *His Girl Friday*, starring Rosalind Russell and Cary Grant, written by Charles Lederer, Ben Hecht, and Charles MacArthur. It's the funniest, fastest-talking, most wonderful thing.

Thank you to my brilliant, patient editor Donna Bray and to the whole HarperCollins team, especially Viana Siniscalchi, Tiara Kittrell, Caroline Sun, Jenna Stempel and Alison Donalty, Renée Cafiero, Janet Frick, Kate Jackson, and Suzanne Murphy. Thank you to my amazing agent, Tina Wexler, and at ICM thanks also to Berni Barta, Tamara Kawar, and Roxane Edouard.

Thank you to Skila Brown, Lindsay Eyre, Erin Hagar, Stefanie Lyons, Kristin Sandoval, Amy Zinn, and all my other Vermont College of Fine Arts fellows and mentors, in particular A. M. Jenkins, Rita Williams-Garcia, and Tim Wynne-Jones, all of whom read an earlier version of this story and offered invaluable advice, guidance, and encouragement.

Thank you to Julia Reischel and Rachel Dry, who both answered my many questions about journalism best practices and ethics, even when I was planning on having my characters not follow them. Their expertise was invaluable, and any errors about reporting and newspaper making are entirely mine. Thanks to Michael Dyer for reading a draft and talking it through with me. Thanks also to Dyan Flores for her thoughts on the manuscript. Thanks to Alison Cherry and the cafés of Brooklyn for being an excellent person to write with and exceptional places to write, respectively.

Thank you to Susan Van Metre, Howard Reeves, Tamar Brazis, Michael Jacobs, and my many other colleagues at Abrams Books over the past 13 years, and thank you especially to all the wonderful writers I've had a chance to work with.

Thank you to my family and friends. You all are the people I am lucky to get to banter with in real life!

And finally, thank you to Kyle and Freddy, the two best dudes.